Lord Rathbone glared at promised to pose as your betrothed for two weeks only. I have satisfied that bargain. I will not continue the charade. You do not own me."

"Don't pretend righteousness with me," Rathbone growled. "No one forced you. And you will help me again should the need arise." His face hovered only inches from her own, an odd gleam growing in his eyes.

"Never, my lord. You do not own me," she repeated, trepidation warring with some other emotion as she saw his pupils blur.

"Perhaps I should," he murmured, dragging her into his arms and kissing her.

Melissa was too surprised to resist, giving excitement a chance to build. His mouth was open, the unexpectedness of it thrilling her as his tongue traced the lines of her lips. This was so different from Lord Helfin's cruel kiss. She felt Rathbone's hands caressing her back, and she arched closer, reveling in the warmth of his embrace.

What was she doing? her stunned mind wondered—even as her pounding heart gave the shocking answer . . .

THE
IMPOVERISHED
VISCOUNT

—⁘—

Allison Lane

A SIGNET BOOK

SIGNET
Published by the Penguin Group
Penguin Books USA Inc., 375 Hudson Street,
New York, New York 10014, U.S.A.
Penguin Books Ltd, 27 Wrights Lane,
London W8 5TZ, England
Penguin Books Australia Ltd, Ringwood,
Victoria, Australia
Penguin Books Canada Ltd, 10 Alcorn Avenue,
Toronto, Ontario, Canada M4V 3B2
Penguin Books (N.Z.) Ltd, 182-190 Wairau Road,
Auckland 10, New Zealand

Penguin Books Ltd, Registered Offices:
Harmondsworth, Middlesex, England

First published by Signet, an imprint of Dutton Signet,
a division of Penguin Books USA Inc.

First Printing, July, 1996
10 9 8 7 6 5 4 3 2 1

Oh, what a tangled web we weave,
When first we practice to deceive!
—SIR WALTER SCOTT, 1808
Marmion, Canto VI, Stanza 17

Chapter One

Lady Melissa Stapleton slipped her needlework back into its bag, finally admitting that tension made it impossible to set even the simplest stitches. She should have gone upstairs with Beatrice, for they were only safe together. But she hated to openly admit fear.

Despite the hot summer evening, she shivered as a burst of laughter erupted from the billiard room. Her brother and his friends were in high spirits. Tobias Stapleton, seventh Earl of Drayton, ninth Viscount Kendall, fourteenth Baron Stapleton—would that he could live up to those exalted titles! If his illustrious ancestors knew who currently held them, they would turn in their graves. A weak, dissipated wastrel, Toby had not been sober since their father's death just after Christmas. He had always called the sixth earl a miser for keeping him on the estate instead of allowing him to live in London. Furious to discover that the coffers really were empty, he had sulked for six months, finally pulling himself out of his stupor long enough to invite three old schoolmates to celebrate the end of deep mourning. There had not been a moment's peace in the fortnight since they arrived.

At least Melissa had the protection of Beatrice, a cousin on her father's side who belonged to the American branch of the family. Bea's husband had met an untimely death two years before, precipitating a melancholy that lingered long afterward. Thinking a change of scenery might help, she had come to England to visit her unknown relatives. But the trip had not gone as planned. Shortly after her arrival, the sixth earl had sickened and died, leaving his two children parentless. Bea graciously offered to extend her visit until Melissa found her feet, but she could not postpone her departure much longer.

Unwilling to brave the Atlantic in winter, she was scheduled for passage six weeks hence.

In the meantime, she and Melissa must cope with Toby's friends.

Mr. Crawford was not too bad. Immaturity was his greatest failing, despite his five-and-twenty years. He alternated between supercilious condemnation of any lapse in rigid decorum, and a youthful vulnerability when his own behavior fell short. Melissa believed he—and everyone else—would be happier if he focused on people's good qualities. But though she found him annoying, he was harmless enough.

Lord Dobson was not so benign. Haughty and lecherous, he spent his time trying to seduce the servants. Even Rose, who was all of fifty, complained of his groping hands. Toby refused to chastise him, despite Melissa's pleas. She tried to keep the maids away from Dobson, but that created other problems. For the last week he had been unacceptably warm with Beatrice. At five-and-thirty, Bea was still a good-looking woman whose light brown eyes could sparkle with delight when she was in spirits. But it was unconscionable that she must fear for her virtue under her cousin's roof.

And Dobson was not the only threat. The worst problem was Lord Heflin. He was both a rake and a scoundrel, his dark, satanic visage increasing his aura of menace. Even Toby admitted that Heflin had a reputation for debauching innocents, and actually apologized for inviting the man into the house. But he refused to end his party. Lord Heflin was stalking Beatrice—there was no other way to describe his conduct. Worse, he insisted on paying unwelcome attentions to Melissa, brushing against her arm as he moved past, standing too close for propriety when they gathered in the drawing room before dinner, and once actually allowing his hand to trail across her chest as she tried to push her way past him when he blocked the exit from a room. The touch raised tingling pains that both terrified and fascinated her.

Melissa tried to decipher such a reaction, but could find no words to describe it, let alone explain it. And she must. Lord Heflin would not be leaving any time soon. She finally turned to Beatrice for advice. One good thing about Americans was their willingness to answer questions, even about subjects society deemed improper. Melissa had taken advantage of that candor many times, questioning Toby's drinking and discussing why people were wrong to excuse it.

"Of course you were terrified," Bea agreed bluntly when Melissa had described Heflin's most recent indignity. "And who can blame you? The British delight in keeping girls ignorant about their bodies."

Melissa flushed scarlet from the top of her head to the tips of her toes. "Ladies never discuss that," she reminded her cousin.

"Nonsense," snorted Beatrice. "You must understand yourself if you are to cope with the rogues your brother cultivates. And you had better learn something about men as well. Heflin is a first-class scoundrel who will try to seduce anyone, and he thrives on depravity. He would derive more pleasure from debauching the innocent daughter of a lord than a widow like me. But he does not rely solely on seduction. Breaking conventions excites him. He loves force, reveling in subduing an unwilling victim. That is why his attentions raise terror. He is a dangerous man, something you know in your heart."

"Then why did his touch seem desirable?" dared Melissa, mortified to admit that she would have liked it to continue.

"That is a normal reaction, Missy," stated Beatrice matter-of-factly. "The human body enjoys caresses. And don't tell me again that ladies do not," she added as Melissa opened her mouth in protest. "I don't care what society deems proper. All women are built alike, regardless of class. Some touches are physically exciting. Brushing across your breasts is one of them. If you do not understand that, a man can easily seduce you. If you expect it, you can control yourself, for the effect goes away quickly. The danger lies in repeated touch, for that can build emotions that overwhelm reason. Never confuse physical pleasure with love."

"Do you mean someone as repugnant as Heflin can excite my body?" squeaked Melissa, appalled at the thought.

"If he takes you by surprise," agreed Beatrice. "If you know what he is trying to do, anger and distaste will cancel any pleasure. That is why information is vital. Of course, in Heflin's case, only avoidance will keep you safe. You haven't the strength to counteract force. But you must be careful around any gentleman. Society safeguards you by demanding that you be chaperoned at all times. But Toby cares little for the proprieties, so you will have to protect yourself. Stay away from Heflin. Don't allow anyone to touch you. And if you do find yourself in trouble, two ways to disable a man are cracking him in the temple with an elbow or fist, and slamming a knee into his groin."

"What did you mean about confusing pleasure with love?" Melissa ostentatiously examined a hideous portrait of her great-grandfather to hide her flaming face.

"Physical reactions cloud your thinking and can make you believe that love exists when it does not." Bea shrugged. "That is why touching is a bad idea. Even an innocuous caress can rapidly lead to shocking misbehavior."

"How does one know if love is real, then?"

"That is always difficult. One clue is whether you put his or your own interests and welfare first. Another is whether you feel as strongly about the non-physical aspects of the relationship. Kissing is fun, but most of your life is spent doing other things. The best proof of love is available only in retrospect. If you truly love someone, intimacy with another is unthinkable. Once the emotions are engaged, you will no longer feel delight from another man's touch."

"Is that how it was with you and Mr. Stokes?" she asked, turning back to her cousin.

Beatrice nodded. "Dear Lord, I miss him," she whispered so softly that Melissa was not sure she had heard the words.

"You loved him." It was not a question.

"I only pray you can find someone to love even half as much, Missy. Intimacy can be enjoyable with many men, but ecstasy is possible only with one you love."

They turned the talk back to Heflin and how to avoid him. As long as he remained at Drayton, Melissa was in deadly danger. His attentions were not the least bit flattering. Only her innocence appealed to the rogue. Although she was eighteen, her body remained flat, with only the faintest hint of developing curves. She did not look a day over fourteen. And a recent bout of influenza had worsened her appearance, leaving her pitifully thin and sallow, her face dominated by dark circles around her eyes.

Another round of laughter sounded. Bea should have returned by now. Melissa bit a fingernail as she tried to pick out voices from the billiard room to see if all four men were there.

Talking to Toby was hopeless. He loved the unceasing gaming and drinking, though she suspected he was losing more than he won. It was all of a piece. Their father had had a head for neither agriculture nor investment. He inherited a purse-pinched estate and left it in worse shape on his death. Toby demonstrated even less ability. Melissa's last slim hope of entering society had died with her father. There were few men living nearby who needed a spouse, and none that she would consider. It was probable that she would spend the rest of her life caring for her irresponsible brother and dodging his dissolute friends.

The laughter was becoming louder, the party turning raucous as more bottles were broached. The servants had better be obeying orders. Only footmen were supposed to answer calls from the men.

She thankfully reached for her needlework when the sound of footsteps announced Beatrice's return. Staying together was their only defense against lechery. But it was Mr. Crawford who staggered through the door. He was halfway across the room before he spied Melissa sitting on the couch. A slack smile did nothing to hide his annoyance.

"Well, if it isn't Toby's baby sister, sitting here alone," he managed to slur between hiccups. His face twisted into a sneer. "No chaperon? How vulgar."

"My cousin will return in a moment, sir," stated Melissa coldly. "Please return to the billiard room. You would hardly wish to be caught alone with me."

"Never," he choked, seeming to gag at the idea. He whirled to leave, but one foot caught on the other, even as his brows raised in agonized surprise. Groaning, he fell with a jolt that shattered all control, casting up his accounts across her feet.

Melissa screamed, jumping out of the way too late. The stench of brandy, sour onions, and sickness wrapped her in a suffocating cloud. She had been unusually sensitive to odors since her illness. As Mr. Crawford continued to retch, she clamped a hand desperately over her own mouth and fled, barely reaching her room before losing her dinner.

Beatrice heard the commotion and rushed in. "My poor Missy, what happened?" she exclaimed, taking in the sopping skirts and the spattered basin as she wiped the girl's face with a cool cloth.

"Mr. Crawford," gasped Melissa, swallowing another surge of nausea.

"Not again," muttered Beatrice. "That boy has the lowest tolerance for wine I've ever seen. Why will he not admit it and stop drinking?"

"What do you mean?"

"Two glasses of claret, and he is as deep in his cups as Toby after two or three bottles of brandy," explained Bea. "When he tries to match the others, he is invariably ill."

That explained those odd odors Melissa had noted lately. "How can he be so uncaring of the servants, if not of his host's furnishings?"

"He usually makes it to his room," explained Beatrice, frowning over the gown she had stripped from her cousin. "He must have left it too late this time. And to give him his due, his valet generally takes care of things. What happened?"

"He came into the drawing room, fell at my feet, and exploded." Melissa grimaced, again fighting down nausea.

Beatrice nodded. "The jolt would do it. He was probably heading for the empty coal scuttle. It wouldn't have been the first time. I think we should spend the evenings up here from now on. We can fix up the next room as a sitting room."

"Why must I skulk in my own house?" wailed Melissa, breaking into tears. "I feel like a prisoner!"

"There, there," Bea murmured soothingly, patting her back. "It is unfair, but there is no reasoning with Toby. If there was somewhere else to go, we would leave tomorrow. Heflin is becoming unspeakably aggressive. He accosted me in my room just now. I had to brain him with a pitcher before he would leave"

"He is dangerous, Bea. Terror chokes me every time he comes near," admitted Melissa. "And he knows Toby won't lift a finger to help me. I am surprised he has not yet resorted to force. Or does he get a thrill from stalking me and gloating over my fear?"

"That is a possibility," admitted Beatrice. "There are men who enjoy such things."

"I wish this party would end!"

"So do I, but think, Missy. Even if you escape his clutches now, he may visit again. Toby is worthless. You must find a refuge."

"But there is no place to go," she protested. "I will have to hire a competent companion."

"Use your head," Beatrice admonished her. "Companions are empty-headed ninnies who cannot take care of themselves, let alone protect you. And as servants, they cannot lift a finger against men like these. You must escape this house."

"How? I know no one but our few neighbors. I never attended school. And the chances of marrying are too remote to consider."

"Have you no other relatives?"

"None that acknowledge us. There is my grandmother, of course, but she and her son repudiated us after Mama died."

"Is that your mother's family?"

"Yes, Grandmama is the dowager Marchioness of Castleton. There were only the two children. She last visited us when I was eight. I remember her as imposing, though she seemed kind enough. But she blamed Papa for Mama's death."

"What happened? He wrote my father at the time, but divulged no details." She had finished helping Melissa into a night rail and now tucked her firmly into bed.

"That is hardly surprising. Lady Castleton's charges increased his own guilt."

"You mean he really did kill her?"

"In a way. Finances have always been tight, especially the year I turned ten. As a result, the staff was cut to the bone. Our only groom was confined to bed after one of the horses kicked him, so Papa drove when he and Mama attended a gala midsummer's ball in Lincoln. Grandfather sat on the box to keep Papa company for the two-hour journey home. Both men were somewhat the worse for wine, but they could not afford to stay over at an inn. I suspect that he dozed off, though he never explained. When they came down Beecher's Hill, the carriage overturned on the corner. Grandfather was thrown into a boulder and killed instantly. Mama was badly injured and died in pain three days later. Papa was unscathed."

"And your grandmother blamed him?"

"Absolutely. She refused to attend the funeral, sending a blistering letter that accused Papa of murdering his wife and announced that she would never speak with him again."

"Yet she is the closest relative you have, Missy. Eight years have passed, and your father is now dead. She might be willing to accept you. I have been worrying about what you would do once I return home. Leaving you in the clutches of so weak a brother does not bear thinking about, especially when his friends are less than honorable."

"I suppose I can write to her."

"Explain your situation. She cannot like having her flesh and blood living in such danger. With luck, she will ask you to live with her."

"Acting as companion to my grandmother would be preferable to staying here," agreed Melissa. "She might even enjoy the company, provided she can afford to support me. As far as

I know, her finances are no better than ours. I have given up all hope of marriage. My looks are against me, and I have no dowry. I suppose putting up with an old lady's crotchets is preferable to fighting off Toby's lecherous friends."

"Write the letter. I will get Toby to frank it in the morning. He will have such a bad head that he will not look at it."

"In the meantime, we must stay together at all times, Bea. For both our sakes."

Charles Montrose, Viscount Rathbone, wiped the water from his eyes and frowned. Rain poured down harder than ever. His sodden cloak no longer protected him, leaving him chilled to the bone. His grays were slipping often enough that his heart was in his throat lest they injure themselves. He would have to stop at the next inn, no matter what its condition.

What was he doing in this godforsaken place anyway? Dorset was not his favorite county. He ought to be heading for Brighton. All his friends were gathered there and the luscious Lady Runyon had signaled that she was ready to welcome him into her bed. He had already laid out the funds to secure rooms at the popular resort, but his grandmother's summons could not be ignored.

He had received the letter two days before. She had taken ill and was not expected to live. At nine-and-seventy, she could no longer shrug off even simple chills, and this one had settled in her chest. Bad news indeed, he agreed, already rearranging his plans so he could leave immediately. But the next paragraph horrified him. She had summoned her solicitor to make revisions to her will.

He had been cursing for two days.

What was he to do? All his life he had been her heir. He had known that she did not approve of his activities, but he had never heeded her criticisms, knowing that he would turn his attention to Swansea when he could address its problems. That was yet impossible. Besides, he was entitled to sow a few oats before he settled down. How he lived was none of her concern. To his credit, and despite his seeming indolence, he had never wasted a shilling. He drank in such moderation that people noticed and eschewed gaming, even for pennies. Fearful of falling prey to his father's failings, he refused even promising investments. He had become adept at maintaining his appearance as a modestly well-to-do peer without resorting to debt. His grandmother must know that.

A run-down inn appeared through the driving rainstorm, and he thankfully turned his weary horses off the road. An hour later he was ensconced in a shabby room that the innkeeper claimed contained the last bed in the house. Huddling near the tiny fireplace, he succumbed to a powerful mixture of anger and fear. Devil take his grandmother! And devil take his father for leaving him to the whims of a capricious woman! He hoped the man was burning. It would be a change from the icy aloofness he had always employed.

But he could not afford to waste time cursing the past. He must decide how to recoup the future. Again he perused the letter, praying he had somehow misinterpreted its message. But the words were crystal clear.

Pouring a glass from his second bottle of nearly undrinkable brandy, he scowled. Heat had replaced the earlier chills. His head swirled. The wine might be awful, but it was potent, especially on an empty stomach. He had been unable to choke down the unidentified glop on his dinner tray.

Lady Lanyard had to be serious. She was not a person to joke about money. He downed another brandy. And another. What did it matter if he drank himself insensible? He stood helpless on the brink of ruin with not a thing he could do to avert disaster. If only there was some way to fight back! Pacing the floor in agitation, he was unaware of the murmur of voices in the next room until they suddenly rose in argument.

"Of course we cannot go back, Bea!" shouted a girl. "Oh, why did Grandmama choose this, of all times, to go to Bath?"

"We could hardly have anticipated that," agreed an older lady. "But what else are we to do? We cannot stay at an inn for a fortnight. There is no money. Nor can we beg admittance to an empty house."

"I won't return," swore the girl. "I will sleep in a ditch first. And we've not enough money to make our way back and return in a fortnight, either. There's no hope of more. We've nothing else to sell. Can we not go to Bath?"

"Of course not! Do you expect your grandmother to welcome you when she is staying with a friend you have never seen? Be reasonable, Missy. Toby must stand up for you after this."

"I am being reasonable. You know how ruthless *he* can be.

And you know what he wants. Toby bends with every breeze. Even if he promises, he will be powerless against his friends."

Charles shook his head, hiccuping loudly into the sudden silence. It sounded like someone was running away from home. Who was Bea? She couldn't be a maid, for she seemed to be giving the orders. The accents were genteel. How far had they already traveled? What would two ladies do for the fortnight before the grandmother returned?

An insidiously attractive idea suddenly popped into his reeling head. Without giving himself time to think, he staggered to the door.

Melissa grimaced as she sipped the worst cup of tea she had ever tasted and tried to identify the food on her dinner tray. Nothing had gone right in days.

She and Beatrice had remained together for two weeks. Arranging a private sitting room meant they saw the gentlemen only at dinner. Lord Heflin had continued his warm remarks, but Bea's presence discouraged his touches. The judicious use of locks and keys also helped. But the atmosphere at the Manor was nearing the explosion point. Toby carried an ever-deepening frown on his face, as did Mr. Crawford. Melissa assumed that both were losing badly at the incessant gaming. Daily she prayed that Toby would dismiss his friends, but he refused to do so. She finally recognized that he could not. When the house party ended, debts of honor must be settled, and he lacked the means.

The ladies retired to the rose arbor after breakfast one morning. It was their favorite place to do needlework, offering escape from the gloomy house. It was also the most relaxing time of day. The men rarely awoke before noon, as their nightly carouses usually lasted until dawn. Thus Melissa was unconcerned when a maid summoned Bea to arbitrate a crisis in the kitchen. But five minutes later Lord Heflin slipped into the arbor, his eyes alight with lust.

"My dear Lady Melissa, you make so charming a picture among the roses," he murmured.

"Hardly," she scoffed, clipping her thread and thrusting the needle into her work.

"So humble." He sat next to her on the bench. She immediately crossed to the other side of the arbor.

"Avoiding me, my dear?" he asked softly, following behind her.

"I am not your dear," she snapped.

"Of course you are." He jerked her against him.

She tried to push him away, but his grip was too strong. "Let go!" she demanded fiercely.

"I always knew that demure exterior hid a heart of fire," he gloated, holding her head so she could not escape his wet lips. His mouth was suffocating. But even worse was her own treacherous body. Her budding breast tautened under his stroking hand.

"See?" he boasted, grinding her lips into her teeth and pulling her closer. "You want me as much as I want you. Enough of your coy teasing. I can't wait another minute."

She squirmed, trying to escape, but the movement only quickened his breathing. Beatrice had spoken truly. He reveled in using his strength against her. She tried to relax, but her body continued to fight.

"Mine at last," he rasped hoarsely.

Screaming, she clawed at his face, but could not break free. At least she no longer enjoyed his touch, a corner of her mind noted. Fury and terror overwhelmed all else. As he dragged her aside, she recalled Bea's words and twisted, slamming her knee into his swollen manhood and stabbing with the scissors that remained in her hand. He doubled over, swearing, as a second stab sliced deeply into the back of his thigh. She ran for the house.

Beatrice followed Melissa upstairs, cradling her until the nausea abated and her stormy tears had run their course. Bea wanted to leave immediately, but Melissa could not agree. She had not yet received a reply from her grandmother. By late afternoon, she convinced Bea to allow one last attempt to talk Toby into protecting her. Melissa had raised her hand to knock on the study door when she heard voices inside.

"I have not got the ready at the moment," admitted Toby. "You will have to wait until the harvest."

"Really?" drawled Heflin. "Judging from your fields, ten harvests will not cover what you owe me, Drayton. But I am a reasonable man. Give me your sister, and we'll call it even. I've a bone to pick with the lady."

"Are you offering for her?" asked Toby in surprise.

"I may as well. She's plain enough that she'll cause no trouble. I need an heir. Once that is settled, she can stay in the country and out of my hair."

Melissa did not wait to hear more, racing back to her room.

"Heflin is demanding my hand," she sobbed. "And Toby will agree. I cannot live with him, Bea! I'll kill myself first."

"Calm down, Missy!" ordered Beatrice. "What happened?"

Melissa took a moment to pull herself together. "Toby admitted that he can't cover his vowels. Heflin offered to take me instead. Toby's only condition is that he marry me."

Bea frowned. "Can he force you?"

"Yes, he's my guardian." She broke into renewed sobs. "What am I going to do?"

"Stop this! I cannot think if you are in hysterics."

By the time Melissa had regained her composure, Bea was pacing the room, muttering about aristocratic stupidity.

"Do you think he has settled anything?" she asked at last.

Melissa frowned. "That depends on Heflin. Toby will do nothing on his own, but will agree if pushed."

"Then we may have time. Heflin will toy with you, the way a cat teases a mouse before the final feast. Can't you see his black eyes gleam while he throws out comments about your future life together?"

"Dear Lord, yes," said Melissa, mopping at her tears. "And every glance will raise the horror of it all."

"Steady, Missy," murmured Bea again. "Nothing is settled. And Toby will likely postpone any agreement if he cannot produce the goods."

"What is that supposed to mean?"

"We must leave tonight."

"And go where?" Melissa scoffed.

"Your grandmother's house." A hand stayed the inevitable protest. "After this she can hardly refuse you, but if she does, you can come home with me."

"It will never work, Bea. It's at least a four-day trip. They will follow and catch us, and I will be worse off than I am now."

Bea joined her on the couch. "Then we must cover our trail. We cannot travel as Lady Melissa and Mrs. Stokes. Nor can we go as gentility. 'Ow's this, me pet?" she cackled suddenly in broad cockney.

Melissa choked. "Where did you learn that?"

"Off'n a maggoty scapegallows workin' in me stables." She changed back to her normal voice. "We'll both be aloof and quiet, but I can carry it off for brief stretches. We'll book as Mrs. Sharpe and her niece Harriet. And we must change your appearance."

Hope raised Melissa's spirits. She threw herself into the game. "Betsy will know how. She was telling me not long ago about a concoction that darkens hair but washes out within weeks."

"Good. And we'll go back into full mourning. Wear that horrid gown, the one that looks like a housekeeper's dress."

"It is the housekeeper's dress."

She laughed. "I'll use that monstrosity I wear for gardening. And I saw a hideous bag bonnet in the attic that will hide my hair."

They continued planning, even while Betsy smeared a dreadful vegetable paste on Melissa's light-brown locks. The girl would accompany them. Even if she had been unwilling, they could not have left her behind to bear Toby's anger.

That evening, they dined upstairs as they honed their plans. The groom—who was utterly trustworthy, for he hated Toby after an unjust beating several years earlier—had agreed to drive them to Lincoln. That way no one they knew would see their disguises. As soon as the men were engrossed in their evening card game, the ladies slipped away. Melissa left a note repudiating any betrothal and announcing that she was going home with Beatrice.

They had to travel by stage, for their resources were unable to stretch even to a mail coach. The second day of the trip was more uncomfortable than the first, with rutted roads and sullen passengers. The third was worse, as the weather turned vilely wet and blustery. The driver finally had to stop at an undistinguished country inn when the road became too mired to proceed. But the worst disaster had been their discovery that Melissa's grandmother was from home.

One of the passengers who boarded at their quick lunch stop was a groom who spent the afternoon in conversation with a clerk from his home village. The groom mentioned a message he was to deliver, announcing that Lady Castleton had decided to stop in Bath for a fortnight instead of returning directly home. Melissa was horrified. She and Beatrice could not afford two weeks of inns. It had occurred to neither of them that a lady of five-and-seventy might amuse herself by visiting friends.

They discussed their predicament after reaching their room, but they could not agree about what to do. The discussion had turned acrimonious, halting only when someone knocked on the door.

Beatrice answered.

A well-dressed gentleman stood in the hall, the cocky smile indicative of advanced inebriation decorating his handsome face. He handed a card to Beatrice and bowed.

"Lord Rathbone at your service," he slurred. "I occupy the next room and could not help overhearing you. May I offer you housing for a fortnight in return for a slight favor?"

Chapter Two

After one look at the room's occupants, Charles wanted to sink through the floor. The lady frowning suspiciously at his card appeared to be in her mid-thirties, her striking appearance demanding a second glance despite the mourning black that swathed her tantalizing figure. Light brown hair framed a heart-shaped face in luscious waves. But she would not do for his purposes.

Shock highlighted her companion's face. And chagrin, for she had been sprawled vulgarly across the bed when he appeared in the doorway. She hurriedly sat up and tucked her bare feet out of sight. But she looked no more than fourteen, her thin, undeveloped figure lost in an oversized, unbecoming black gown, and her black hair hanging limp and lifeless. Dull eyes surrounded by dark circles stared from a pinched, almost skeletal face that appeared yellow in the wavering light. She looked like a waif. But perhaps he was being unduly harsh. The tiny room was lit only by two tallow candles. Could he pass her off? A second piercing look at that flat chest almost sent him running. He should have waited until morning and examined his neighbors first. But here he was, and here he would stay. Desperation could find hope in even the most unpromising situations.

"Lord Rathbone?" echoed the older lady, puzzlement clear in her musical voice.

"At your service," he repeated. "And you are . . ."

"Mrs. Sharpe," she responded. "This is my niece, Miss Harriet Sharpe."

She nodded at the girl on the bed who reluctantly curved her lips into the parody of a smile. Stony hostility glared from her eyes. "What is the favor you seek, my lord?" Harriet demanded harshly.

"It depends." Nervousness robbed his voice of composure. The girl's tone was as quelling as that of the haughtiest dowager. Paradoxically, her patent antagonism hardened his resolve. "How old is Miss Sharpe?"

"Sixteen." Belligerence stiffened Mrs. Sharpe's back.

"This may work, then." He fought to keep surprise out of his voice. "I occupy the next room. As you can see, the rooms were originally one and the partition is thin, so I could not help overhearing your exchange. You two stand in need of a fortnight's lodging. I need help for that same period of time. Perhaps we can assist one another."

"How?" demanded Harriet.

"It is a long story," he admitted, looking pointedly at a chair. He would fall if he did not soon get off his feet. It had been years since he had drunk so much.

Mrs. Sharpe motioned him to sit, even as Harriet opened her mouth, apparently to protest.

"My grandmother is Lady Lanyard," he began. "She declared me her heir when I was still in short pants, and has frequently assured me that her considerable fortune would come to me on her death. Through no fault of my own, my financial position is precarious, and Grandmama's money is essential if I am to rescue my estate from ruin. I just received a letter informing me that she is ill and not expected to live. She has summoned her solicitor to make revisions to her will, and for the first time ever, she has stated that I will be her heir only if I am married."

He paused for a response but none was forthcoming. The barest expression of polite interest showed on Mrs. Sharpe's face, and her niece appeared totally bored. He had never had a less attentive audience, but he slogged ahead, trying to force his renowned charm into his words.

"I know no one whom I would consider for a wife, nor is it likely that I could contract an alliance until next Season. I had thought to point out the impossibility of my grandmother's request, hoping that she would agree to leave me the inheritance contingent upon marriage. But my argument will carry more weight if I can produce a prospective bride. I would like Miss Sharpe to pose as my betrothed during my grandmother's final days. Lady Lanyard can die happy, and I will have the necessary time to make a wise choice of spouse."

Harriet was frankly staring. "You belong in Bedlam," she snapped. "Do you expect me to willingly employ deceit so you can win a fortune? I presume there is no question of continuing the charade beyond a fortnight."

"It would only be for a few days, Miss Sharpe," he hastened

to assure her. "I don't know how Grandmama came by this idiotic idea. She can hardly expect me to jump blindly into a marriage that will remain in effect for the rest of my life. Such a hare-brained scheme would produce no benefit to either party and would contradict one of her own favorite adages. *Marry in haste, repent at leisure.* I suspect that her mind may be slipping, though she has been uncannily prescient until now. But I cannot risk my future by arguing with her. I must produce a candidate for my hand."

"How do we know you speak the truth?" asked Mrs. Sharpe. "You might fabricate such an unlikely tale when your real goal is to cut out a rival for her fortune."

Fury sparked in his eyes. "I am a gentleman, madam," he growled.

"I have had too many dealings with so-called gentlemen to believe anyone's protestations," stated Harriet firmly. "A more dishonorable bunch of animals I cannot imagine. What other family members might be in line for this inheritance?"

"None."

"You have no other relations?"

"Only a cousin, but he is wealthy and has never desired Grandmama's money. Nor has she ever been partial to him."

Absently chewing a fingernail, Harriet stared wordlessly at her aunt. Goose bumps skittered down Charles's spine. Why couldn't he have presented this scheme to someone who understood what being a gentleman meant? He despised begging.

"What would such a charade entail?" Harriet demanded at last.

"You would pose as my betrothed. We would have to decide how we met, be prepared to relate our plans, and devise a suitable background for you. You would meet with Lady Lanyard once or twice, possibly alone. And we must keep up the pretense of a betrothal at all times. The servants report everything to her. She should not live beyond a few more days, but regardless of her health, you would be free to leave in a fortnight."

Harriet frowned, looking to Mrs. Sharpe for assistance as she resumed nibbling a finger. All her nails were gnawed to the quick. Charles shuddered at the sight, his head resuming its swirling so that he lost track of the conversation.

"I deplore deceit," Harriet murmured to her aunt.

"If the facts are as stated, it is not that bad," Bea countered.

"How do we know he is truthful? Toby's friends often lie when they want something."

"Do we have a choice?" asked Beatrice. "Where else can we go?"

Harriet pressed her hands over her face, blotting out the sight of Lord Rathbone. His looks were disconcerting. His physique was ideal for displaying current fashions—the shoulders unusually broad and the waist elegantly slender, giving his coats the proper nipped-in appearance without the aid of either padding or corsets. Long, muscular legs made the most of his tight pantaloons. His blond curls were arranged negligently around a handsome face dominated by beguiling aqua eyes. But there was nothing of the dandy about him. His shirt points did not endanger his eyes, and his cravat was modestly elegant. She pegged him as a Corinthian for his muscularity and the graceful athleticism that showed despite his inebriation. And he was tall. His head had brushed the lintel of the door.

Why must so well-set a man beg favors from a stranger? But perhaps that was the appeal. He might not dare approach a friend. If his grandmother recovered, she would mention the supposed betrothal to others, forcing him into marriage. Harriet did not believe that he would look for a wife the following Season. He must hope that producing a candidate now would remove all conditions. Using a stranger would leave him free. If word leaked out, he could always claim his intended had jilted him. He would have no qualms about blackening Harriet's reputation.

But that was a point in her favor. Unbeknownst to him, she was already engaged in a charade. The nonexistent Harriet Sharpe could disappear without a trace, never seeing Lord Rathbone again. And there was no guarantee that her grandmother would take her in. She might yet go to America with Beatrice. The possibility actually appealed to her, for here in England her prospects were dim. Toby would never be in a position to bring her out, nor would Lady Castleton. Although the dowager was currently engaged in an unfortunate round of visits, her lack of funds would prevent her from presenting a granddaughter to society. Her father's constant complaint before his wife's death had been her family's inability to help them financially.

Rathbone belched, spewing brandy fumes into the room and reminding Harriet of all the distress of the past month. She had hoped to never again set eyes on a dissolute gentleman. Was this one another irresponsible drunkard who needed saving from the consequences of his actions? Hadn't she put up with enough of this from Toby?

"Please, Miss Sharpe?" His voice interrupted her thoughts.

She ignored him. "I have trouble with the idea of deceit," she stated, again frowning as she addressed her aunt.

"We could at least explore the situation," pressed Beatrice. "If he has lied, we will disclose the truth and depart, leaving us no worse off than we are now. Otherwise, no one would be hurt."

"You have always been the pragmatic sort." Harriet scowled. "But this is going too far. Dishonor is intolerable."

"I suspect he is truthful," mused Beatrice. "He is worsening his own situation if he is not."

"You will find that everything is exactly as I stated," Rathbone interrupted to assure them.

Harriet continued to frown. Bea was right about one thing— they had no place to go. "All right, Lord Rathbone. I will help you as long as I am convinced that the situation warrants it."

He relaxed into an easy smile. "Thank you, Miss Sharpe, Mrs. Sharpe."

"You are welcome," said Beatrice. "What time will we leave?"

"It depends on this storm." He shrugged. "Will you breakfast with me at eight?"

"Until then, my lord." Harriet's voice was dismissive.

He rose to depart, but stopped at the door. "If we are to pretend a betrothal, Harriet, you must call me Charles."

Mindful of the thin wall, the argument that followed was waged in whispers. Melissa feared the proposed masquerade. If her identity became known, it would destroy her reputation. And there was something frightening about Lord Rathbone. He reminded her of Lord Heflin, for he exuded the same sense of power, awareness of his own appeal, and arrogant determination to ride roughshod over anyone who thwarted his desires. And Rathbone's intelligence was also suspect. Who would choose a conspirator while roaring drunk? He had to have been planning this since he received word of his grandmother's illness. And choosing her was just plain stupid. Harriet stood little chance of convincing his family that a London Corinthian wished to wed a country miss who looked like nothing more than a little girl playing dress-up.

Beatrice countered Melissa's arguments with the oft-repeated observation that if anything proved to be amiss, they could call off the deception and leave, though where they were to go was never addressed. Bea considered Rathbone's offer just another example of aristocratic stupidity that they might as well milk for their own benefit.

Much as she liked Beatrice, Melissa got tired of hearing about American democracy and tolerance. It was easy for Bea to be tolerant, for she had nothing to lose. Whatever happened, she could return home with no one the wiser. But Melissa faced the possible destruction of her life. In the end, however, she gave it up. She had already agreed. Honor would not allow her to renege unless she had proof of perfidy.

"Good morning, Harriet," said Charles, smiling as the ladies arrived for breakfast. The smile covered a grimace. He had awakened with a pounding head and a prayer that it had all been a nightmare. But here she was, looking even worse than he remembered, in a hideous lavender gown. In the wan light that filtered through the single filthy window, her face was even more sallow, almost jaundiced, and its skeletal appearance was accentuated by the tight knot into which she had pulled her hair. He shuddered. How could he convince his usually astute grandmother that he was in love with the chit? But it was much too late to call off the charade. The stage had already left.

"Good morning, my l— Charles," Harriet replied.

"I understand you have a maid with you."

"Yes."

"We must wait until my baggage coach catches up, then." He sighed. "My curricle cannot hold five. Even the three of us would be uncomfortable, for it is three hours from here to Lanyard Manor."

Seating the ladies at the table, he again hid a grimace. The top of Harriet's head was at least two inches below his shoulder. She appeared little more than a child. He had never been attracted to petite females, preferring taller wenches whose bodies molded to his own in bed. And he abhorred the schoolroom set. His eyes refused to remain on her pinched face.

They ate in silence. If anything, the food was worse than it had been the night before. Harriet gave up after the barest taste, and Mrs. Sharpe managed just one helping. But Charles ate greedily, starved despite his pounding head. He had consumed nothing the previous day except brandy and hoped that food might counter the alcohol's effects.

"I believe that we should claim your age as seventeen," Charles began once he had pushed his plate away. "Grandmama will not think kindly of someone still in the schoolroom."

"That is reasonable," she agreed.

"You are in mourning?"

"My father died seven months ago."

"That can explain why you skipped the Season, and it gives us an excuse for not wedding immediately. We will tell her that our betrothal will be announced when you are out of black gloves. The wedding will be at the end of next Season to give you an opportunity to acquire some town bronze before settling down."

"How did we meet?" She grimaced, replacing her cup on the table.

He hoped her expression was for the atrocious coffee and not for his suggestions. "Might I have attended your father's funeral?"

"Unlikely. Country funerals in midwinter involve only family and neighbors, even among the aristocracy. Where do you live?"

"Kent."

"Very unlikely, then. Perhaps we met at the estate of a mutual friend."

"Who?"

"Pick someone." She glared. "I doubt I know anyone in your circle, my lord."

"Charles," he reminded.

"Charles."

How stupid of him, he reminded himself. She sounded genteel, but she could not hail from the aristocracy. That gown could only belong to a rustic, for it bore no trace of style. Nor did he know in which part of the country she lived. Her voice was undistinguished, while her aunt's held a subtle accent he could not place. His eavesdropping had left the impression that the ladies had traveled a considerable distance before fetching up at this inn. But at least Harriet seemed sensible. Most girls her age were giddy gigglers.

"We must invent a suitable background." He sighed, running a hand through his hair and further disarranging his curls. Fabrications risked exposure. "You are the daughter of

Eleanor Harrison, youngest daughter of Lord Beverly. He is a hermit, having shown his face to no one in nearly fifty years, and his sons follow in his footsteps. His estate is somewhere in Yorkshire. Your father was the younger son of a vicar. Your mother died when you were born. You know little of Lord Beverly as he turned your mother off when she married beneath her."

"What sort of lord is Beverly?"

"A baron."

"All right," she agreed. "My father was Howard Sharpe. We can claim that he inherited a small estate from his great-uncle, Lord Purvey—he was a viscount who died with no heir, so the title and entailed estates reverted to the crown. Father could not accede to the title as Lord Purvey was his grandmother's brother. The estate produces little income, so the Sharpe family has never entered society. How did we meet?"

"It must have been recently." He frowned in thought.

"It must have been before my bereavement," she countered.

"No. I would scarcely have come in contact with the school-room set. That long ago you would have been there, even if we claim an age of seventeen now. I can hardly push it further. No one would believe you to be eighteen." He rose to pace the floor. Where had he been in recent months that he might have encountered her without the knowledge of anyone else? "I have it. While visiting friends this past February, my horse stepped in a rabbit hole hidden beneath a crust of snow, throwing me into a wall. You were passing, observed the incident, and assisted me to your house, where I remained for some hours until my friends could send a carriage. My horse was lamed by the accident."

"Did such a thing really occur?" she asked, sounding surprised that a Corinthian would admit such ignominy.

"Actually, yes. Fortunately, Charger's injury was not serious. I suffered concussion and a sprained wrist."

"And where did this take place?"

"Lincolnshire. Do you know the area?"

"I have been there," she admitted. "It is pretty country."

"Good. You can describe your home if necessary."

"Where was this party?"

"Willingford House, near Market Rasen. Is that near where you visited?" She was gnawing her fingers again. He grimaced. It was a deplorable habit.

She nodded. "I believe I have passed through there. Is it northeast of Lincoln?"

"Yes." This was going to work, he exulted silently. What a coincidence to discover a chit who knew Lincolnshire! He thrust down his trepidation at the look on her face. Was there an unfortunate memory attached to that journey through Market Rasen? "I was impressed with your nursing skill and your character, returning several times during my visit to speak with you. I paid a further visit at the end of the Season, at which time we agreed to an unofficial betrothal. Should anyone care to check on my movements, I was absent from my usual haunts for a week at the end of June." He had actually been combing the attics at Swansea for something to sell that would finance his summer in Brighton. His circumstances were daily becoming more precarious. "We reluctantly parted at the end of a week, not seeing each other again until I fetched you when I learned of Grandmama's last illness."

"Good. That visit would coincide with my emergence from deep mourning. Now what should I know of you, my lord?"

"Charles," he reminded again. "Please, Harriet, you must remember to call me Charles."

"Very well, Charles. What must I know of you?"

"First tell me of Mrs. Sharpe."

"I am her father's sister-in-law," lied Beatrice calmly. "I visited them after my husband was killed. When Howard died, I stayed to help Harriet, but must now resume my own life. I am escorting my niece to her grandmother's house, after which I will depart."

"And what part of the country are you from, Mrs. Sharpe?"

"No part. My home is in America. I return in one month."

"I see." That explained her accent. He resumed pacing the floor, his forehead creased in thought and pain. Perhaps he should incorporate the move into his story. He would hardly have had time to travel to Lincolnshire and back since receiving this summons. He had pressed his team harder than usual just to get this far.

"Do you have any other family?" he asked.

"Only a brother," murmured Harriet.

"Why, then, are you leaving home?"

"I need a chaperone until such time as I can seek a husband."

"We will use that in our story," he decided. "You are staying with your grandmother until our marriage—it must be the vicar's wife, now a widow. Lord Beverly is a widower. I was already escorting you there when this summons arrived."

Charles grimaced. That was a lot of people to keep straight. But he had no choice. "We had already left your home and received Grandmama's summons on the way." Could he expect anyone to have followed him with the news? No. But his grandmother would not know that. He must have a word with Renfrew. And Harper. A dangerous number of people must know of this charade. If only he had thought this through before proposing it. *But you were drunk . . .* He needed to calm his throbbing head.

"What must I know of you?" asked Harriet for the third time, as he took a long pull from a flask of brandy.

"My full name is Charles Henry Montrose. I am a viscount, acceding to the title eight years ago when my father died. My estate, Swansea, is in Kent, though it is in poor repair, as I mentioned last night. I have no house in London, but keep rooms there. My mother died when I was three. Father never remarried so I am an only child."

"What are your interests, Charles?"

"Sports of all kinds. And art," he admitted, almost sheepishly. A love of art had never conformed to his image of the ideal Corinthian.

"Do you draw?" Her brows lifted in surprise.

"Some."

"You must show me your work. We need to have something in common."

"You also enjoy art?"

"Very much."

"Do you ride, Harriet?"

"Quite well, though it has been a couple of years since I have had access to a quality mount."

"How about driving?"

"Equally well, though I've driven nothing worthy for some time."

Who was this girl? he wondered suddenly. How had an impoverished chit come to be a good driver by age fourteen? Of course she might be exaggerating her skills. He must test her before arriving at Lanyard Manor. It was crucial that he not misstate her expertise, for that was one area in which he was unmatched. He had always rued the lack of funds that prevented him from supporting a coach and four. Membership in the Four-in-Hand Club was his fondest dream.

Harriet already felt trapped in a web of deceit. It had been foolish to agree to so ignoble a venture. She lived barely three miles from Willingford House and now recalled details of Rathbone's February accident. Everyone had laughed over the discomfort suffered by one of London's noted Corinthians. But there was more. That house party had included a number of highborn families, gathered for a celebration of Valentine's Day. If the Draytons had not been in deep mourning, they would have been included as well. Lord Willingford had planned a fortnight of activities, hoping his daughter might form an attachment and eliminate the need for a London Season. But the only attachment to arise involved his wife. She had been discovered in an indecent embrace with one of the guests, who precipitously departed. His name was Lord Rathbone.

Harriet watched as he restlessly paced the room. This was going to be even trickier than she had supposed. Many people must contribute to the charade—herself, Rathbone, Bea, and Betsy, as well as Rathbone's groom, coachman, and valet. Success would be less likely with each new player. But she must concentrate on her own role. Double deceit would make it doubly difficult. While she was convincing Lady Lanyard of her attachment, she must prevent Lord Rathbone from discovering her real identity. And on top of everything else, there was no reason to trust the man. He had been drunk the night before and was already imbibing brandy at breakfast.

Harriet Sharpe was a figment of the imagination and must remain so, for giving Rathbone the means to contact her would place her reputation in jeopardy. In order to keep her stories straight, she must stick to the truth whenever possible. But that was dangerous. If she built up too clear a picture of her life, someone might stumble on to her identity. Her father had been reclusive, out of necessity rather than choice, and had not been near London since his marriage. But Rathbone had friends in her neighborhood. Then there was Toby. He had not attended a university, but some of his schoolmates had, and Rathbone looked about the same age. He would know Toby's friends, for they all frequented London. It was going to be tricky to build her background as a real person without revealing the truth. She hoped that her mention of her former neighbor, Lord Purvey, would not come back to haunt her.

The arrival of Rathbone's groom postponed further conversation.

"The roads are passable," Charles reported when the man had left. "Mrs. Sharpe, you will ride in the carriage with your maid and my valet. Harriet will ride in the curricle with me and my groom. We must continue this discussion if we are to carry off the masquerade with any hope of success. And I need to see how developed your driving skills are, my dear."

She glared at him but offered no response. Insufferable toad! How dare he imply she was guilty of exaggeration! *He thinks you a country nobody*, she reminded herself. *Why should he believe you?* It was going to be an interminable two weeks.

Chapter Three

Harriet sat in silent trepidation as Lord Rathbone tooled his curricle along a muddy road. Second, third, and even fourth thoughts were rampaging through her skull. How had he talked her into this farce? She deplored deceit. She despised greed. Yet she was helping an arrogant toad fraudulently acquire a fortune.

After an hour alone with him—for the groom perched up behind hardly counted—she had decided that he was even more odious than Lord Heflin. Admittedly, he had made no move to force attentions on her, but he treated her like a half-witted child who knew nothing of society, or even of polite manners. She bore it as long as possible, reminding herself that he believed her to be a member of the lower classes. It was doubtful he could know how upset she was, since she was wearing an old-fashioned, deep-brimmed poke bonnet that masked her features unless she stared directly at the observer. But his condescension finally became too much for her always fragile temper.

"You are insufferable, my lord," she snapped, looking at him for the first time since leaving the inn and letting the full force of her fury blaze in her eyes. "I am no longer in the nursery. Nor am I ignorant of basic manners. It would be better to use this time to teach me about your grandmother's household."

He stared, then turned on a charming smile. "I am sorry, Harriet. But you made no mention of an aristocratic background."

"Odious toad! What did you take me for? A scullery maid? The nobility does not hold a monopoly on politeness, my lord. Only on arrogance and condescension."

"Enough!" *What a termagant*! he thought as she turned her attention to a colt kicking up its heels in a distant meadow. He shook his head, trying to relax before his own temper shat-

tered. His temples pounded, and the foul-tasting breakfast
churned unpleasantly in his stomach. Perhaps appeasement
would soften her ire. "We cannot afford to brangle, my dear.
We will be there in a couple of hours. Suppose you drive now.
I believe I've taken the freshness off the horses."

"Meaning they are practically dropping in the traces," she
muttered darkly. But she accepted the ribbons, taking a moment to get the feel of his team before setting them to a spank-
ing trot that kept them well into their bits. It was obvious she
had some experience, which soon quieted the groom's muffled
protest.

"Ah, but you're a bang-up pair of nags," she murmured.
"Jake would have loved you, lads."

"Watch the cant," snapped Charles, temper again close to
exploding. "Ladies do not use such language."

He remained tense for several minutes, but had to admit that
she was a competent whip. Whatever her current situation, she
had been taught by a master. He still did not know her background, but decided to quit brangling over social skills. She
would never pass as a paragon anyway. Her gestures were too
broad and her voice too strident.

His mind wandered as the curricle bounced over the rutted
road. It had been years since he had suffered from too much
wine, and he had forgotten how unpleasant it was. He would
have done better to spend the morning in bed. And it had been
lunacy to burden himself with the inn's unidentifiable breakfast.

Harriet drove for half an hour before reluctantly returning
the ribbons to Lord Rathbone's control. It had been marvelous
to handle a quality team again, and equally enjoyable to ride
with a competent whip. She had watched his hands when they
first left the inn. Rumor of Rathbone's horsemanship had not
been exaggerated, which would have made his accident all the
more embarrassing.

"You had best describe your grandmother, my lord," she
said now, turning to look at him. If only she had another bonnet. This one hindered her vision. "Tell me whatever you
would expect your betrothed to know on a first visit."

"You must practice calling me Charles," he reminded.

"Yes, Charles." She sighed. "But such familiarity is difficult, especially toward one I don't particularly like."

She saw his anger at her words, but had no time to repent

before his face blanched. He looked so much like Mr. Craw-ford had on that night at Drayton Manor that she gasped.

"Here!" He jerked the team to a stop, thrust the ribbons into her hands, and vaulted to the ground. He had barely disap-peared into a copse when the sound of retching wafted back on the breeze.

Harriet shrugged at the groom and signaled him to help. She had eschewed breakfast, not liking its very peculiar taste. Now she wished she had mentioned her suspicions. It had probably been tainted. Was Bea all right? The carriage was nowhere in sight.

Harper helped Rathbone back to the curricle.

"You drive," he moaned, slumping into the seat and closing his eyes. He looked like death.

"Your grandmother?" she prodded half an hour later when he appeared to perk up.

"She was a beauty in her youth," he began. "Blue eyes, tall, with glorious golden hair. I will show you her portrait tomor-row. It is the most arresting picture in the gallery. She was un-doubtedly one of the reigning diamonds of her day. Age has been kind, though her health has deteriorated over the last two years. She has been a loving person all of my life, supporting me even when she disapproved my actions."

"I take it you are prone to deplorable escapades," she com-mented curtly.

"No more than anyone else," he denied. "Her marriage to Lord Lanyard was her second. The first was to a wealthy busi-nessman. They had no children, so he left his entire fortune to her, tied up so that even remarriage left her in control. Lord Lanyard was also very wealthy. When he died, everything went to their only son, so she declared that hers would ulti-mately go to their only daughter, my mother. Within the year, my mother died. Grandmama had never liked my father, so she announced she would leave it directly to me."

"Why?"

"If you mean why did she dislike him, the man had a posi-tive genius for funding ventures doomed to failure."

Harriet wondered if he were different, but did not ask the question. His financial acumen was none of her business.

"Describe her household, please," she commanded instead.

"She still lives at Lanyard Manor, occupying a separate wing from my uncle. He has four children, of whom two nom-inally live at home. But only Edith is sure to be there. She is fifteen. You must remember that you are supposed to be seventeen and out of the schoolroom. Don't get too chummy with her. She is the worst sort of prattlebox."

Where did an uncle come from? She stared at him in trepidation. His white face told her better than words that his concentration was elsewhere. Already he was confusing his stories. He had claimed only a cousin as an alternate heir, yet he now admitted to an uncle and at least four cousins. How many other relatives would turn up? Harriet added lying to Charles's already long list of foibles—drunkenness, greed, arrogance, condescension, questionable intelligence, debauchery. He had probably fudged other details to convince her to help him.

But just now he was suffering from the tainted breakfast. Four more times Harper helped him out of sight. Between stops she tried to learn as much as possible, as it was likely he would be confined to bed for a couple of days. She asked about the estate, which was just east of Bridport. So Harriet was not moving out of her way at all—she and Bea would have changed coaches there for the last leg of their journey to her own grandmother's house.

As they rode, they discussed her fictional background again, reviewing the names and relationships, and expanding the details of their February meeting. By the time she turned his curricle through the impressive stone gates of Lanyard Manor, she felt almost as nervous as if she really were meeting a prospective husband's family.

The park was beautiful, displaying the stamp of Capability Brown, though Charles claimed the landscape was actually designed by an assistant. Not until some minutes later did they top a rise and see the house. Harriet gasped. At least three times the size of Drayton Manor, the Elizabethan central block was flanked by Palladian and gothic wings. Despite their contrasting styles, the whole was harmonious, nestling into a valley that was protected by a row of hills from the nearby coast.

Wealth was everywhere evident, from the manicured perfection of the park, to the extensive gardens laid out around the house, to the house itself, which glowed with care. It made her feel the untutored rustic Lord Rathbone had assumed. But at least he would not find her a cringing schoolroom miss. Years of running Drayton Manor had given her the confidence to carry off this impersonation, despite her misgivings.

The carriage pulled up behind them, even as the groom ran

around to take the horses' heads. Charles helped her down, then turned to assist Beatrice.

"Chin up, my love," he murmured as they mounted the steps to meet an imposing butler.

"Of course." She pasted a false smile on her face.

"Masters." Charles nodded at the butler. "Is my uncle about?"

"He is with the dowager Lady Lanyard, my lord."

"I will see him as soon as I have cleaned up. This is my betrothed, Miss Harriet Sharpe, and her aunt, Mrs. Sharpe. Am I in my usual room?"

"Yes, my lord." Not a flicker of his eye expressed surprise at the unexpected guests.

Charles turned to Harriet. "As soon as you are recovered from our journey, have someone show you to the crimson drawing room. I will meet you there and introduce you to my grandmother."

"Thank you, Charles." She smiled, then went thankfully upstairs. How long would Rathbone be? His white face was again covered with cold sweat, the now-familiar anguish blazing from his eyes.

Her room was a delight, decorated in blue and gold, and holding the most comfortable bed she had ever seen. Bea occupied an adjacent room done in green and gold, and a connecting door allowed them easy access for consultation. A maid bustled in with a can of hot water, followed by Betsy and two footmen carrying luggage. Her shabby valises contrasted sharply with her surroundings.

"Are you all right, Bea?" asked Harriet, joining her cousin once she had washed and changed into her best dress. "Breakfast was tainted."

"I know." Bea sighed, stretching out on a couch. "But I should be fine. And you?"

"I did not eat it, but Rathbone is suffering."

"That explains how we arrived together."

"I should never have agreed to this farce," moaned Harriet. "How can I be a party to defrauding these people?"

"We've had this out before, Missy," countered Beatrice. "Have done with it. And it has already improved our lot. Can you imagine being on that stage after a tainted meal? There is no reason to back out unless we discover that someone is being hurt. So far, there is no evidence of that." Personally, she cared nothing for a family squabble over money. Keeping a roof over their heads was worth bending the honor of the fictitious Sharpes.

"He never mentioned his uncle," pointed out Harriet. "And the unmentioned uncle has four very-much-alive children."

Bea frowned. "Betsy will discover how the family is situated," she said at last.

"His new story is that the uncle inherited a fortune from his own father, allowing Lady Lanyard to leave hers to the sister, Lord Rathbone's mother."

"We will see."

"And Bea, do you remember that scandal in February involving Lady Willingford?" asked Harriet, pacing nervously before the fireplace.

"Vaguely. I paid little attention, as I do not know them. What does that have to do with anything?"

"Lord Rathbone was the gentleman who seduced her."

Bea frowned. "I see what you mean. But we need a place to stay. When you meet this grandmother, see if you can discover her real feelings. I cannot believe anyone in full possession of her senses would make these demands. Despite his lordship's denials, I suspect something havey-cavey. But whether by her or him, I do not know."

"Yet another level of deception." She sighed. "I only hope I do not slip and allow them to discover who I am. My reputation would never recover." Leaving home and traveling by stage was enough to tarnish it, she silently conceded, despite the presence of a maid and a widowed cousin. But there had been no acceptable alternative.

She rang for a servant and was soon entering an elegant Adam drawing room. Scarlet silk blazed from wall panels separated by gilded moldings. Each panel displayed a painting or formed a backdrop to a statue. Elaborate cornices framed an Italian stuccatori ceiling, its pattern mirrored in the Axminster carpet. Scarlet and blue upholstery decorated chairs and couches. Rathbone looked almost drab as he stood near the fireplace, despite his blue coat, gold-striped waistcoat, and buff pantaloons that disappeared into gleaming Hessians. At least his face showed a little color. With luck, they could complete this introduction before he succumbed to another bout of illness.

"You'll do," he shrugged, noting that she had changed into gray and had loosened a few wisps of hair to soften her face. The dress lacked style and was poorly constructed, but it was better than the lavender. Explaining his attraction to this girl would prove difficult. She would make a perfect governess if she was not still a child herself.

"Here." He dropped a small emerald ring into her hand. "If we are betrothed, you must wear a ring. This is hardly worthy of my intended, but my finances cannot be expected to stretch very far."

"Where did you find a lady's ring?" she asked, shoving it onto her finger, where it fit surprisingly well.

"It belonged to my mother and was still in her old room. I only hope that Grandmama does not recognize it."

There was nothing she could say. Reluctantly placing her hand on his arm, she allowed him to lead her away. They traversed several corridors in silence before he drew in a shaky breath and rapped on the double doors of a large suite.

"Uncle Andrew," he said, smiling at the imposing gentleman who answered the door.

Lord Lanyard's hair was still gloriously golden, in marked contrast to his dour expression. "Welcome, Charles. It took you long enough to get here," he complained.

"I could hardly drag Harriet through the mud," Rathbone answered calmly. "You know what the weather has been like. We had not planned to introduce her to the family until she is out of black gloves, but Grandmama's illness gave us no choice. Harriet, this is my uncle, Lord Lanyard. Uncle, my intended wife, Miss Harriet Sharpe."

"My lord," murmured Harriet, curtsying properly.

"Miss Sharpe." He was blatantly staring, a disbelieving frown marring his face. "And how long have you known my scapegrace nephew?"

She ignored his rudeness. "Since February, my lord. He had the misfortune to lame his horse near our house, and crack his head."

Lord Lanyard's eyes relaxed slightly. Evidently he knew of the accident.

"Is Grandmama able to receive visitors?" interrupted Charles.

"Yes. She is anxious to see you."

"You will excuse us, then." he patted Harriet's hand and smiled into her eyes. "Come, my love."

Lord Lanyard frowned as they disappeared into the next room.

Harriet's first impression of Lady Lanyard was of weak

frailty. As Charles voiced greetings and expressed disbelief that she would dare succumb to a mere chill, Harriet was able to examine the lady whose decree had led to this deception. The classic bone structure that had made her a diamond in her youth still gave her beauty, but her hair was now as white as her lacy bedcap. Her skin varied, stretched thin in some places, falling in parchment folds in others, its translucence a product of age and illness. But it contained fewer wrinkles than one would expect of a woman approaching eighty. The eyes were a pale, wintry blue, but when they turned on Harriet, the girl nearly gasped. They were not the eyes of terminal illness, muzzy and filled with pain. Intelligence flared there. And calculation. But what dominated their expression was anger.

Why?

Lady Lanyard was angry at the appearance of her grandson's betrothed, though she had demanded that he marry. Harriet doubted it was anything personal, despite her uninspiring appearance. Her ladyship knew nothing of her. Perhaps Beatrice was right. If Lady Lanyard's demand was designed to test Rathbone's worthiness, anger would indicate that he had failed. But whatever the truth, Harriet must carry out her own promise with the honor her birthright demanded.

"Grandmama, this is Miss Harriet Sharpe, my intended bride." Charles's voice dragged her attention back to the niceties. "Harriet, Lady Lanyard."

"My lady," murmured Harriet.

"And how long have you been betrothed?" the dowager demanded immediately.

"It will not be officially announced until my mourning period is concluded after Christmas," answered Harriet steadily. "But we have been unofficially promised for the past month."

Calculation thrust the anger from her eyes. "And how long have you known my grandson?"

She repeated the story of their meeting.

"Is that supposed to be a betrothal ring?" she asked sharply, holding Harriet's hand up to the light.

"No." Charles injected an amazing amount of charm into his voice. "Merely a small token of my affections, given on the acceptance of my hand. She will receive the Rathbone ring in December."

"Hmph," snorted her ladyship. "Nothing to prevent the announcement earlier."

"I could not so dishonor my father's memory, my lady," declared Harriet. "And there is no need to rush. I am only seventeen."

"I must rest," announced Lady Lanyard suddenly. "This cursed chill saps all my energy. Charles, you will attend me for tea when I awaken. I will speak with Miss Sharpe following dinner."

They left, Harriet marveling at how well Rathbone had managed when he must be dropping from weakness and pain.

Lady Lanyard summoned her son from the next room.

"What do you think?"

"She is certainly no high-flyer," he replied in a ponderous voice. "Nor is she an actress. Your fears on that score would seem unfounded. I wonder where he found her. She barely looks old enough to be out of the schoolroom."

"You do not believe the tale of his winter accident, then?"

"The tale is true, for I have heard it before. And it is possible that she might be the one who rescued him. But I cannot believe that he could develop a *tendre* for so drab a chit."

"My thoughts exactly. I am disappointed in the boy, for I thought he had more strength of character. I'll not leave my fortune to be dissipated on frivolity. But it is early days yet. Keep an eye on them when they are not in my august presence. And you might as well see what you can discover about that accident. Where did it occur?"

"Lincolnshire, I believe, Mama."

"Good. I will see if Miss Sharpe knows anything of the country thereabouts."

Sweat again coated Charles's forehead by the time they reached the brighter light of the family wing. "You had better lie down, my lord," Harriet murmured softly. "I can find my way back alone."

He nodded wordlessly, desperation flaring in his eyes. No servants saw him bolt for his room.

Harriet checked on Bea, who was feeling better, and described the scene in Lady Lanyard's suite.

"I would swear she was furious," she finished. "You were right to suspect her motives. There is more going on than even Lord Rathbone believes."

"We need to understand his lordship's character before we can begin to guess what is happening," mused Beatrice.

"It would serve him right if she cut him off," snapped Harriet.

"Watch yourself, Missy," warned Bea. "You must be doubly careful that your behavior is faultless. If his plans fail, you must give him no cause to blame you."

She gasped, for that possibility had never occurred to her. "I am expected to speak with Lady Lanyard after dinner tonight. I suspect it will be a private chat."

"Mind your tongue, and not just with her. Rathbone could prove dangerous if you rile his temper."

"We had best warn Betsy again," decided Harriet. "She must not give any hint of our real identities."

"I will take care of that now," promised Bea. "It is time I changed anyway."

Returning to her own room, Harriet stretched out to relax, but she was allowed no respite. A footman summoned her to meet Charles.

"Allow me to show you the house, my dear. You will feel more at home when you know your way about."

"Thank you, Charles. You are always so thoughtful." She smiled for the benefit of the butler, who was positioned just outside the door.

"Shouldn't you rest before meeting your grandmother?" she asked when they were alone.

"Later. This is more important. Besides, I believe the problem is waning. I swear I'll never overindulge again."

"But, this has nothing to do with last night's excesses," she said, raising surprise on his face. "Breakfast was tainted. Did you not know? Bea is also ill."

"Devil take it," he grumbled.

"It hasn't killed you," she observed cheerfully. "You should be right as rain in a day or two."

That earned her a glare. But she enjoyed the hour that followed. The house was magnificent, offering a delightful feast for the eyes. Not until they reached the conservatory did Charles relax into a frown.

"She will see you alone tonight, Harriet," he reminded her.

"I expected it, my lord."

"Damnation!" he exploded, pulling her into the shadows cast by several orange trees. His voice lowered to a hiss. "Will you cease this constant 'my lording?' Have you no sense at all?"

"Stubble it," she snapped. "I will not slip when anyone is around, but you hardly deserve such kindness."

"I don't deserve . . . ," he sputtered, fingers clutching as though he wished to strangle her. "I grabbed you off the street and offered you a roof over your head. Don't you dare tell me what I deserve."

"What arrogance! I'm doing you a favor that will mean the difference between poverty and affluence for the rest of your life. You need me far more than I need you."

"Without me you would be sleeping in a ditch."

"Only for a fortnight."

Anger blazed in his eyes, reminding her of Bea's warning.

"Enough of this brangling, Charles," she said in a calmer voice. "It is too late for either of us to debate who owes the other more. I suspect the servants will report it if we get into an argument. They cannot allow us to remain alone for long."

He drew in a deep breath, letting it escape with exquisite slowness as he visibly fought to control himself. "You are right, Harriet. But I am worried about you spending so much time with my grandmother. She is unnaturally canny. You must watch your step."

"I know she is canny. Her eyes reveal a great deal. She already suspects something havey-cavey between us. You were noticeably strained earlier. You must tell her of your illness or she will draw the wrong conclusions. Eating at tea will do you no good, anyway. But beyond that, she can hardly believe our tale. You would never choose a bride as unprepossessing as myself."

"Not for a marriage of convenience, certainly. But I am madly in love with you, my dear. Don't forget that. It is your inner beauty that attracts me." He nearly choked on the words.

"If you repeat such a taradiddle in that tone of voice, no one will believe you," she commented wryly. "You sound as though you are taking a purge."

He laughed suddenly, his natural charm surfacing. "That bad, is it? I must practice."

She giggled at the vision of a Corinthian standing in front of his mirror, practicing words of love while painstakingly examining his face. But his charm frightened her. She must guard against any real attraction.

"Perhaps it is your horsemanship that caught my admiring eye," he continued.

"That seems more plausible. I do ride well. I wonder why I

consented to marry you. Arrogance has never appealed to me, and I have yet to meet any lord who does not harbor odious traits I would never consider living with."

"My looks, perhaps? Women seem to like them."

"Hardly. I deplore handsome gentlemen. They are always so self-centered. Though perhaps I can pretend. Shall I become the sort of giddy chit who would fall for looks and a title? But that is unbelievable. Such girls demand a fortune as well."

"Few people realize my financial woes," he said gratingly, temper again close to exploding.

"Really? But that is hardly surprising in one so eager to embark on deceit. I should have realized it is a way of life for you. There must be something about you I can admire. You say you are fond of art?"

"Yes."

"I take it you have examined the paintings at the Royal Academy?"

"Of course."

"Perhaps it was your descriptions of those that first attracted my attention. A person who loves beauty cannot be all bad."

"All right. Let me escort you to the stairs. It is nearly time for tea." He shuddered. Under her questions, he described the current exhibit at Somerset House, demonstrating a genuine interest.

Dinner brought a host of new introductions. The entire family had gathered to spend these final days with Lady Lanyard. In deference to her illness, they assembled in the more intimate green salon preparatory to a meal in the family dining room. Harriet was grateful. She did not have a gown suitable for a formal dinner, and even her best was woefully inadequate compared to those worn by the other ladies.

Charles joined her when she appeared in the door, touching her hand to his lips as he held her eyes with his own. He must have been practicing. He actually looked smitten.

"At last, my love." He smiled. "Come and meet my family." Placing her hand on his arm, he led her to Lord Lanyard's side, with Beatrice trailing behind.

"You already know Uncle Andrew. This is his wife, Lady Lanyard, my Aunt Agnes. My betrothed, Miss Harriet Sharpe, and her aunt, Mrs. Beatrice Sharpe."

They exchanged suitable greetings. Lady Lanyard was approaching fifty, her salt-and-pepper hair adding a touch of iron to an already austere expression. Harriet could not imagine two more dour-looking individuals than the Lanyards. No trace of warmth lit their eyes, and she was grateful when Charles led her toward another group by the fireplace.

"My oldest cousin, Edward; his wife, Josephine; and my cousin, Lucas," said Charles.

Edward was a younger version of his father, complete with dour face and frosty wife. But Lucas offered more promise. Dressed in the high shirt points, elaborate cravat, and brightly colored jacket of a fop, he quizzed her with his glass before breaking into a grin.

"Where have you been hiding Miss Sharpe, cousin? I swear she's not been near London."

"Naturally not," rejoined Charles. "Can't you see she's in mourning?"

"As we all will be soon," intoned Edward, his glare erasing the smile from Lucas's face.

Another couple joined them.

"This is my cousin, Charlotte, and her husband, Sir Harry Ruskin," said Charles. "They arrived even later than we did and have barely had time to remove the dust of travel—or mud, in this case."

Harriet smiled, though Charlotte looked nearly as cold as Edward. She hoped it was not a family trait, but perhaps their grandmother's illness accounted for it. She had not thought her ladyship at death's door, but she was no doctor.

Her initial impression softened as the group dissolved into general conversation. Charlotte was an unexceptional lady whose daughter shared the nursery with Edward's son. Once she embarked on describing dear Mary, animation drove all hint of toploftiness from her face. Beatrice was locked in a lively discussion of America with Lord Lanyard that made the man seem approachable. Charles was enduring good-natured teasing from his cousin Lucas.

"Does this mean the ladies of London are finally safe?" asked Lucas with a chuckle.

"Watch your tongue, cuz," warned a noticeably irritated Charles. "But yes. Harriet will have my head if I look at another female. Not that I want to."

Lucas stared. "Are you serious?"

Charles's eyes turned slaty with anger. "Are you implying something you shouldn't?"

"Never, Charles," denied Lucas, speculation lighting his face.

Harriet continued her conversation with Charlotte while admiring Rathbone's performance. He was quite an actor, his anger over the sideways jab at her drab appearance sounding genuine.

"Excuse us, please," interrupted Beatrice. "Missy, Lord Lanyard wants to hear the details of Lord Rathbone's mishap last spring." Harriet sighed, even as she set a smile on her lips and turned to comply. If he had heard tales of the accident, had he also heard rumors of why Charles had left Willingford House so precipitously?

Charles had dreaded introducing Harriet to the family, and having everyone gathered around a deathbed made it worse. It wasn't just her unknown social background that worried him. She was just sixteen! Could she carry off an evening with his toplofty cousins without stumbling? But she did. He grimaced to find her seated with his uncle and Edward, while he was at the far end with his aunt and Josephine. Between fielding his aunt's pointed questions and straining to hear Harriet's conversation, Charles forgot to accept only the blandest dishes. Yet everything seemed fine. Harriet even drew a smile from Edward and a chuckle from Uncle Andrew over some tale she was telling.

Charles fretted over the formalities of after-dinner port, wanting nothing more than to instruct Harriet on her upcoming interview. But when he reached the drawing room to find her gone, dinner turned to lead in his stomach, giving him no choice but to retire ignominiously to his room. Devil take the chit for not warning them that breakfast was bad!

Harriet's interview with Lady Lanyard was not nearly the ordeal she had feared. Whatever had prompted that earlier flash of anger had vanished. It turned out that her ladyship had often visited friends in Lincolnshire. Fortunately, they lived at the other end of the county, so Harriet hoped that her descriptions would not pinpoint Drayton Manor. It was bad enough to admit living near Willingford House.

She had given considerable thought to her charade. It would not do to paint a false picture of obsessive adoration. Aside from the impossibility of looking the part, she could never play so alien a role. She would admit to loving her supposed betrothed, but she would also admit to his faults. Wherever possible, she would stick to the truth of her own life, including the problem that her brother was not the sort of man she could live with in peace, even for the remainder of her mourning. That would explain why Charles was escorting her to her grandmother's house, where she would remain until her marriage.

So Harriet spoke of her home and of her brother's disreputable friends. She admitted hesitancy about putting herself in the care of a man whose own past contained some rather unsavory incidents—Betsy had heard of several already—but she believed his claim that such behavior was part of his youth and no longer relevant to his life.

And so the first day passed. Harriet went directly to bed after being dismissed from Lady Lanyard's room. Her only new fear was the impression that her ladyship was not as ill as she claimed. If her indisposition was not fatal, Lord Rathbone was in a pickle. But that was none of her concern.

Chapter Four

Harriet woke at her usual early hour. The morning sun was so enticing that she took a turn around the gardens before breakfast. It was a more formal setting that she preferred, but it offered sorely needed relaxation. Rows of Italian cypresses separated a series of reflecting pools, their shapes repeated by box hedges and regimented flower beds. After circling an eight-pointed star with plots laid out like a compass, she encountered another young lady.

"Who are you?" asked the girl, astonishment flickering in her eyes as Harriet appeared around the corner of a hedge.

"Miss Harriet Sharpe, betrothed of Lord Rathbone. And you?"

"Edith Lanyard, Lord Lanyard's youngest daughter. You hardly look old enough to be betrothed."

"I am seventeen."

"Really? I am only fifteen." She sighed.

Harriet could understand the question. Edith was already well endowed, her curvaceous figure the envy of one who remained flat and straight.

"Do you not like bonnets, either?" Edith asked in a conspiratorial whisper. "I despise them, though Mama will have twenty fits if she sees me."

"Normally I wear one," lied Harriet. "But I only slipped out for a moment to enjoy the sunshine, and did not anticipate meeting anyone."

"You know, my maid has a marvelous concoction that can add shine to even the dullest hair," the girl continued brightly.

"Th-thank you," stammered Harriet, her mind racing. That was another problem she had not anticipated. Darkening her hair and using a bonnet that shaded her face was an adequate disguise for escaping on the stage, but it would never do in bright light. The dye left her hair dull and lifeless, and there was danger that sharp eyes might note the stratagem. The color was not as even as she would have liked. Wearing hats in the house was so eccentric it would draw comment. But for her own peace of mind, she must avoid brightly lit rooms. The dining room had been somber, whether from clutchfistedness or in deference to Lady Lanyard's illness, she could not say. With luck, that would continue.

"Forgive my impudence," Edith said, misunderstanding Harriet's chagrin. "My governess chides me for my unbecomingly forward tongue. *A lady must never disparage another's appearance*," she quoted with a grin.

"Forgiven. Does your governess allow you to roam unaccompanied?"

"Actually, no. But she was called away, and I could not resist such a beautiful day." She giggled.

"Or the opportunity to read something forbidden?" guessed Harriet as she spotted the corner of a hastily hidden book.

Edith laughed. "So knowing. Yes, I do love a good book, though Miss Bekins and I disagree on just what fits that description."

Gothic novels, Harriet decided. "I take it that she is the improving sort?"

"Alas. Maria Edgeworth's *Moral Tales for Young People* is as exciting as she gets. But are you really betrothed to my dashing cousin?" demanded Edith, eyes shining with excitement. "You are the luckiest girl in the world."

"Yes, we are betrothed, and yes, I consider myself lucky. He is a wonderful man who shares many of my interests."

"You like sporting? But you must. He is a well-known Corinthian who delights in mills and races. And he is the best rider I have ever seen. Oh, how I wish he would take me to Newmarket! Perhaps you could ask?" Pleading blue eyes turned toward Harriet.

"Hardly. Races are not suitable for ladies, as you must know. The company is remarkably low."

"I suppose it is even more hopeless to ask to watch a mill. Oh, to be a boy!" She sighed. "Is his lovemaking as exciting as one would expect from a libertine of his experience?"

"Miss Bekins is right. You are an impudent young lady." Harriet prayed that she had not blushed. "Surely you know the limitations placed on couples, even those who are betrothed. And you must have been taught what constitutes proper conversation. I cannot picture your parents hiring an inept governess."

"Sorry, but you must know his reputation."

"Of course." It must be worse than she had imagined. Was he another Lord Heflin?

"Then you can hardly act shocked when I speak of it." Her eyes sparkled. "He is the most romantic of men. They say he has loved most of society's ladies, even those who claim him a scoundrel. No one ever terminates a liaison with him. His charm is legendary, as is his prow—" She broke off as it finally dawned that one did not repeat such stories to the betrothed of the gentleman in question. "You are right. I need to review acceptable topics of conversation. And now I must go, or Bekins will assign some dreary lesson as punishment."

"Which you will greatly deserve," said Harriet laughingly. She watched Edith scurry back to the house. The girl was at least as much a hoyden as she herself. The book had indeed been a gothic novel.

But her face snapped into a frown as she reviewed Edith's disclosures. So the incident with Lady Willingford had not been an isolated case, or even one born of country boredom. Rathbone was a libertine and scoundrel who had probably seduced half of London. No wonder he was so certain of his attraction. And no wonder his grandmother disapproved of his activities. Edith might find him romantically heroic, but in truth he led a sordid life. Shaking her head, she headed for breakfast. She must warn Beatrice. They had another rake on their hands.

Charles was enjoying a hearty breakfast. He had slept like the dead after one last round of illness, awakening in good spirits and feeling like a new man. But that lasted only until Harriet arrived. He grimaced as his eyes took in yet another shapeless gown, this one in the unbecoming lavender that made her look like an invalid. He sneezed.

"Haven't you anything decent to wear?" he murmured as he seated her at the table. He instantly regretted the words. She appeared to have no awareness of the constantly hovering servants.

"You knew what I looked like when you proposed," she said crossly. "And you know my circumstances. I haven't the means for a new wardrobe. Which would you prefer? Ignoring mourning to wear my own gowns, or observing mourning with makeovers of Mother's old dresses?"

"Surely you have something better. Grandmama will wish to see you again today."

"Don't turn toplofty on me now, Charles," she commanded, fire flaring in her eyes. "You've always claimed that my lack of a dowry made no difference, and that my looks were acceptable. You know very well you've never seen me in anything but mourning. Am I to suppose you were lying? You act ashamed of me."

Fury washed over him. As soon as the footman slipped a plate in front of her, Charles signaled him to leave.

"Watch your tongue," he hissed once the door was closed. "The servants will repeat everything you say to my grandmother."

"Then she will know that we are a normal couple who occasionally have spats," she said, raking him with a supercilious glare. "Radiating sweetness and light all the time is unreal. I am a young lady who is sensitive about my looks and my lack of money. Accepting the hand of a handsome lord must increase my own sense of inadequacy. You, on the other hand, are a haughty prig who had better think of a reason why you would overlook all your natural instincts to wed so dowdy a miss. And the reason had better be good. If you truly loved me, you would never embarrass me in front of the servants by criticizing my dress."

His fingers clutched air and his arms shook with the effort not to strangle her. "You must be a cit," he growled at last. "No lady would ever act thus."

"My background is irrelevant," she countered, her own eyes flashing. "Either you call off the charade right now, or you start treating me like a prospective bride. One thing I am not is biddable. I'll be no man's chattel, even in pretense."

"Jade!" he snapped, thrusting his plate so violently aside that it tipped over his coffee cup.

New anger over his clumsiness sent him storming from the room. Infuriating infant! How dare she criticize a man who was so far above her? The ten years difference in age alone should have prompted her to follow his lead, to say nothing of the vast gulf that separated them in position, in looks, in experience. She must be a cit. Nothing else could explain her brash manner. Yet she had lived in the country. Perhaps she was a squire's daughter. But where could any poverty-stricken country chit acquire so haughty a manner? She acted as though her standing were higher than his.

But a hard ride to the sea and back calmed his nerves. By mid-morning he admitted that his conduct had been unacceptable. Regardless of her background, he dishonored himself by so public a humiliation. She was right. As a guest in his grandmother's house and his supposed betrothed, she deserved better. He must ignore his personal repugnance if they were to have any hope of carrying off this masquerade. And he must never lose sight of the ultimate goal—without the inheritance, he would be chained to his estate forever. There would be no more Seasons in town, no more excursions to races or mills, no more opportunities to satisfy his hunger in the beds of London's loveliest matrons. And he could hardly blame Harriet for putting him in this position. He had initiated their bargain, insisting that she help him and ridiculing her objections.

But it was only for a fortnight. Heaving a sigh of resignation, he sent word that he wished to show her around the estate. They must stage a public reconciliation to counter their fight. And he was feeling worse again. Nothing had gone right since he met her.

Harriet stared into her tea, a frown wrinkling her forehead. The message had been necessary, though he might have listened better had she delivered it in a less confrontational manner. What would he do now? With luck, he would admit that his behavior was counterproductive if he meant to make this farce believable. Or he might call it off and toss her out of his grandmother's house.

She prayed that reflection would cool his temper. The thought made her grimace. Despite her abhorrence of the deceit upon which they were embarked, she recognized a selfish desire to continue it. Lanyard Manor was amazingly comfortable, and the food was both abundant and delicious. Her previous life had produced nothing even close, despite the fact that she was higher up the social scale than Lord Rathbone and much higher than Lord Lanyard. It would seem that she was just as devious as he. The thought of abandoning this refuge was unacceptable.

Polishing off two plates of breakfast, she returned to her room to discuss the latest developments with Beatrice.

Lady Lanyard pushed her breakfast tray aside and regarded the stiff footman who was standing just inside the door.

"Yes, James?" she prompted.

"They had quite a row at breakfast, milady," he reported. "He complained of her gown, and she set him down right smartly." He repeated the gist of the discussion. "Then he signaled me to leave. I couldn't hear what they said after that, but he slammed out of the room in a proper taking not five minutes later."

"Thank you, James. You may return to your duties."

She frowned for some time after the servant had gone. Whoever the girl was, she was not spineless. Few ladies dared deliver setdowns to charming gentlemen. She had rarely known a young girl to do so. And Harriet was frugal. That maid, Betsy, had served her for years and described some of her life, including tales of how she had run their estate for the past four years in the face of a weak father and a dissolute brother. Even this argument over clothing revealed a thrifty character. Lady Lanyard did not for a moment believe that her profligate grandson was in love with the chit. The girl was not his style. Nor did she know how he had talked her into either a betrothal or the pretense of one. The thought that she was a victim of seduction did not tally with the way Harriet put Charles in his place. Starry-eyed adoration was alien to Miss Sharpe's character. Lady Lanyard's inclination upon their arrival had been to cut the boy off without a penny. Now she was not so sure.

Charles reined in after a hard gallop across the fields. Harriet's habit was another horrendous creation. The brown velvet was worn bare with use and nearly splitting its seams. Her figure was even more off-putting than he had feared. And she again wore that concealing bonnet.

But she had not exaggerated her skill. He had taken her at her word, mounting her on a spirited bay mare that would give a fine ride to an excellent horsewoman but would inevitably toss anyone else. Harriet proved equal to the challenge, displaying a neck-or-nothing skill despite the limitations of using a sidesaddle, taking even high walls in stride, and rapidly developing rapport with her mount. For the first time since they had met, he felt in charity with her.

"You ride beautifully, Harriet," he complimented her now, leading them out of earshot of the groom.

"It has been one of my few pleasures," she admitted.

They walked in silence for several minutes until the horses were cooled enough to halt. He helped her down and led her to the top of a rise from which they could see the Channel.

"Gorgeous," she breathed.

The day was sunny and clear, with only the faintest hint of haze showing in the distance. Several fishing boats bobbed about, some already returning to port from a night's work. Out on the horizon, a ship of the line surged westward, the sight less menacing now that the war with France was finally over.

"You like it?" he asked idly, dabbing at his nose with a handkerchief. He feared he was catching a chill from driving an open curricle so long through a torrential downpour.

"Of course. The sea is even more majestic than I expected. I could drink in the view for hours." She climbed onto a low boulder, as if the added height might improve the already spectacular scene. What it did was bring her head level with his.

He cringed at the desire that suddenly erupted. He was in worse shape than usual and needed to find an excuse to ride into Bridport. But with the groom as an audience, he could at least snatch a kiss. He loosened her bonnet and bent his lips to hers.

Harriet stiffened. "What do you think you are doing?" she hissed.

"The groom is watching," he reminded her, sliding an arm around her shoulders.

If anything, she became stiffer. "That's enough of a show, my lord." Though she was whispering, anger and determination rang through the words. "There is no need for vulgar displays."

"Kissing one's betrothed can hardly be called vulgar."

"I might have known," she sighed, turning her head away to retie her bonnet. "Gentlemen are all alike. You are no better than Lord Heflin."

Shock snapped his face into a scowl that he barely remembered to keep turned away from the groom. "I refuse to occupy the same sentence as that reprobate," he spat, the force of his anger ruined when he sneezed.

"Why? You've a similar reputation."

"To paraphrase your breakfast comment, my background is none of your business, though you may rest easy. I draw the line at seducing innocents. But how did you become acquainted with him?"

"He visited our neighborhood," she murmured, relaxing though his arm still circled her shoulders. Her face was turned away as she watched a pair of gulls swooping over the sea.

"Did he accost you?"

"He tried, but I managed to escape. After that, I made sure I was never alone."

"You escaped him?" Disbelief was obvious. His arm tightened. "How?"

She giggled. "With a rather unladylike maneuver of the knee, accompanied by two stabs with a pair of scissors."

"My God!" exploded Charles, overwhelmed by laughter that turned into choking coughs. "What I would have given to see that! The man is insufferable."

"He is indeed. But be warned, my lord. I will not tolerate your attentions, either. I am no man's toy."

Humor faded from his eyes, and he sighed. "I would never dream of inflicting unwanted attentions. But you must recall that we are betrothed. I cannot ignore you. As you pointed out at breakfast—and I apologize, for you were right—we must carry out this scheme to the best of our abilities. If I am to convince people that we are in love, I must take every opportunity to touch you, and that includes the occasional stolen kiss."

"You need not do that in public. It will be sufficient if we slip away once in a while. What happens in private is between you and me alone. And since you dislike me, and I abhor arrogant fools, what happens in private will be a necessary counting of the minutes until we can thankfully return to company."

He grimaced, but offered no further argument. And why would he wish to argue, anyway? Harriet Sharpe was not attractive. She was barely sixteen, without a figure, and with minimal experience of life. He was hardly so desperate that he would consider raiding the nursery for a companion. He had no need to kiss her.

They returned to the horses and headed back to the house. Whatever charitable feelings her riding skills had raised rapidly disappeared. On dismounting she exchanged a comment with the groom that set them both laughing. Or rather, Billy laughed. Harriet brayed. Like a mule. Even worse was their return to the house. He shook his head. She did not walk. She strode. There was little difference between her and his groom. She might have learned table manners, but she exhibited none of the graces one expected of a lady. She did have a fine seat, though.

*   *   *

Lady Lanyard requested Miss Sharpe's company that afternoon. Despite her initial trepidation, Harriet soon relaxed under her ladyship's charm.

"My mother died in an accident when I was ten," Harriet replied to a question. "After that, I had little formal learning. We had not the means to pay for a governess, though a neighbor did invite me to study with her daughters for a year. I am untutored in the ways of society, but Charles will teach me what I need to know."

The neighbor was Lady Willingford. Harriet suppressed a shudder at the memories. Not of the pea-brained Willingford daughters, though being in their company was penance. But she had spent much of the year caught in an impossible tangle. Lady Willingford ostensibly accompanied her home each day, and Melissa was expected to support that story. But in fact, her ladyship was carrying on with another neighbor at the time. The catechisms Lord Willingford routinely conducted left Melissa with a permanent abhorrence of any deceit. Yet here she was.

"Perhaps it would be better to engage a companion who can help you feel more at home," suggested the dowager, pulling Harriet's thoughts back to the discussion.

"I will look into that, but I am not sure that Grandmama can afford it. She is elderly and has little income."

"I will speak to Charles on the matter. Even if he were to pay the lady's salary, it would be so small an irregularity that it would hardly count. And the benefits are obvious. But why are you not remaining with your brother?"

"He is weak and has acquired all manner of dissipated friends. It is unsafe to remain at home without protection, but my brother's funds do not extend to providing me with a chaperone. Now that Aunt Bea is returning to her own home, I must make other arrangements. Grandmama is the best choice. And I will not be much of a burden on her. I have been running my family's house since my fourteenth year, so I can assist her."

"How did Charles come to know you?" Lady Lanyard asked.

Harriet repeated the tale yet again. Was her ladyship growing forgetful? But those wintry eyes showed too much intelligence to accept that premise. Perhaps she was looking for inconsistencies. Suspicion of this all-too-fortuitous betrothal had to be expected.

"Excuse me for mentioning it, Harriet, but I have trouble believing that Charles is attracted to you. You are so different from his usual tastes."

"You are not alone. I too cannot believe he loves me as he claims," she admitted candidly. "It can't only be my horsemanship, or even my appreciation of art. Who would predict that so handsome and sophisticated a gentleman could offer for someone as dowdy and homely as myself? I hardly look a day over fourteen and despair of any change."

"As to that, do not give up hope," chuckled Lady Lanyard unexpectedly. "I too was late growing up. When you begin to develop, you will be amazed at the speed with which you catch up to the other girls. I'll show you what I mean. Bring me the painting that is in the drawer of my escritoire."

Puzzled, Harriet complied, retrieving a foot-square canvas of a family grouping.

"That is the Earl of Watts, Lady Watts, and his four children," commented Lady Lanyard. "This is me." She pointed to the youngest child, who appeared to be about thirteen. The tight lacing and wide skirts fashionable at the time in no way hid that straight, girlish figure.

"Your sister and brothers are considerably older," Harriet ventured.

"Actually, we are all two years apart. I was eighteen when this was painted. It is not a fact I am proud of, which is why this picture has never hung on display. It was done on the occasion of my betrothal. My appearance was largely responsible for the marriage my father arranged with my first husband, a wealthy manufacturer who was hoping a young bride might provide him with the family his first wife failed to produce. Don't misunderstand," she continued as Harriet gasped. "Despite the forty-year gulf in our ages, Thomas was a good man and we became close friends. But my father despaired of me, deciding I would never cut the sort of dash in society that was expected of Lady Abigail. By the time he discovered his error, it was too late. You must have Charles show you the gallery. There is a painting of me that you will like. It was done when I was nineteen, just after my marriage."

"I will certainly do so, my lady," promised Harriet. "And thank you for the encouragement. Perhaps I am too sensitive about my appearance."

"One must make the most of whatever the good Lord blessed us with," stated Lady Lanyard. "But having done that, never waste time or energy bemoaning that which cannot be changed. And Harriet—." The blue eyes sharpened as they caught her gaze. "You should beware. Those of us who suffer from late development often share another problem. The body's rush to catch up can result in a confusing mix of emotions that plays havoc with your common sense and leaves you susceptible to seduction. Be careful. Charles can be overly charming at times."

"Thank you, my lady. I am familiar with his reputation, but he knows better than to turn his wiles on me until we are wed. He values his life too much."

Lady Lanyard chuckled, relaxing in relief. "A girl after my own heart," she murmured.

"I will leave you now, as I believe you need to rest," decided Harriet. They bade each other farewell, and Harriet sent in the maid.

Lady Lanyard was again staring at her youthful portrait. "Hand me the letters in the left-hand slot of the escritoire, Simms," she ordered as the woman appeared. "And my lorgnette."

Harriet finally ran Charles to ground in the stables.

"Your grandmother suggested I look at the family," she stated baldly. "You had best show me the gallery, for she is sure to ask questions later. And it looks like you will be confined to bed for at least the next week." His nose was red, his eyes watered, and his cheeks were flushed with fever, all symptoms of a severe chill.

"All right," he agreed, his voice already scratchy. He sneezed.

It would not do to show any personal interest in the paintings. And she certainly could not let on that she was the same age as Lady Lanyard had been in the earlier picture. But Lady Lanyard's official portrait was so different that Harriet nearly gasped. Gainsborough had painted her life-sized against the riotous greenery of one of his rustic exteriors. Lady Lanyard had grown tall, and her tight, low-cut bodice revealed enticing curves and an almost voluptuous bosom. Even with the powdered hair and elaborate gown, she was beautiful.

"I wish I had known her then," murmured Charles, half to himself, as he stared at the painting. One hand hesitantly reached out as if to stroke that painted cheek. "She was so incredibly beautiful. Of course, she was probably just as dictatorial then as she is now. She picked up too many odd notions from her first husband. And she had to be conceited. All beauties are."

It was a good likeness, Harriet agreed, ignoring his comments. There was an almost ethereal quality about that image, as if it might at any moment step off the canvas; and the alluring half-smile seemed ready to break into an intimate chuckle.

Charles was still engrossed, his face radiating some emotion Harriet could not identify. Not awe or love. Worship perhaps? But that did not fit either.

She turned her thoughts to the lady herself, barely nineteen and betrothed a year earlier to an elderly manufacturer because she was too dowdy to show her face in London. What must she have felt to find herself beautiful? Conceit would have been absent. Aside from her previous lack of beauty, it was hard to reconcile self-centeredness with the woman she had become. Lady Abigail had made the most of so unpromising a start, growing fond of her husband, earning the regard that prompted him to place his fortune permanently in her hands, and eventually returning to the society to which she belonged. It was an encouraging tale of accomplishment.

With a start, Harriet realized that several minutes had passed in silence. Charles still stared at Lady Lanyard, his gaze riveted to that painted face as though it held the key to eternal life. She shivered.

"She was lovely," Harriet said aloud. "Who else is here?"

Charles jumped at the sound of her voice, a sheepish look stealing into his eyes.

"This was her second husband, the seventh Baron Lanyard," he wheezed, pointing to a portly gentleman in his mid-forties.

She paid little attention to the other paintings, beyond noting that Charles's mother bore no resemblance to his grandmother. Lady Rathbone appeared as dour and toplofty as her brother.

By the time they left the gallery, Charles could no longer hide his frequent use of a handkerchief. He retired to his room and spent the next fortnight in bed with a raging chill. For the sake of the servants, Harriet sent him encouraging messages, but in truth, she enjoyed the freedom to relax, away from his intimidating presence. Despite the act he adopted of loving her, she could feel his disapproval. With familiarity, others would surely notice.

Lord Lanyard made her welcome, no longer trying to probe

her background. Lucas insisted on flirting, though never seriously, so she was able to respond in kind. Even the servants accepted her as part of the family, no longer straining to hear every word she said. Lady Lanyard spoke with her daily, but without the suspicion that had characterized their early conversations. Edith was occasionally allowed downstairs for tea, and even for dinner one night. In company, the girl seemed less hoydenish, closely minding her manners and refraining from praise of her cousin's dissolute lifestyle.

Morning rides formed the highlights of Harriet's days. It was pure heaven to have access to quality mounts again. Her father had sold the last of their horses two years before in order to pay his most pressing debts. She often wondered what had become of Firefly, her favorite mare. She hoped the new owner was kind.

Her biggest complaint was that life was growing too relaxed. The pleasant routine made it difficult to maintain the constant watch over her tongue that would guard against revealing her true identity.

Chapter Five

L ord Lanyard joined his mother for breakfast one morning.
"I have heard from a friend about the accident at Willingford House."

"And?" she prompted.

"Willingford arranged the gathering to find a suitor for his
daughter. It was to last a fortnight. Charles often eschewed the
formal activities and rode off on his own. It was while he was
engaged in a solo ride that he lamed his horse on the second
morning, but his own injuries were confined to a concussion
and sprained wrist. He was tended by a neighbor for several
hours until Willingford fetched him back. Unfortunately,
Knightsbridge has no idea who the neighbor was."

"So we still know nothing." Lady Lanyard sighed. "He
could have fed her that story."

"Personally, I think he must have," he declared. "There is
more."

"What?"

"Charles did not remain for the entire fortnight, but packed
up abruptly midway through the party. He claimed an emer-
gency at Swansea, and several guests believe that he bolted to
avoid a leg-shackle, however the more persistent rumor is that
Willingford threw him out for dallying with his wife—something about being discovered in the folly."

Lady Lanyard's eyes flashed. "I must talk with hi—." She
cut off the words and frowned. "No. Summon Miss Sharpe."

"You wished to see me, my lady?" asked Harriet when she
reached Lady Lanyard's room.

"Yes, my dear. I just heard a most disturbing tale about
Charles and hoped you could enlighten me."

What now? Had someone backtracked them to that inn?
"Anything," she murmured.

"My son had a letter from a friend, mentioning that Charles

left the Willingford party early, ostensibly on orders from Lord Willingford. Did such an event occur?"

Harriet forced herself to laugh lightly while her mind raced. Obviously they had been investigating the tale of how she and Charles met. She wondered how much they knew. It did not take long to invent a mixture of truth and fiction to explain those rumors. If it did not fit, they could presume that the tale had been diluted for the ears of young innocents like herself.

"Yes, it did," she admitted, shaking her head, "though for once Charles was not the instigator. Lady Willingford followed him to the folly one afternoon and kissed him. They were discovered almost immediately by her husband. Charles is lucky it was no worse. Willingford has resorted to challenges more than once. His wife is a disgrace."

"You mean Lady Willingford did it?" echoed an amazed Lady Lanyard.

"That is the tale I heard. I am not surprised. Her affairs are legendary. She even tried to use me to cover one a few years ago, swearing that she was looking after the poor, motherless neighbor chit when she was really visiting Sir William."

"Scandalous! Are you sure Charles was innocent?"

"Of course not. You must know his reputation. But I also know hers. She would never allow so handsome a man to ignore her. And she would have had many opportunities to approach him. He loathed her empty-headed daughters and avoided them whenever possible. Manners prevented him from spending too much time with me. I was appalled to learn why he left and refused to see him when he first returned to the area. But he swears he was the victim. That I can accept because it was in the past. He also claims no interest in anyone else. I am willing to give him a chance to prove himself, for love can be a powerful force for change. But believe me, he'll rue the day he was born if he strays in the future. I'll not tolerate a tomcat."

Lady Lanyard accepted the explanation, and Harriet departed.

She had to tell Charles of this latest problem, but he was still tied to a sickbed. She bit her thumbnail in indecision, but there was no choice. When she was sure the servants were elsewhere, she rapped on his door. He was alone, with the draperies of his windows drawn against the brilliant morning sun in deference to his pounding head.

"What the devil are you doing in here?" he demanded hoarsely.

"Be quiet and listen," she snapped. "Your grandmother knows why you left Willingford in such a hurry."

"What?" he choked, staring at her through the gloom. He looked perfectly miserable propped up in bed, a scarcely touched breakfast tray pushed to one side.

"She knows Willingford caught you in the folly with his wife and kicked you out. I claimed you were only kissing her—any more and it would have been pistols at dawn. I also said that she had approached you. I don't care if it's true, but it's likely, given her history. You'd been there nine days, so it couldn't have been the first time. What else were you to do? I doubt you liked spending time with her hen-witted daughters, and there cannot have been anyone interesting in attendance. The Willingfords would never include a guest who might outshine their own girls. Frankly, I can't understand why you were there in the first place. But because of the scandal, you had to do some fast talking to get me to see you when you returned."

His mouth was hanging open in shock. "Harriet, I—"

"Stubble it, my lord. I couldn't care less what really happened. But you need to think of a tale to reconcile my story with the truth. There's always society's reluctance to sully young innocents with the lurid details of a rake's life."

Without waiting for a response, she slipped back into the hall, grateful that no one was there. The last thing she needed was for someone to cry compromise and decide that a special license was called for.

Charles's mind was whirling in chaos. Still groggy from his stuffy head and flaming throat, he was hardly able to take in Harriet's words. He should never have raised the specter of that disastrous house party. Of course his grandmother would have checked on it. And it would have been easy. Knightsbridge had been another guest and was his uncle's closest friend. His stupidity was appalling.

Harriet had come very close to the truth. Lady Willingford really had followed him that day, not that he had objected. Shaking his head, he stifled the memories, only to sit up in shock as a new question crashed into his mind.

How had Harriet learned Lady Willingford's propensities? That was not something either his uncle or his grandmother would have told her. And she had deduced the makeup of that party perfectly. He had never mentioned Willingford's purpose for the gathering. Who was the chit and how well did she know Lincolnshire?

His throbbing head forced him to lie down, but the questions continued. If Harriet knew that much, perhaps she also knew what else had occurred. Could she actually be one of Willingford's tenants?

Grumbling, he reached for the bellpull. His untasted cup of tea had spilled onto the bed, and cold liquid was now running beneath the sheet to pool near his right hip.

"Lord Rathbone has been behaving himself, hasn't he?" Bea asked when she joined Harriet for morning chocolate.

"Of course. He is still tied to his bed. And even if he weren't, I doubt he would try anything. He stole a kiss early on, and I told him how I had dealt with Lord Heflin." Her body's reaction on that occasion had been so much stronger than she had expected that she was grateful for his illness. It kept him well away from her.

"You didn't!" laughter lighted Bea's eyes, belying her shocked expression.

"I'm afraid I did. I only hope they are not too close, though he seemed furious that I would consider them alike." She frowned. "He also knows that I know about Lady Willingford. Why?"

"That's all right then." She sighed in relief.

"What happened to bring this up, Bea?" asked Harriet sharply. "He is a blatant libertine but is confined to quarters."

"Not entirely. Last night he cornered me in the conservatory and tried to press attentions on me, though to give him his due, he did not use force and accepted my refusal."

"That is still unconscionable," glared Harriet. "You are a guest in his grandmother's house. Whatever his ideas about our background, no honorable gentleman should pursue you under such circumstances."

"This is hardly a usual situation," protested Beatrice. "I suspect he was merely stretching his legs and was not aware that I was there until he arrived. Given the opportunity, he was testing the bounds. Now that he knows, he will leave me alone. I am only grateful he has not pressed you."

"You act as if attempted seductions were acceptable. I don't know what passes for manners in America, but in our present situation it is simply not done." Beatrice opened her mouth to protest, but Harriet cut her off. "Don't remind me of how much infidelity goes on in society, for we have discussed it before. This is different. We are guests at a family gathering around a deathbed, and he is relying on us to provide him a fortune. Trying to seduce you is idiotic and shows that he is even more arrogant and self-centered than I thought. Honestly, I don't know how anyone can stand gentlemen. They seem to believe that inheriting a title, which they have done nothing to earn, should give them carte blanche to behave however they wish."

"That is surprising, coming from the daughter of just such a man. You've a title of your own, if you recall."

"Courtesy only. Lady Melissa hardly wields the same power as ruling lords. But it is because I have rubbed shoulders with them all my life that I feel able to criticize. My father was a weakling who did nothing to improve his precarious position. My brother is worse. Why should they deserve fawning respect just because a remote ancestor did a favor for the ruling monarch?"

"You had best come to America," suggested Beatrice. "Democratic ideas are applauded on our side of the Atlantic. If you stay here, you could jeopardize your future with such statements."

"Relax, Bea. I would not dream of repeating such a thing to anyone else. You are a safe outlet because you are American. Besides, there is little chance I will ever marry, so my odd ideas will not matter. I can become a country eccentric."

When Charles officially rose from his bed, Harriet was noticeably cooler. She avoided him, remaining polite but distant in the drawing room before dinner. He puzzled over the change, but she successfully sidestepped a tête-à-tête so he was unable to question her. He supposed it was his affair with Lady Willingford. He still wondered what she knew, but he could think of no way to ask.

Lady Lanyard's solicitor finally arrived and spent several hours closeted in the sickroom. Charles wandered the house, too nervous to sit for more than a minute and too fearful to absent himself in case his grandmother took it into her head to summon him. She had already demanded an explanation of the Willingford scandal, but seemed satisfied with his story. As near as he could tell, Harriet knew more than his grandmother did, raising further questions about the girl's past.

The servants avoided him. His temper had grown testier during his illness, which the uncertainty of his situation did nothing to improve. His future was in Harriet's hands, but he had not been in a position to supervise her. And his irritation had increased hourly since his recovery.

The chit crawled under his skin like no one else. She treated him like a recalcitrant child. Her refusal to acknowledge their different stations annoyed him no end. She showed no awe of his title, no appreciation for his elegance, no interest in his looks, and no envy of his superior social skills. When she wasn't avoiding him, she criticized everything he said, haughtily enough to be a duke's daughter. He had received more setdowns from her than he had in his entire previous life.

His usual appetites were also interfering with thought. Illness had prevented that trip to Bridport but had done nothing to depress his needs. He dared not approach the servants or any of the village lasses. Word would immediately reach his grandmother's ears. Years earlier, she had made it clear that she would never countenance interference with her dependents. Hoping that Mrs. Sharpe might be amenable, he had sounded her out. After all, she was both a handsome woman and a widow. With luck, she would have needs of her own. But she had proven to be the prudish sort, leaving him ready to explode with frustration. And that was dangerous. Runaway passions could cloud his judgment. He had barely escaped disaster several times before.

The Willingford party had been just such a close call. He knew the husband was possessive, yet he had continued the liaison. Willingford had returned early from a jaunt into Lincoln to find the delectable Carla with her dress down around her waist. If he had entered the folly even five minutes later, Charles would have been facing him at dawn instead of just nursing a bruised jaw. He had already enjoyed Carla's lustful charms several times that week. The lady was insatiable.

His groin tightened painfully. Just such a situation now loomed. Nothing else could account for his growing desire to kiss Miss Sharpe. She was as unattractive a package as he could imagine. Every time she chewed her nails, he wanted to shake her. And she was the only female he had ever met who openly disparaged his touch. Even in the drawing room, when she could not object to him kissing her fingers, he could feel her fury. So he paced the house, his mind cycling between his grandmother's demands and his unaccountable attraction to a dowdy schoolroom chit. *Please let this be over.*

The solicitor finally retired to draft Lady Lanyard's last will and testament. The dowager immediately summoned Harriet to her bedside, and Charles's nervousness increased. His future was in the hands of an immature, lower-class stranger. He belonged in Bedlam! He should have stuck to his original plan, pointing out the impossibility of his grandmother's demand and suggesting that she either bypass him or leave the inheritance in trust until he wed. But there was nothing he could do about that now.

"We need to have a serious talk," Lady Lanyard began as Harriet seated herself in a chair. "You will make a satisfactory wife to my scapegrace grandson, but there are things you must understand."

"Yes, my lady?" she responded in surprise.

"Are you aware of his financial standing?" she asked.

"Yes. He has been open about it since the beginning," she truthfully stated. "It was what finally prompted my acceptance. He could hardly afford a dowerless wife, given his own need, yet he insisted upon marriage."

"He has always known that he would inherit my fortune."

Harriet raised her brows.

Lady Lanyard continued in a hard voice. "But I will not tolerate a continuance of his frivolous ways. His grandfather gamed away much of his inheritance. He made himself a byword in London, losing so consistently that it became a standing joke in the clubs. Anyone needing money need only challenge the ninth Lord Rathbone to cards and his troubles would vanish. Charles's father was shamed by his predecessor's excesses and vowed to recoup the family fortunes. It was why we allowed Althea to accept him. What a mistake! He may have eschewed the tables, but he was as much a gambler in his own way, losing the remains in bad investments that even the most obtuse cloth-head should have seen were doomed to failure. His only virtue was dying before he mortgaged Swansea. Charles claims to despise them both, but he has shown little inclination to assume responsibility. Since leaving school, he has spent his life in London, doing the pretty in society, lolling about the clubs and sporting circles, and sowing more wild oats than are seemly."

Harriet blushed but nodded agreement.

"My first husband taught me a healthy respect for achievement," continued her ladyship, pinning Harriet with an icy stare. "I believe you share that view."

"I do. I prefer to judge men on character and accomplishments—and that does not necessarily mean money. Our neighbor, Lord Mitchel, has a love of learning that prompted him to become an expert on Chaucer and other medieval writers. He has recently completed a book on the subject that will share his insights with others. One can applaud his expertise regardless of how little interest one has in his subject. Even the wealthiest peer should not believe that setting a good steward over his lands frees him to idle about town the rest of his life."

"I have judged you well, then. I expect you to challenge Charles. See that he does something useful with his life. First he must learn how his estate operates. It will not be easy, for he has shown no interest there in eight years of ownership. Once he accomplishes that, you will have to decide what to encourage next. You will know where his interests and abilities lie, probably better than I. Despite our blood relationship, he spends only a short time here each year. But I love him dearly. He inherited the charm and vivacity that bypassed my son and daughter. Take care of him, Harriet."

"I will do what I can," she promised.

"You will also raise your children to accept responsibility," ordered Lady Lanyard.

"Certainly, my lady."

"We must leave the world a better place than it was when we were born," she declared. Though still firm, her voice was noticeably weaker.

"Lady Tanders's favorite saying," murmured Harriet without thinking, her mind focused on terminating the conversation before her ladyship tired.

"You are also related to Lady Tanders?" asked Lady Lanyard. "She was my grandmother."

"No," lied Harriet, cursing herself for forgetting her role. "You are not the first person to quote her. I met a lady in Bath some years ago, who often talked of Lady Tanders. Her philosophy influenced my own thinking."

She was fighting off panic as she groped with a horrifying realization. Her grandmother, Lady Castleton, was also a granddaughter of Lady Tanders, which made her Lady Lanyard's first cousin. Thus Charles was her third cousin. *Dear Lord, please let the two branches of the family be estranged!*

Fancy almost revealing her identity by absentmindedly repeating her mother's favorite adage. She hoped her claim was vague enough to satisfy Lady Lanyard.

Talk wandered idly for another hour. Lady Lanyard reminisced about Lady Tanders, a forceful, opinionated woman dedicated to good works. She had loved her family with a deep devotion, spending many hours with the children. They passed her ideals on to their children, and so on. Only Charles lacked training in the Tanders philosophy of dedication, self-reliance, achievement, and frugality. His mother had died when he was three, depriving him of that influence, and his father was no pattern card.

Charles accosted her as soon as she emerged from Lady Lanyard's room, hauling her into a dimly lit state apartment where they would not be overheard.

"You are spending too much time with my grandmother," he charged angrily. "How can you maintain the fiction for so prolonged a period?"

"Jealous?" she snapped, unwilling to put up with his arrogance another minute. "How do you suggest I refuse her commands, my lord? *My dear lady, I cannot sit with you any more because his toadship fears I might inadvertently reveal what a scheming bastard he is, and upset his plans to inherit your fortune.* Is that what you want?"

Her biting condemnation seemed unexpectedly to soothe his temper, for he smiled.

"Forgive me, Miss Sharpe. This uncertainty is amazingly frustrating."

"I suppose you are unused to waiting for anything," she observed tartly, wandering across the room to examine a portrait of a typically dour Elizabethan Lanyard. "A little disappointment would probably improve your character."

"You wouldn't!" He sounded aghast.

"Do you think me capable of dishonoring a vow, sir?" Her voice was again hard. She shrugged. "Of course you do. Your opinion of me remains unspeakable."

"Nonsense," he swore. "I spoke without thinking, out of my own fears. Your performance has been marvelous, and I am grateful. But what do you talk about for so long?"

"Today she was reminiscing about her childhood, recounting tales of her grandmother, Lady Tanders."

His shoulders relaxed and he joined her before the fireplace. "Ah, I might have known she would wish to talk of the past

now that she has reached the end. And thank you for sparing
me that. She can become remarkably tedious, for all I love
her."

Selfish prig. His devotion to his grandmother was rooted in
avarice. But it was not her place to judge. Nor would she continue this masquerade any longer. For good or ill, the will was
written. She would apprise him of her impressions, and then
wash her hands of the whole sordid mess.

"I wouldn't be too sure the end is near," she warned.

"What do you mean?" He turned her to face him.

"How long has it been since you visited her?"

He frowned. "Yesterday, briefly. And a fortnight ago. I've
been ill."

"Did you really look at her?"

She could feel his hand trembling. "I'm in no mood for
games, Miss Sharpe."

"She may well be at the end of her life, but I doubt if this
chill will kill her," she stated firmly, her eyes holding his.
"She is much better than when we arrived, her skin less trans-
parent, her eyes clearer. Her relief that you are well situated
has restored her will to live. She could linger for months or
even years."

"Damnation!" he exploded, dropping her arm and striding
furiously away. She watched him reach the door and turn
back, his brows creased in desperate thought.

"Are you sure?"

"Of course not. I am no doctor," she demurred. "She is elderly and frail. This chill could still prove fatal, or something
else might claim her tomorrow. The body has an unfortunate
habit of wearing out with age. But you must be prepared for
any eventuality."

"What should we do now?" His fingers were tangled in his
hair.

"There is no question of *we*. This is your problem, my lord.
Our agreement is concluded. My grandmother should have
reached home by now. I plan to leave tomorrow."

"But what will I tell her?"

"You will think of something."

"You can't leave me in the lurch like this," he protested,
grabbing her arm and shaking it. "You promised to see that I
received my inheritance."

"You twist our agreement," she accused him, hardening her
tone and pulling free. "I promised to pose as your betrothed

for two weeks in exchange for a roof over my head. I have sat-isfied that bargain. You do not own me. Nor will I continue this charade in the future. I should be shot for joining so dis-honorable a scheme at all."

"Don't pretend righteousness with me, my girl," he growled. "No one forced you. And you will help me again should the need arise." His face hovered only inches from her own, an odd gleam shining in his eyes.

"Never, my lord. You do not own me," she repeated, trepi-dation warring with some other emotion as his pupils blurred.

"Perhaps I should," he murmured, dragging her into his arms and kissing her.

For a moment she was too surprised to react, which gave excitement a chance to build. His mouth was open, and the un-expectedness of it thrilled her as his tongue traced the line of her lips. This was so different from the terror Heflin had raised. His hands caressed her back and she arched closer, rev-eling in the warmth of his embrace.

What was she doing? He despised her!

Furious, she fought free. "Arrogant oaf!" her hand flashed up, leaving a red print on his face. "Do you really think your-self so irresistible that you can seduce me into continuing this deceit? I owe you nothing, my lord."

"It need not be a deceit," he said rashly, his voice rasping as he gasped for breath. His fingers brushed across her breasts. "Marry me."

"I would sooner live in hell than with someone who would wed for money," she snarled, ignoring the tingles radiating from that feather-light touch. Oh, treacherous, untrustworthy body! "Find some other poor fool. Surely there is someone so desperate for a title and fortune that she would overlook the selfish conceit that rules your life. As for me, I will never wed a greedy fribble, and you have shown no inclination to any-thing else."

Turning on her heel, she slammed out of the room, heading upstairs to inform Beatrice of their imminent departure. She should never have agreed to come. The only worthy person in this entire family was Lady Lanyard, yet Harriet had spent a fortnight deceiving her.

Guilt assailed her for stooping so low. She had allowed a charming rogue to seduce her will and had continued lending her support despite everything. He had twisted facts to elicit her agreement. His reputation as an unprincipled libertine should have warned her off, yet when he had insisted on touching her more than was seemly, she had only halfheartedly protested. Even when he tried to seduce Bea, she had done nothing. Why? Because she was enjoying her stay too much to face leaving. She was as selfish as he. Bitter and ashamed, she set Betsy to packing and sat down with Beatrice to plan how they could depart without leaving a trail to Lady Castleton.

"He is your cousin?" choked Beatrice when Harriet had recounted her latest conversation with their hostess.

"I am afraid so. And that complicates matters. I have no idea if Lady Lanyard and Lady Castleton are close. Nor is there anywhere else I can go for shelter. We must trust that Rathbone does not turn up on the doorstep."

In the end they decided to continue traveling as Mrs. Sharpe and Miss Harriet as far as Bridport. There they would change inns, resume their identities of Lady Melissa Stapleton and Mrs. Stokes, and take the further precaution of traveling separately. Melissa and Betsy would take the mail to Exeter, then double back on the stage to meet Beatrice and proceed to the Castleton dower house.

Charles remained in the state apartment for some time. What devil had possessed him? It was bad enough to maul an innocent under the protection of both himself and his uncle, but it was insufferable to have offered marriage to an insignificant nobody. How could he have been so stupid? *You were on fire for her*, whispered a voice. Dear Lord! He was rapidly losing his mind. It was time he moved on to Brighton.

He visited his grandmother as soon as his temper cooled. Harriet had been astute. Lady Lanyard looked better than he had seen her in at least two years. He hid his horror, keeping up a flow of inconsequential chatter during his brief visit, referring to Harriet only to refuse his grandmother's suggestion that they schedule their wedding at Christmas. He insisted that his betrothed deserved a formal come-out before settling down.

"Who will be sponsoring her?" asked Lady Lanyard

His heart sank. "Her grandmother."

"And she is?"

"Mrs. Sharpe," he murmured, hoping that she had forgotten that the fictitious lady was the poor widow of a country vicar who could never hope to launch a granddaughter in London.

"Of course," she agreed, a half-smile pulling at her lips.

He took his leave, new worries haunting his thoughts. And he insisted on escorting Harriet and Beatrice to the coaching inn.

"Good-bye, my dear," he murmured over Harriet's hand as he helped her out of the carriage in Litton Cheney. He had scarcely seen her since they had parted the previous afternoon. Nor could he see her now. Her bonnet concealed her features, and she refused to look at him. "Where can I reach you?"

"There is no need," she insisted firmly. "I have no desire to meet you again, and you have no further claim upon my time. This adventure has been dishonorable enough without prolonging it. Let it go, my lord."

"You are hard."

"And you are selfish. It has been quite an education, but not a course I care to repeat. Good-bye."

He turned pleading eyes to Beatrice, but she merely bade him farewell and turned away.

Chapter Six

April 1817

Lady Melissa Stapleton rose from her dressing table and dismissed her new maid, Willis (Betsy had married one of her uncle's tenants). She paused to look in the mirror before gathering her reticule, fan, and gloves for an evening at Almack's. The face that stared back was so different that she still had trouble believing it was hers.

The black of her disguise had long since vanished, and even the usual dull brown color was gone. Frequent lemon rinsings had lightened her hair, raising golden highlights that turned it a rich, honey blonde. Matching reflections made her light brown eyes glow like amber. Nine months of safety and relaxation had likewise left their mark. Gone were all signs of strain—the worry lines, the haunted eyes, the rigid shoulders. Gone too was the sallow thinness that had characterized her last year at Drayton Manor, when illness and short rations left her looking like a waif. Smooth, creamy skin now glowed with care. But the biggest difference was in her figure. Lady Lanyard had been right. She had already shown signs of maturing before she left home, but the changes since then astonished her. She was five inches taller, with curves in all the right places and a bosom best described as bountiful.

Lady Castleton had been shocked at her sudden appearance on the doorstep. The lady had barely returned from Bath and had not yet perused the mail that had accumulated in her absence. Thus she did not know of Melissa's situation.

Melissa's first look at her grandmother revived memories of the summer ten years before when that lady had visited Drayton. Tall and spare, with silver hair and a classical bone structure, Lady Castleton did not look anywhere near her five-and-seventy years. Even now her face displayed few wrinkles. As a girl she must have been a beauty. But there was no doubt she would make a formidable opponent if she chose to counter one's ideas. The dowager Marchioness of Castleton could be remarkably haughty. That was why Melissa had originally balked at approaching her, but now that she had no choice, she decided to trust her fate to the Tanders philosophy of judging people on deeds rather than breeding.

Lady Castleton looked her granddaughter up and down, a frown creasing her forehead. "You're not much to look at."

"As was your cousin, Lady Lanyard, at my age," countered Melissa.

Eyebrows rose. "You know Lady Lanyard?"

"We met recently. She agreed that I was probably like herself."

"Your mother was the same. As was I." No emotion showed in her voice.

"I did not know that." Melissa shrugged. "She died when I was ten. There was no reason for her to mention it."

"Why was it necessary to leave home?" she asked.

"I feared for my reputation and my virtue. Toby is weak, given to gaming and drinking. He has been entertaining a group of friends that includes Lord Heflin. I managed to avoid him much of the time, but his attentions were growing insistent. Toby owes him vast amounts of money and wants to use me to settle the debt."

"Just like his father," muttered her ladyship.

"Grandmama," stated Melissa firmly, her own iron will showing. "My father may not have been the most upstanding gentleman of my acquaintance, but I will tolerate no aspersions on his character. I know that you disapproved of him and tried to prevent my mother's marriage. You refused to help him financially and blamed him for her death. You are entitled to your opinions. But if you cannot refrain from venting them in my presence, then I must find some other shelter. He is dead and can no longer defend himself, nor can I be held responsible for his failings, for I was never in a position to influence his behavior. I ask that you judge me on my own merits."

Lady Castleton stared piercingly at her granddaughter. "Well said, Melissa. You have inherited the best from your ancestors. We will speak no more of the past. But we must counter this threat from Tobias. Is he your legal guardian?"

"Yes, he is. There was a provision in Father's will for a guardian to us both should Toby not be five-and-twenty, but he had just passed that milestone when Papa died. The wording left him in sole control of everything, including me."

"How do you know of his plans?"

"I went to his study to beg him to send Lord Heflin away, but they were inside talking. Heflin was furious that I had again refused his advances. He offered to forgive Toby's debts if he could have me."

"What did you do?"

"That was when Beatrice and I decided we could not wait for a response to my letter. We left that night. I wrote a note to Toby denouncing Heflin and implying that I was going home with Beatrice. I am not usually quite this hideous, you know. We dyed my hair and dug out an old gown of the housekeeper's to hide my identity, then traveled under assumed names. I feared that Toby would follow and drag me back."

"Very resourceful. I will send my secretary to talk to the boy. Saunders will convey my horror that any member of my family could consider selling his sister. With sufficient pressure, he should drop the idea. Heflin is an evil man; society has shunned him for years."

"Thank you, Grandmama. If you will excuse me now, I am tired and wish to retire as soon as I see that all is well with my cousin. She has done much to help me in recent months."

And so she had been able to relax at last, free from her fear of Lord Heflin. But new fears quickly emerged. Lady Castleton was far from being the elderly pauper Melissa had envisioned. She may have refused to help a worthless son-in-law, but not because of poverty. Nor was she a stay-at-home. She spent most Seasons in London and had just returned from successfully launching a goddaughter. Her credit was high, and she had the ear of every influential gossip and hostess in town.

Her first pronouncement was that they would repair to London the following Season. Melissa tried to protest, but she quickly discovered that Lady Castleton did not sway with the breeze as her own family had always done. And there was no way she could voice her real objection—Lord Rathbone. Admitting an acquaintance would reveal her stay at Lanyard Manor, which she was loathe to do.

"Bea, what am I to do?" she begged her cousin a week after their arrival. "Grandmama insists on bringing me out. How can I go to town after everything that has happened?"

"Are you afraid of seeing Heflin there?"

"Yes, though I do not think Toby will involve himself again. But that will not stop Heflin. You know how he is."

"Yes, I do. But Lady Castleton will make a formidable champion. I shouldn't waste time fretting over him."

"But what about Lord Rathbone? That is my biggest worry. He can ruin me with a word. I had not seriously feared it before, for I thought never to meet him again, but he is always in London."

"Why should he go to the trouble of ruining you?" asked Bea, veering away from the maze, where gardeners were trimming its hedges.

"What if we were right and he has failed a test set forth by Lady Lanyard?" demanded Melissa. "He would blame me instead of himself. Aside from his conceit, he was confined to his bed much of the time, while I saw her ladyship daily. We quarreled on that very subject just before we left. Our parting was anything but cordial."

Bea's brows lifted. "Was that the only reason?"

"No." She blushed. "He wished me to be available to continue the charade. I refused. He then pressed attentions on me that forced me to slap him. His blood was up enough that he actually suggested marriage. I turned him down in unflattering terms and left him. He may decide he has a grievance against me even if Lady Lanyard leaves him the money. At the very least, I have injured his pride."

Beatrice examined her cousin's face with shrewd eyes. "You do not fear only injured pride, Missy. It is the man himself who intimidates you, is it not?"

"Yes," sighed Melissa. "He is dangerous, for he is so very attractive. I found his kiss too pleasant, yet I cannot trust that enjoyment. He embodies so many traits that I abhor. You spoke once of a physical attraction that had nothing to do with love. I fear such a connection exists between myself and Lord Rathbone. Should he ever turn his wiles on me, there is little doubt that he would seduce me. So what am I to do? He can ruin me in multiple ways."

Bea was silent for several minutes, her forehead creased in thought. "I do not believe that he would," she ventured at last. "His temper before we left was admittedly short, but you must remember that he was laboring under considerable stress. He had been ill for the better part of a fortnight, something few men handle with aplomb. The tension surrounding his suddenly uncertain future made it worse. When he has had time to reflect, he will be grateful to you. After all, you carried off your role better than he had any right to expect."

"Do you really think so?" Her eyes lit.

"Yes. If you do meet in London—and remember that he may be in mourning by then—let him set the tone. Bringing this up in public will hurt him just as badly as it would you."

"I had not considered that. He has violated the gentleman's code of honor and may choose to forget it, regardless of his feelings for me."

"As to the other," said Beatrice as they turned back toward the dower house. "I do not think you need worry unduly. Whatever you believe, Rathbone considers himself a gentleman. He may be selfishly immature—most British men are at his age—but he is not another Lord Heflin. Seducing the unwed daughter of an earl would never occur to him. I may not approve of the ridiculous rules you live by, but they will protect you. He is the son of a viscount and grandson of a baron. You are descended from an earl and a marquess. That puts you above him."

Melissa giggled. "Not by much, for I lose by being both female and common, while he is a lord. But you are right. He would not treat Lady Melissa the same way he treated Miss Sharpe." She refused to identify a tug of regret at the words.

Beatrice left the next day. Melissa had enjoyed the intervening months. They lived in the Castle Windcombe dower house, but she had the run of the castle as well as the grounds. She was welcomed by her Uncle Howard, the current Marquess of Castleton, whose wife had died three years before. He was a quiet man, with little interest in socializing or government affairs. It took her a while to discover that he was nearly as stodgy as Lord Lanyard. Cousin Eleanor, now sixteen, and Cousin Clarissa, fourteen, lived at home. Melissa's newfound relatives were absurdly correct in thought, word, and deed, making her feel hoydenish in their company, especially after they accepted the duty of correcting her behavior to prepare her for London.

It was Lady Castleton who insisted on an improving regimen. Appalled at Melissa's lack of training, she drilled the girl mercilessly, correcting her walk from a stride to an elegant glide, teaching her how to sit (don't sprawl, knees and feet together), how to rise and move with grace, and how to hold her hands primly in her lap instead of gesturing broadly. Most importantly, Lady Castleton banned all nail biting, so Melissa's hands now bore the fingers of a lady. And her voice sounded soft and silky instead of sharp with irritation.

She threw herself energetically into the lessons, surprising even her grandmother. Her mother had trained her well until her death, but since then Melissa had spent much of her time in the stables and had unconsciously patterned herself after Jake. Even her language and conversation had become vulgar. Mortified at what the inhabitants of Lanyard Manor must have thought, she was determined to never again embarrass herself in such a way.

As her social skills improved, she felt less like an outsider. Each day she visited the castle, studying flirting with her cousins, learning the latest steps with the dancing master, practicing court curtsies with the governess, and devouring much of her uncle's library. After years of ignorance, she welcomed knowledge.

Castle Windcombe was located just east of Exeter, nestled in a narrow valley surrounded by steep hills. The winter was milder than she was accustomed to, so she balanced the interminable lessons with riding, reveling in the sparse beauty of the countryside. She was delighted to learn that one of Uncle Howard's friends had bought Firefly, and her grandmother was able to repurchase the mare.

Lady Castleton and Melissa arrived in London in March. The first two weeks were spent on fittings for an extensive wardrobe and on daily calls on society's matrons. Several carefully chosen activities were added the third week. With the official opening of the Season, their social schedule overflowed. It started with her presentation at Court and the year's first Almack's assembly, followed immediately by Lady Jersey's annual ball. Since then, they had attended as many as six events a day, from morning calls and promenades in the park, to breakfasts and museum visits, to balls, routs, soirees, and musical evenings. She rarely arrived home before two, and had only managed a morning ride twice.

But London was not all frivolity. Melissa's lighthearted facade hid continuing fears. The first was of meeting Lord Rathbone, who could hardly fail to recognize her. One word of their previous association and she would be ruined. But so far he had not appeared, and she dared not ask anyone where he was. There was no way to explain her interest, but somehow she must learn, for meeting unexpectedly in public could ruin them both. In the shock of the moment, he could easily reveal their association. She briefly considered writing him, but that could ruin her too if the correspondence ever came to light.

An even worse fear was that of running into Lord Heflin. But at least she did not have to worry about seeing him at marriage-mart entertainments, for he would never be invited. Shocking tales of his escapades made the rounds of Mayfair drawing rooms whenever current scandals lagged. The most frequent speculation centered on why he was away. He had eschewed London since the previous Season, a longer absence than ever before, yet no one doubted that he would soon return. So there was no way to avoid revealing her presence. Would he seek revenge for the pain she had caused him? He had plenty of complaints—refusing his advances, inflicting injury, Bea's attack, Toby's mountain of vowels . . .

Shrugging aside her thoughts, she grimaced at her reflected image and headed downstairs.

Almack's was crowded, as always. Lady Sefton and Princess Esterhazy were doing the honors in the receiving line. After passing their scrutiny, Melissa and Lady Castleton joined Lady Stokely, whose youngest daughter, Lady Helena, was also making bows this Season. She and Melissa had met at a winter house party and were now bosom bows.

"Good evening, Helena," murmured Melissa. "You look lovely tonight." Helena's blonde hair and blue eyes glowed above white muslin trimmed in pale pink.

"As do you," responded Helena.

Melissa was wearing white silk embroidered in gold and green, over an amber slip, with pearls at her throat and in her hair.

Helena's face suddenly snapped into a horrified glare as an elegant gentleman entered the room. "Did you hear about Lord Thornhill? You will have to cut him."

"No, what?" Edwin Morris, Lord Thornhill, was heir to the Earl of Waite and a member of Melissa's court. He still seemed a silly boy, but he had a way of twinkling his eyes that always raised shivers. She had decided it was due to one of those unfortunate physical attractions that Beatrice had warned her about, for it was rumored that all Morrises were rakes at heart.

Helena suddenly flushed. "Maybe I shouldn't tell you."

"Nonsense," swore Melissa, her curiosity piqued by the words. "He's too young to be interested in marriage, and I'd not accept him anyway. What did he do?" She doubted cutting would be necessary. Helena was too proper to discuss anything really bad.

"I'm not supposed to know," admitted Helena, lowering her voice until Melissa could barely hear the words. "It's amazing what people try to hide. The scandalously fast Cavendish ball was last night. Thornhill was discovered in an anteroom with two dancers, all of them unclothed. He forgot to lock the door, and Lord Dobson walked in, looking to entertain his own friend."

"Helena!" gasped Melissa. "How did you learn such a lurid story?"

"I overheard my brother and a friend laughing about it in the library this afternoon. They actually sounded envious."

"No doubt," hissed Melissa. "But don't tell anyone else. You'll ruin your reputation."

Helena nodded, her blue eyes blazing with offended propriety. The conundrum vexed her: How could one deplore depravity when one could not mention it? She sighed. "Here comes Lord Rufton."

Melissa turned to her most persistent suitor and smiled. "Good evening, my lord." George was a good-natured man and a close friend. Whether their relationship would warm she could not yet decide. Only a couple of inches taller than herself, his bright blue eyes glistened below a mop of reddish-brown hair.

"My dear Lady Melissa." He smiled as he led her out for a waltz. She had been approved for the dance the previous week.

"I've not seen you for a couple of days, my lord. What have you been doing?"

"My friend, Lord Hartford, and his wife just arrived. I spent last evening with them. You will like them. Caroline is much like you."

"Will they be here tonight?"

"Probably. Would you visit Somerset House with me tomorrow?" They had already discovered a shared interest in art.

"I would love to, but not tomorrow. We are already committed to visiting Lady Covington. How about Friday?"

"That is agreeable. I will speak to Lady Castleton. Perhaps the Hartfords can accompany us."

They finished the dance in amity, exchanging the latest gossip. Rufton appealed to her intellect, but there was nothing more. Would that missing spark ignite in time? She wanted a husband who was more than just a friend.

"You haven't forgotten that we are to drive in Hyde Park tomorrow, have you?" wondered her next partner, Mr. Parkington, when they came together in a country dance. She had again mentioned Lady Covington.

"Of course not, sir," she protested with a smile. He was a handsome man, with black hair and gray eyes that could turn stormy in anger, or soft and seductive. At the moment they were soft. "How could I forget so delightful a treat? Will you be driving those marvelous bays I saw you with the other day?"

"Yes. Beautiful animals, are they not? I still cannot believe I managed to buy them. They are just the sort that Hartford usually outbids me for."

"Is his stable so extensive?"

"He breeds horses," he informed her. "And his are the best to be had. But he did not attend the auction when Sir Henry Oglethorpe disposed of his stable."

She raised her brows.

"The man is rolled up," he explained. "Lost a bundle at White's last month. Rumor has it that he is selling everything portable in an attempt to pay his creditors. It is possible he will make it, though the betting still favors him fleeing the country."

They shook their heads over such profligacy, and she smothered a reminder of her equally profligate brother. It was doubtful he could ever pay what he owed Heflin. "I hope he does not have a family dependent on him for support," she commented.

"Only an elderly mother, and I believe she has enough income of her own that his antics will hurt only himself. But enough of others. Are you attending Lady Barnsleigh's Venetian breakfast next week?"

"I think so, but I would have to check with my grandmother before I dared swear to it."

"Perhaps I can escort you."

"Perhaps."

Lord Thornhill led her into a quadrille, and she decided her earlier thoughts were correct. She reacted quite strongly to his twinkling blue eyes and crooked smile, but that reaction arose from Helena's scandalous tale. If she truly cared for him, she would have been furious over his misdeeds, but she was not.

The tale was funny. And titillating, though she refused to admit that.

Lord Rufton waltzed with her a second time, then introduced her to the Hartfords. Lady Hartford was an elegant matron in her mid-twenties whose warmth struck an immediate chord. Lord Hartford was amazingly handsome, with black hair and vibrant green eyes. After seeing him, Mr. Parkington's gray eyes seemed nondescript.

"What do you think of George?" asked Lady Hartford when the gentlemen were engrossed in discussion.

"He is a good friend," admitted Melissa. "Beyond that, it is too early to tell."

She smiled. "I find him delightful. We have been close for years. He deserves the same love and happiness I have found with Thomas."

Melissa smiled back. "A lovely thought. My cousin and I often spoke of marriage before she returned home. I cannot imagine so close a relationship without love."

"Would I know your cousin?" asked Lady Hartford.

"I doubt it. She is American."

"Is it true that Americans are more candid than we are?"

"I cannot speak about all Americans, but Beatrice was openly informative." She blushed.

"Ah," said Lady Hartford, understanding that look. "Good luck in finding the right husband, dear. The rewards are infinite."

Lord Englewood arrived to lead her into a cotillion, terminating the conversation. Heir to the Marquess of Thorne, he was also affording her noticeable attention. He was tall and dark, though not handsome, and her only complaint of him so far was that he was rather high in the instep, reminding her of Lord Lanyard.

Her fortnight of deceit returned to tease her mind that night, holding sleep at bay. Memories of that visit remained surprisingly vivid. Her behavior had been reprehensible and dishonorable, and she shuddered at what must happen if any of it became public. Perhaps that was why she could not forget. Surely there was no reason to recall the interlude with longing.

Chapter Seven

Lord Rathbone sprawled across the chair in his study, staring at the glass of brandy in his hand. He steadfastly refused to look at his surroundings, needing no reminder of how bad things were. A leak had allowed water into both this room and the adjoining library, damaging a century's worth of estate records and destroying most of the books. The only saving grace was that the books were old sermons that he had no interest in reading anyway. But this wasn't the only leak. Unless he found the money for a new roof, the entire house would rot.

The estate was in worse shape than he had ever imagined. The aesthetics were bad enough—formal gardens so overgrown that he could only raze them and start over, a lake so choked with weeds that fish could not survive, outbuildings fallen into ruin after half a century of neglect. But all that could be ignored. What had sent him to the brandy decanter was a recital of the more basic problems.

Of seventeen tenant farms, six were abandoned, their fields fallow for years and their fences and buildings destroyed. Four others were on the verge of ruin, the cottages unworthy of human habitation, and the rest needed major repairs.

His steward had been a hidebound incompetent. Without crop rotation, the soil was exhausted. Even the timberland had been overcut, producing most of his limited income in recent years and leaving no possibility of further production for at least a decade. The flocks were decimated, for inbreeding had created an unusual susceptibility to hoof rot that a wet year had exploited. Specialty crops had never been tried. The orchards were on the decline because aging trees had not been replaced with younger ones. The woolen mills had wiped out most cottage weaving, leaving those remaining in the village on the verge of starvation. The Rathbones had done nothing for their dependents, and he was no better than his father and grandfather had been.

Unwillingly, his thoughts returned to the charade he had played out the previous summer. It had seemed so simple in the beginning. He had decided that his grandmother's orders arose from the understandable longings of a lady whose grip on reality was slipping. So when the opportunity arose to comply—at least on the surface—he had grasped it with both hands, grateful that he could ease her mind in her final days. He would not have done it had he been sober, but even after his head had cleared, he did not truly regret his actions. Certainly he could never have produced a real betrothal on such short notice. Yet he could only assume that he had been mad.

Harriet Sharpe. Her image floated before his eyes, as it had so often of late. All had gone well. She had played her part better than he could have hoped, even managing to defuse potential disaster over the Willingford scandal. And though they had parted on acrimonious terms, she had done nothing to disabuse his grandmother of the notion that they were betrothed. Perhaps it would have been better if she had.

"You have chosen well," Lady Lanyard declared the day Harriet left. He had come to explain the summons that had sent Miss Sharpe to her grandmother's sickbed. "The girl is sensible and shares my ideas about many things. She will see that you cease frittering your life away."

"I expect so," he agreed. "We have been discussing what must be done to turn Swansea around."

"Has she seen it?"

"Not yet." He should have stopped there, of course, but the charade had almost become real. "I will invite her down for a week before the Season. She can order what improvements she wants to the house. The worst of the estate problems will have improved by then."

"Excellent."

He was to rue that conversation many times over the following week. Both she and Lord Lanyard pestered him daily for details of his estate, details he could not provide because he had spent little time there since reaching adulthood and had rarely talked with his steward. The only trips to Swansea in four years had been to pick up items he could sell to augment his meager income. He was hard-pressed to describe problems, but pride prevented him from admitting ignorance.

His grandmother assumed that he would join Harriet once he left Lanyard Manor, pressing a letter on him to deliver to her. Every day found him mouthing new lies and dancing to recall the old ones. The falsehoods piled atop one another until he felt buried under their weight. His fondest dream was to suffer a relapse that would keep him abed for another week.

And Harriet had been right, devil take her. Lady Lanyard had not succumbed to her chill, surprising her doctor by regaining so much strength that she was able to rise from her bed and join the family at dinner. Talk had touched too often that night on his future plans.

He left the next day, ostensibly to see Harriet. Messages and good wishes echoed in his ears. When he promised to deliver them, Lady Lanyard smiled that secretive half-smile that appeared in her portrait, and he shocked himself by praying she would die soon.

Prayer was not his reaction four months later. His blasphemy had been rewarded as he deserved. Lady Lanyard sent a new message, again summoning him to her side, and Harriet too. She wished to celebrate Christmas surrounded by her family, but she was disappointed that Harriet had not replied to her letter.

His heart plummeting, he dug the missive from his desk and read it. It was exactly the sort of letter he would expect to a new member of the family, containing enough questions and suggestions to demand a reply. A string of lurid curses reverberated through the study. His stupidity was appalling. He should have read it at the time and formulated a response, of course. But he could not answer without inviting another letter. And where could he have that sent? Falsehood inevitably bred further falsehood. His head spun.

Not once had he considered what would happen if his grandmother did not die. Nor did he have any idea where to find Harriet. Not that it mattered, for she would never consent to repeat her impersonation. It was Christmas, for God's sake! They had promised to make their betrothal public when her mourning was over. Lady Lanyard was undoubtedly planning a party for the occasion, probably a full-fledged house party and grand ball, if past experience could be trusted. He could not produce Harriet unless he was prepared to marry her. He shuddered.

Lies, deceit, pretense. Where did it all stop? But he could not confess now. If the truth came out, he would forfeit every penny of the inheritance. And after four months at Swansea, he knew the full extent of his dilemma.

He lived through two weeks of hell, making and discarding

plan after plan. He finally decided that Harriet was ill and unable to make the journey. To appease his grandmother, he produced a letter in a feminine script that Harriet would send to Lady Lanyard, begging forgiveness both for skipping Christmas and for neglecting to reply earlier. It was yet another layer of dishonesty, but he had no choice. He desperately needed his grandmother's approval. His financial position was increasingly precarious. He had fired his steward and much of his staff, and had even given up his rooms in London to save money. Swansea demanded a large infusion of cash if he was to have any hope of reaping a profit from it any time soon. His only recourse was to ask Lady Lanyard for help, describing his problems and his plans for dealing with them. But if she was angry over Harriet's absence, the chances of getting her agreement were slim. It was bad enough that he could no longer remember what he had told her on his last visit. Nothing remotely correct, he was sure, for he had known next to nothing. His former ignorance was embarrassing.

He arrived at Lanyard Manor to a scene of grief. Lady Lanyard had passed away in her sleep two days before. Relief overwhelmed him, an emotion he immediately thrust aside in shame. He had genuinely cared for his grandmother, yet even as he observed the rituals of mourning, his mind was busily planning. Building projects. Competent steward. Expanded staff. New roof. Repairs. Decorating . . . *Greedy.* Harriet's echoing accusation sounded like an epithet. But she did not understand. He had obligations to his tenants and employees that could not be met without the inheritance. And relief at the resolution of his problems did not mitigate his sorrow over Lady Lanyard's demise.

But grief disappeared a week later when Mr. Andrews arrived, and shock trapped Charles in a hell he had still not escaped. The solicitor's dry voice droned through Lady Lanyard's will, not seeming to care that the words affected people's lives. After leaving various bequests to her faithful servants and other grandchildren, the dowager had willed *the remainder of my estate to my loving grandson, Charles Henry Montrose, eleventh Viscount Rathbone, provided he marries his betrothed, known to me as Miss Harriet Sharpe, within twelve months of my death.* If for any reason the marriage did not take place, the bequest would be divided among the charities listed in a codicil held by her solicitor. She further requested that mourning be terminated within three months.

Charles heard nothing else, sitting in shock long after the rest
of the family exited the library, unaware of the glare directed
at him by Lord Lanyard.

Hoist by his own petard. Charles departed in the morning,
faced with the impossible task of finding Harriet and convincing her to marry him. He had spent the four months since that
day alternating between fury and resignation.

His first step had been obvious. He inquired at the Litton
Cheney coaching inn, asking for her destination. Learning that
she had gone to Bridport, he had immediately followed, but
there he had lost her. He made a sketch of Harriet and her
aunt, but he was not very happy with it. Mrs. Sharpe looked all
right, but he could not seem to produce Harriet. And it would
have done little good if he had. Few people would remember
so unprepossessing a pair five months after the fact. The
records showed no tickets issued to them and no other parties
who resembled them. But the hope that her grandmother lived
near Bridport was quickly quashed. It was not a large town
and no one he met in three days of asking knew of anyone
named Sharpe.

He had next returned to the inn where they met, but though
the proprietor recalled the storm, he had no memory of indi-
vidual travelers, even failing to recognize Lord Rathbone.
Backtracking the stagecoach proved fruitless as well. Harriet
had boarded it the day of the storm but no one recalled how
she had arrived at the inn.

Based on his impression that she might have lived or visited
near Willingford House, he had scoured that area, but no
Sharpes emerged. He discovered that Lord Purvey had lived in
Lincolnshire and wondered if they might have been related,
but he could discover no connection. When a search of coaching records turned up no parties that could include Harriet, he
gave up and returned home.

Since then he had stayed at Swansea, assigning his secretary
to the search, though he had little hope of success. She had
been on her way to her maternal grandmother's home, so the
name Sharpe was of limited use. He tried locating the aunt,
checking passenger manifests for ships at several departure
points covering many months, without luck. He searched death
notices for her father's obituary, but without knowing where
she came from, it was difficult. No nobleman was named
Sharpe, nor were any baronets. He could only surmise that his
initial impression was correct. She was the daughter of a vicar

or squire or other low-ranking gentry. Such folk would be unknown outside their immediate community, and without knowing what county she had lived in, the chances of success were nil.

He briefly toyed with finding some other unfortunate to pass off as Harriet, but the idea rapidly died under scrutiny. He was done with deceit. Besides, it would never work. Andrews had met Harriet. To get the inheritance, he would have to marry the chit, but a marriage using an assumed name would be invalid. If it came out, he would lose everything. Even if it didn't, it would cast a permanent cloud of uncertainty over his heirs. And hiding the truth would be impossible. His family knew Harriet. Given his illness during that fortnight, they probably knew her better than he did.

And so he faced a future different from the one he had been raised to expect. His estate was a wreck, with little chance of improvement. He drained the glass in one long swallow and refilled it. He should not even be drinking. His cellars were nearly empty, and he had not the means to replenish them. But a long day in the fields, trying to finish the spring planting with less than half the men he needed, had left him too blue-deviled to sleep.

Another memory nagged at the back of his mind, and though he tried to refuse it entry, it surfaced anyway. His grandmother's last letter had contained more than her order to produce Harriet for a family Christmas.

I will doubtless succumb before many more weeks have passed, she wrote. He had thought she was making sure he appeared as commanded. *Do not continue mourning me into the Season. I must insist that your plans move forward as scheduled.*

He might have known from that what she had done, he groused to himself. But that was not all.

As long as you will accompany dear Harriet to town, I must ask a favor of you. My cousin, Anne, will be bringing out a granddaughter this year. Not only was Lady Melissa delayed in making her bows by the unfortunate death of her father, but she has the misfortune to be Lord Drayton's sister, so will need all the help she can get. Will you introduce the girl around? Anne assures me that she is nothing like her wastrel brother, but his reputation will still tarnish hers.

Damnation! He had no desire to dance attendance on some chit merely to satisfy his grandmother. And how could he go

to town? He had no place to stay. Poverty prevented him from
moving back into Albany, and living anywhere else would
cause comment and speculation. Mourning explained his current absence. Would it excuse lodging elsewhere?

With a shock, he realized that he was not swearing over the
idea of helping Lady Melissa, but was already planning ways
to accomplish the deed. Why? He had no duty to an unknown
third cousin. He ran his fingers through his hair as he traced
the relationships again. Yes, she was a third cousin. And Lady
Castleton could be the starchiest matron in the *ton*. She would
wonder at his interest. He could hardly claim to be head of the
family. Yet the reference to Lord Drayton bothered him. He
had never met the man, but he had heard of him—a gamester
and drunken sot who would sell his own mother if he could
gain anything by it. No girl deserved to be tied to so unworthy
a brother.

His mind returned to the problem of Harriet. Where was
she? Who was she? He reviewed everything he knew about
her. There was Toby. He had been mentioned only in that
overheard argument at the inn. He might be a brother, an
uncle, or a cousin. Charles suspected that the man occupied a
position of authority. She had also mentioned a brother, but he
was almost certain that she had lied about her background in a
deliberate attempt to mislead him, not that he understood why.

Then there was Lord Heflin, though inquiring about that
man's movements would be ticklish. There was no way to discover whether Harriet had stabbed the fellow, for the accompanying low blow would prevent Heflin from ever mentioning
the incident. And there was no guarantee that the confrontation
was recent. It might have been two, or even three, years before. Heflin was not averse to misusing children.

And finding Harriet would be the easy part; convincing her
to wed him might prove impossible. She had a poor opinion of
his character and a tongue like an adder, though if truth were to
be told, he found her intriguing if he ignored her looks and unladylike mannerisms. There was something excitingly sensual
about her, an aura that raised heat in his loins. If she had looked
better, he might have made a serious push to court her. He grimaced over that cow-handed proposal. His relief when she refused had been profound. Yet he had been on fire for her.

Fustian! he snorted into his wine. Such an alliance would
have been unthinkable. She would have to be a member of the
aristocracy to be eligible to be his wife. Of course, now he had

no choice. If he did not wed her within the next eight months, he was doomed to poverty.

And he deserved it. Dishonorable masquerade. He had been mad to conceive the idea. Even if it had worked, it was beneath his dignity as a gentleman. How much it had cost him.

It was time to start behaving like an honorable gentleman, he decided, heading upstairs to bed. And his first act toward making amends would be to fulfill his grandmother's last wish. He would go to London, sell the rest of the Rathbone paintings, and make a last effort to find Harriet. Perhaps someone in town knew of a family named Sharpe.

Chapter Eight

Melissa jumped when a footman rapped sharply on her door. She and her grandmother were scheduled to be at home for the afternoon, but not for another hour.

"Lady Castleton asks that you hurry, milady," Willis reported, rapidly twisting Melissa's hair into a high knot that spilled wisps and curls around her face. "Lord Rathbone is in the gold drawing room."

Melissa froze. Her second worst nightmare. His mourning period had several weeks to run, so she had ceased worrying about him. Lady Castleton would be furious if the truth came out. Melissa had lied by omission, implying that she had come straight to Castle Windcombe upon leaving home. Even worse, she had demanded that she be judged on her own merits. Could Rathbone control his surprise when he recognized her? She hadn't changed *that* much.

How should she greet him? she wondered as she descended. She must prevent all mention of the past. *Let him set the tone,* Bea's voice echoed. He was enough of a gentleman to wait until they were in private to bring up their mutual deceit, for he could also be damaged by exposure. But intelligence had never been his strong suit, and she had no idea if shock might loosen his tongue. In that case, she would have to deflect the conversation and pray her very astute grandmother would not pounce on the ploy.

Had he changed? Her heart beat a little faster at the memory of his blond hair and aqua eyes. Few men compared favorably with his physique. But entertaining such thoughts was unproductive. Infatuation with his admittedly handsome exterior would never do. At least she was no longer a hoydenish rustic. Her afternoon gown of green-striped muslin set off her figure, its primrose ribbons emphasizing the amber highlights in her eyes and turning her hair to spun gold

"It has been some time since you last called, Charles," complained Lady Castleton as Melissa approached the drawing room. It sounded like they were still exchanging greetings but the words confirmed Melissa's impression that Charles was not the sort to pursue family obligations.

"I have been at Swansea, my lady," he responded. She could hear the smile in his voice. "But my grandmother requested that I look in on you this Season, so here I am."

"Dear Abigail," said Lady Castleton sadly. "How I miss her. She was the best of my cousins."

"We all miss her."

He had done very well by her death, fumed Melissa, picking up a hint of ambivalence in his tone. She drew a deep breath to steady her nerves, and glided into the drawing room.

"There you are, Melissa," exclaimed Lady Castleton. "We have spoken of my cousin, Lady Lanyard. This is her grandson, Charles, Lord Rathbone. My granddaughter, Lady Melissa Stapleton."

Charles berated himself for acquiescing to his grandmother's demands. Speculation was already flaring in Lady Castleton's eyes. It was too late to back out, but he would conclude this duty call as quickly as manners allowed and then wash his hands of them.

But he swallowed hard when Lady Melissa entered, hardly hearing the introduction. She was the image of his grandmother's portrait. Tall. Golden. Voluptuous, yet innocent. His cravat dug into his neck, restricting the flow of air to his lungs. If the picture was fascinating, how much more was the living, breathing woman?

His hesitation lasted only a moment. Stepping forward, he led her to a chair. "I had no idea the family was hiding such a beauty."

"You sound a shocking flirt, my lord," she murmured.

He was stunned. There was no other word for it. Her eyes were only inches below his own. His arms trembled with the effort to not drag her into an embrace. Dear Lord! He had never met a woman who affected him thus. It was all he could do to limit himself to a light kiss on her elegant hand. Forcing his attention elsewhere, he seated her and retired to lean against the mantle, a safe eight feet away. A deep breath allowed him to address commonplace remarks to Lady Castleton while he fought to regain his composure.

* * *

Melissa saw that flash of recognition and the accompanying shock, but his greeting remained coolly formal. The familiar web of pretense closed around her, and she bit her lip in anger. This was not the same as the deceit they had perpetrated in the past. As soon as they managed a private word, they would agree to forget their earlier association and put it behind them.

Why had Lady Lanyard asked him to call? Surely she had not known the truth. He would have inherited nothing in that case; and gossip being what it was, everyone would have heard if he had been cut off.

With a start, she realized that Rathbone was talking and had been doing so for some time. It would not do to call attention to herself by woolgathering. That could only pique Lady Castleton's interest and bare the very scandal she sought to avoid.

" . . . your son not here?" he was asking.

"You know he hates London," replied Lady Castleton. "He will not subject himself to town until Eleanor is ready to make her bows. Certainly not this Season."

"I understand that your brother is Lord Drayton," Charles commented, turning his eyes to Melissa.

She sighed. "That is true, my lord, though thankfully he has no plans to come to town."

"Thankfully, indeed. His weakness for wine and gaming is well-known. The connection could mar your standing."

"My own countenance has already countered such nonsense," declared Lady Castleton. "But your support is welcome."

"You have gentlemen to escort you?" he asked.

"Not this Season. My grandsons are otherwise occupied. Edwin is still at Oxford, and Henry stayed home to study estate operations. He is to take over one of Castleton's small holdings next fall."

"It is a complicated subject. I have spent much of the past year doing the same."

"You are interested in estate management?" asked Melissa.

Despite his claims, she had not believed he would actually involve himself in Swansea's operation. It was more in Rathbone's character to use his inheritance to hire an efficient steward, leaving him free to pursue his indolent life in town. Of course, he might be merely passing the time until mourning was over, though he had not even managed to do that. He displayed his usual casual elegance with no sign of black. His bottle-green jacket fit tightly across muscular shoulders. Buff pantaloons clung to equally muscular thighs before disappearing into dazzling boots. His blond curls raged in deliberate dishevelment around his face. Even his indolent pose against the fireplace could not mask his athletic conditioning. He could be the model for Corinthians everywhere. She shivered unexpectedly as memories returned of being pressed against that masculine body.

"I must be," he answered, aqua eyes unexpectedly serious. "Swansea has never been in good condition and needs considerable attention."

"Do you enjoy the work?" she asked.

"More than I expected," he admitted, surprised both at the question and at the continuing attraction she exerted for him. Her voice was pure velvet, stroking seductively across his skin. But it would not do, he reminded himself sharply. He could not seduce an innocent, especially one of his relatives. And he certainly could not court her. He must find Harriet.

"My uncle has a fascinating book detailing Coke's experiments at Holkham Hall. Have you seen it?"

"Yes, I've studied it in detail. My former steward did not hold with 'new-fangled notions,' as he called them, so I've had to learn everything on my own." He mentioned several specifics, leading to a delightful exchange lasting some time.

"Will you be in town long?" asked Lady Castleton when the visiting hour approached.

"A fortnight, perhaps. Since you have no escort, perhaps I might offer my services," he heard himself saying, as surprised at the offer as Lady Castleton. Lady Melissa was frankly staring. His mind reeled off a string of oaths for his stupidity.

"That will be charming," her ladyship accepted. "We attend the Sefton ball this evening. Would you care to dine with us first?"

"Delighted."

The arrangements were quickly made, much to Melissa's discomfort. What game was he playing? Surely he could not wish to continue their acquaintance beyond a duty call. Perhaps he intended to maneuver a moment alone to agree to forget the past. Or maybe he was plotting to retaliate by embarrassing her in public. But that was unimaginable. He knew that she would fight back. His own reputation was tarnished enough; revealing his deceit would ruin him.

She stifled all questions as the first of their callers was announced and a footman set a tea tray before her. Within minutes the drawing room was crowded with gossips, friends, and beaux.

Unaccountably, Charles stayed through the entire afternoon, his status as a distant cousin hardly stretching to cover this breach of good manners.

"How handsome you look today, George." Melissa smiled an hour later as Lord Rufton bowed over her hand. "Is that a new waistcoat?"

"Yes, it is," he admitted, his eyes lighting as he took in her own appearance. "Beautiful, as always, my dear."

"I will become hopelessly conceited if you continue such exaggerations," she countered lightly.

"Fustian. Have you heard the latest? Kemble announced that he is retiring from the stage."

"Oh, no! He will be missed."

"His last appearance will be next week. Would you like to attend?"

"Very much. Make the arrangements with Grandmama. Who else will be in the party?"

"I thought to ask the Hartfords and possibly another couple. But who should I include to balance numbers?"

"Perhaps my cousin. He just arrived in town. Are you acquainted?" She gestured at Charles, who was exchanging *on-dits* with Lady Debenham.

"Yes, but I had no idea you were related." He frowned.

"Only distantly. Our respective grandmothers were cousins. He will not be here long, for he is still technically in mourning, but he will escort us in the meantime."

George was still frowning, but had no right to object to the arrangement, so he held his tongue.

Charles fended off Lady Debenham's curiosity even as his eyes returned to Lady Melissa. What was so intriguing about her? It went beyond her similarity to his grandmother's portrait. He was too old to be taken in by a pretty face and had never been interested in the annual influx of young girls, though at nineteen she could hardly be categorized with the twittering seventeen-year-olds that flooded London every Season. He grimaced as he recalled that Harriet would be barely seventeen, if that. Lady Melissa seemed at ease, surrounded by admiring swains.

It took him a moment to identify what had caught his eye about the scene. Though she qualified as a diamond and at least six gentlemen were staring as if they would devour her, she affected none of the airs of an incomparable. The conceit was missing. She did not play her suitors off against one another, made no move to create competition between them, and derided no one. Even Lord Ampleigh, whose shyness and obesity repelled many young ladies despite his title and fortune, was joining in the conversation, laughing and teasing with the rest.

He excused himself from Lady Debenham's side when Matt Crawford arrived. They had long been close friends.

"Matt." Once Crawford had greeted his hostess, they retired to a relatively quiet corner. "It's been an age."

"You begged off your usual rounds last fall," Matt reminded him.

"My grandmother fell ill." Charles shrugged. "I would not be here now if she had not commanded me to leave off mourning after three months and look after her cousin."

"And who might that be?"

"Lady Castleton, of course. That is why I am here. I only arrived last night."

"Ah." Matt looked speculatively at Charles. "So the delectable Lady Melissa is your cousin. I am amazed that you have not already snapped her up. She is your type."

"Hardly." But his loins protested the lie. "My tastes do not run to innocent maidens, as you well know. Nor had I met her before today. Her brother is definitely not my type."

"Nor mine, though at one time we were friends," admitted Matt. "I spent a month at his estate last summer, along with several others, including one who was sharping cards. Not something I care to repeat."

"Who?"

Matt shook his head. "You know better than that, Charles. Without proof, I cannot blacken any man's reputation."

"No wonder Lady Melissa moved in with her grandmother," murmured Charles to himself. Something nagged at the edges of his mind, but he could not bring it into focus. He hoped she had left upon the death of her father. If she had been in her brother's keeping at the time of that house party, publicizing it would tarnish her reputation. Who had been dishonorable enough to cheat at cards? He could understand Matt's reluctance to name names, for such a charge would ostracize the perpetrator. And without proof, Matt would face a duel and the blackening of his own name. But he could not let the incident die. Somehow he would discover the villain and bring him to justice. It should not be difficult to learn who had attended that party.

"Yes, she has suffered from association with such a weak, dissipated fool," agreed Matt, not pretending that he had missed the aside. "But those who know her will never hold it against her. She is a delightful young lady and will make a wonderful wife."

"You sound infatuated. Are you pursuing her yourself?" asked Charles.

"No. We would not suit. But I consider her a friend."

Charles let his eyes return to Lady Melissa. Lord Rufton was taking his leave, his eyes betraying how much he cared for her. Hers also contained warmth. Rufton was an unexceptionable suitor, heir to an earldom and wealthy in his own right. Charles examined the rest of her court. Ampleigh was unworthy of such a beauty. Thornhill could be ignored; he would not consider settling down for years. Parkington could not seriously court her; as the younger son of a baron, he was far beneath her touch.

He scowled at the arrival of Lord Graffington. Here was another whose eyes betrayed his interest, but he was not an acceptable suitor. Too many black deeds lurked in his past, and not just his unrestrained raking. He delighted in roughness and had been banned from several quality brothels in consequence, though that was not common knowledge. Charles only knew about it because he had witnessed a contretemps in which Graffington was physically ejected from Madame Filette's for injuring one of the girls.

He forced his attention back to Matt.

"You figured that out in the short time she's been in town?" he asked.

"Of course not. I've known her for years. As I said, her brother used to be a friend."

How was he to discourage Graffington? wondered Charles as he turned the conversation to horses and last month's mill near Dover. Whether the man was serious or not was irrelevant. It would not do for him to hover around her. His mere presence could damage her reputation. It never crossed his mind to wonder why he felt responsible for her future. He paid not the slightest attention to any of his other relatives.

Matt took his leave, first arranging to drive Melissa in the park. Charles grimaced when Lord Englewood arrived to flirt with her. There was another who was unworthy of the lady—a prosy bore who dampened the spirits of everyone around him.

By the end of the afternoon, Charles had decided to stay in London for the rest of the Season. Before he returned for dinner, he sold the last of Swansea's paintings, moved out of his cheap hotel, and rented a dilapidated room whose only virtue was its proximity to Mayfair.

Melissa enjoyed the afternoon once she realized that Charles would not bring up their sordid past. She deliberately steered her eyes away from his sartorial splendor, and concentrated on her suitors. Not much had changed in two weeks. She still could not summon the excitement for any of them that might grow into love.

George headed the list, as he had from the first, though the glow he raised was nought but relaxed friendship. Perhaps it was his unprepossessing appearance that kept her heart from pounding. His bright blue eyes were his best feature, but it was difficult to develop paroxysms of pleasure over a stocky physique topped by a mop of red hair, especially when compared to tall muscularity and blond curls.

Stop it! she admonished herself. She was not such a shallow ninny that she judged a man by his shell! But she had to concede that George did not raise thrills. And she refused to admit that Charles did.

Lord Graffington was new to her court but she found him intriguing. He had a delightful sense of humor that had lightened several boring evenings, including Lady Osterley's dull musicale two days earlier. And he was certainly pleasant to look at—tall and blond, with warm brown eyes. Perhaps too warm. He exuded the same powerful masculinity she had noticed in Heflin and in Charles.

The other regulars were mostly friends, and she must work to keep that relationship. None would make an acceptable husband, but none was shopping for a wife. Matt Crawford fit neither category. Though he only occasionally approached her, she often felt his eyes on her, almost in a paternal way.

Charles was the last to leave, promising to return for dinner. Whatever his game, she must distance herself from him. He was not a man she could ever accept, yet he still exerted an unwanted attraction on her. She feared where it might lead.

"I cannot believe you would allow Lord Rathbone to accompany us," she protested when everyone was gone. "The man is an unprincipled libertine whose presence can only tarnish my reputation."

"Nonsense!" scoffed Lady Castleton. "It is true that he sowed his oats with abandon when younger, but he is now seven-and-twenty. It is time he married and settled down. He inherited a considerable fortune from my cousin. You could hardly do better, dear."

"Absolutely not," stated Melissa, horrified at the direction her grandmother's thoughts had moved. "I'll not wed a libertine no matter what his fortune. Don't encourage him. I would hate to have to repudiate him publicly."

Lady Castleton agreed, but with a look in her eye that Melissa mistrusted. It gave her yet another worry.

The Sefton ball was a sad crush, expected for any affair hostessed by an Almack's patroness. Lady Sefton was delighted. Charles was less happy, for he had never enjoyed the marriage-mart rounds and was already having second thoughts about squiring his cousin for the Season. Granted, she was lovely and there was something about her that haunted him. But he should be hunting for Harriet so he could begin the monumental job of convincing her to marry him. Yet he was helpless as Melissa drew him unwillingly to her side. He had often had the unsettling thought that his soul was bound up in that portrait of his grandmother, trapped in the painted half-smile of her creamy face. The feeling had now returned with a vengeance, concentrated on his cousin.

"You will grant me the first dance, of course," he stated as they descended the staircase into the ballroom.

"I'm sorry, my lord," she apologized with a smile. "I have already promised that one to George."

Scowling, he grabbed her card, surprised to find most of the dances already allocated. He rapidly scrawled his name next to two open sets.

"Your arrogance is showing," she chided him softly, steel spiking the words.

Rufton was approaching, so Charles had to content himself with a curt "Until later." He felt as if he had just been whipped. It was a familiar sensation, though he could not identify why. Collecting a glass of punch, he joined a group of friends who were practicing looking bored while offering humorous critiques of every dancing couple.

Melissa was furious that Charles could be so dictatorial

when he must remember that she despised that trait. That had been the cause of most of their fights. But she curbed her anger, for she was unwilling to become the subject of speculative *on-dits*. By the time George joined her, she was calm.

An hour passed in lighthearted pleasure. Mindful of the expectations of society's dragons, she kept her smile coolly polite. Why had the *ton* decided that boredom was de rigueur? It seemed ridiculous to plan exciting entertainments when the guests must appear disinterested. Sometimes she longed to burst into laughter. Like now. George was relating a story that had her sides aching.

"She had hardly recovered," he continued blandly, "when a squirrel appeared—a candidate for Bedlam if I ever saw one; the nearest tree was thirty yards away. The dog took off with no thought to Miss Appleton, who had foolishly wrapped the lead around her wrist. She hadn't gone three steps before she tripped, sprawling headlong into a flower bed where she succumbed to hysterics. Pansies lodged in her bonnet, and ivy looped around one ear. The dog tried to soothe her, administering exuberant kisses, but all he accomplished was tangling her in the lead. It took three gentlemen to rescue her."

Melissa thrust aside the vision lest she burst into laughter. "You are hoping I'll make a cake of myself, aren't you, George?" she charged, her eyes sparkling in unison with his. "Why can't you save stories like that for informal occasions?"

"Sorry, my dear," he lied, winking at her.

She rapped him sharply with her fan.

Two sets later, she smiled as Lord Ampleigh tried one of the more intricate patterns of the quadrille. Considering his girth, he was surprisingly graceful, but dancing was not his forte. She had already complimented him on his elaborately embroidered waistcoat, but believed he would look better if he chose more restrained cravats and a more conservative line to his jackets. His figure did not display his wardrobe to advantage. But he was a knowledgeable and amusing companion, regaling her now with a description of the telescope at the Greenwich Royal Observatory. She knew little about the heavens, but his words were easy to follow. He would make a good teacher. And when he discussed something he enjoyed, his shyness fled.

When Charles claimed his first dance, Melissa's anger over his arrogance resurfaced. He had signed for two of her waltzes, dances she usually sat out as she distrusted such closeness. It raised disturbing sensations that were best left dormant. She could not afford clouded judgment and did not want to encourage anyone's attentions until she had decided who she wished to attach. So far, she had waltzed only with George.

"You dance very well," he smiled as they twirled around the room.

"You sound shocked," she countered. "And I am not pleased with the way you thrust yourself forward tonight, my lord. I rarely waltz and resent anyone demanding the privilege."

He raised his brows. "Are you setting yourself up as a puritan?"

"Not at all. But waltzing implies a closeness that I do not wish to encourage, especially with you."

His eyes suddenly glared, though his lips retained their social smile. "And what have I done to draw your ire, cousin?"

He honestly did not recognize her. What a relief!

"I do not know you," she responded, wondering how to rectify her error. She must not instigate a fight that might trigger his memory. Her voice lightened into teasing. "Nor am I sure I wish to. Your reputation is not what I would look for in a friend."

"I thought most young ladies were attracted by rakes." He smiled charmingly.

"I am not 'most young ladies.' You may be as debauched as Lord Thornhill, for all I know. Imagine being caught *au naturel* at a ball with two ladies of the evening!"

"Where did you hear that?" he demanded in shock.

"I imagine everyone in town has heard by now. It's been two weeks. Most gentlemen sound envious when they laugh over it."

He sighed. "You made your point, cousin. You're no prude. I presume you know enough not to mention this to others."

She mentally kicked herself for forgetting her training. Being close to Charles made her regress to Harriet's vulgar behavior. "Of course, my lord. And you know enough not to commandeer my dance card."

He nodded. "Surely waltzing with me is not that bad."

"On the contrary." It was far too pleasing, she conceded. And for that reason alone, it must never happen again. "I am uncomfortable in your company. The way you stare is rude."

"My apologies, Lady Melissa," he begged. "I will restrain

myself in the future. But you look so much like a youthful painting of my grandmother that I cannot help myself. It does not seem possible."

That accounted for that blaze of shock, she acknowledged silently, and it was another reason to hold him at arm's length. Continued scrutiny must surely reveal her identity. "I can understand your surprise, my lord. But staring in public makes you look like a mooncalf. I'll not have my name linked to such behavior. Nor am I attracted to fribbles."

"That was part of my youth," he protested. "I have spent the last nine months working on my estate."

"The exigencies of mourning mean nothing, my lord. And you can hardly plead mourning when you are here now."

"My grandmother ordered that mourning cease after three months," he stated firmly. "I loved her dearly and will mourn her in my heart for much longer, but I can hardly counter her expressed wishes."

"Very well, my lord. I will grant you that. But I expect you also to honor mine. You will not behave in so highhanded a fashion again, or I will not suppress my natural desire to rake you over the coals, even in public. Nor will I dance with you at all if you do not squire other partners. I will not be singled out in such a manner." She was the first one he had led out.

He sighed. "You win, Lady Melissa."

She pondered their exchange several times during the evening when she caught him staring at her. She had not thought of that portrait since leaving Lanyard Manor and had never realized that she resembled it. He was abnormally attracted to it. His indecipherable expression as he gazed upon the painted face returned to mind. And many of the names linked to Lord Rathbone's were women who shared characteristics with Lady Lanyard—tall, well-endowed, light-haired. What did that mean for her?

Chapter Nine

Covent Garden was packed the night of Kemble's last performance, excitement surging as people flocked to witness the end of an era. Kemble might not project the magnetic intensity that Kean had recently brought to the stage, but he had been part of theatrical circles for more than thirty years. His career had been characterized by stiff, studied mannerisms and a coldly oratorical delivery, even when playing opposite his sister, the incomparable Sarah Siddons. But he had chosen a perfect vehicle for his adieu—the haughty, arrogant Coriolanus.

Melissa enjoyed the play, but the crowd was as inattentive as ever, paying more attention to one another than to the stage. Few had any real interest in the theater, attending only because it formed part of the social rounds. The excitement on this occasion arose from earning bragging rights in Mayfair's drawing rooms.

George had filled his box to capacity. Charles dutifully escorted Lady Castleton, though he often turned a disapproving eye on Melissa. And that was ridiculous! Why was he upset? he wondered, cringing as she laughed at one of Rufton's sallies. The man had no known vices; he drank and gamed in moderation and only occasionally dipped into the muslin company. His main interest was horses, which made him an excellent match for Melissa. Charles had already discovered her expertise, accompanying her on morning rides twice. She rode even better than Harriet, although she exuded the grace that Harriet had lacked. He had never expected to find a lady who could combine both femininity and skill. Away from London's rigid decorum, Melissa would be a neck-or-nothing rider. And Firefly was one of the best horses he had seen. His irritation flared.

It had done so with increasing frequency. George leaned close to murmur something in Melissa's ear, and Charles forced his fists to relax. She responded with a comment that set them both laughing. Charles determinedly turned aside to address a remark to Lord Hartford, and was soon engrossed in a discussion of horses.

"Don't make me laugh during the performance," George begged when he had recovered himself. "I'd hate to be thought rag-mannered."

"You asked for that one," Melissa riposted with a grin. "If you hadn't compared me to Titania, I never would have mentioned it."

"At the risk of offending your dignity, would you like to visit Astley's next week? I have promised to take my godson."

"I hope that I never use dignity as an excuse to avoid fun." She glared at him, but her twinkling eyes gave her away.

She spent the first interval talking with Lady Hartford. They had become fast friends. Caroline also believed in accomplishment, assisting others to achieve their own goals, particularly the crippled veterans who still littered London two years after Waterloo.

"Did George invite you to accompany us next week?" she asked now.

"Yes. Are you also part of the group?"

"Of course. George is Robbie's godfather. Robert is three and a half and anxious to see the performing horses. He already rides so well that I fear he may try to duplicate their tricks." She grimaced. "But Thomas promised, so here we are."

Melissa laughed. "I suspect that if he tries to mimic their stunts under Thomas's eye, he will rapidly become as expert as the performers." Lord Hartford had long been acknowledged the best rider in the *ton*, though Charles was nearly as accomplished, as was George.

"You are good for George," said Lady Hartford, her voice now serious. "He has become much too solemn in recent years."

"I have done nothing for him," protested Melissa. "And I doubt he has changed. It is true that he smiles more than when we first met, but that is mostly for show. There is an urgency beneath his surface that belies pleasure."

Lady Hartford frowned, her eyes studying George as he laughed with Thomas. "I see what you mean. There is an element of determination in his frivolity. I must talk to Thomas. He might know what is the matter."

It was Melissa's turn to frown. "I may be wrong. It would be mortifying if my unthinking words started a groundless rumor."

"Fustian," snorted Lady Hartford. "This is not for public consumption. You are astute and merely focused my own impressions. George is too dear a friend to do anything that might hurt him. But neither should he try to bear burdens alone. Not when he has others with whom to share them. That's what friends are for."

"I hope the problem is a small one."

"Do you care for him?" she probed, then slapped herself on the wrist. "Forgive my impertinence, Melissa. But I would hate to see him hurt. He is clearly infatuated with you."

"There is nothing to forgive, Caroline," sighed Melissa. "I care very much for him, but I cannot decide how." Blue eyes flashed before her own, but instead of the bright sapphires that blazed below George's russet locks, she saw a beguiling aqua complementing riotous blond curls. She frowned. "How can one choose a husband in so short a time? There is little chance for serious discussion. I don't feel like I really know any of them, including George."

"You must remember that the London Season evolved when marriages were arranged solely for dynastic and financial reasons," said Lady Hartford. "It allowed both parties to meet before the nuptial agreements were signed. Many marriages are still based on those principles. But for those who want to marry for love, it does pose frustrating restrictions."

"How did you manage?" asked Melissa. She had already discovered that the Hartfords were as close a couple as she had ever encountered, sharing an emotional bond that often allowed them to read each other's minds.

She laughed. "Actually, we were involved in a coaching accident and inadvertently compromised. Luck sometimes plays a large role. But not everyone is so fortunate. Be sure before you choose. This decision will be with you for the rest of your life."

Melissa nodded. How did she feel about George? He was amusing, comfortable, intelligent, and respectful. He had a serious nature and a long history of responsible behavior. He was generous with his assets but never wasteful. She could not imagine him becoming a dissipated weakling like her brother.

She cared deeply for him and wanted him to be happy. Was that a good enough foundation for marriage? His attentions were so marked that he would certainly offer for her. And his underlying urgency made it likely the offer would come soon. She pondered her emotions as the second act opened on stage. How would she feel as this man's wife? Her eyes peeked sideways at him, taking in his solidity and recalling his protectiveness. He had never kissed her. Her skin prickled. Was it from love or was it just another manifestation of physical infatuation, brought on by a sudden image of a man's hand brushing her breast?

Charles commandeered her for a stroll during the next interval, leaving George trapped in a ponderous discussion with Lord Peregrin.

"You aren't seriously considering Lord Rufton, are you?" he scoffed, leading her away from the crowds.

"Yes, not that it is your concern," she replied.

"He is too stuffy for you."

"And how would you know?" she demanded. "You are hardly qualified to judge, being an irresponsible fribble with a reprehensible reputation. No lady could consider you a suitable spouse."

"And what does that mean?"

His steely voice and heavy glower ran shivers along her arms. She had never expected aqua eyes to look so menacing. But they were no longer aqua, having darkened to slate. She had forgotten that tendency, though it had been less noticeable at Lanyard Manor. Their quarrels had usually occurred in dimly lit rooms. Perhaps that was why he did not recognize her now.

But she had no time to reflect on the past. As so often happened in his company, her temper was rapidly fraying. He had no right to criticize her. "You've hardly been subtle in your choice of companions or in your indolent way of life, my lord," she riposted. "Lazing about town every Season, lolling in Brighton every summer, frolicking through hunting parties every fall that no decent lady would tolerate."

"Hardly every year," he denied. "In fact, I skipped most of that last year."

"Only because you were dancing attendance on your grandmother during her summer illness," she returned, forgetting that Lady Melissa would not know of his movements.

His brows raised in surprise. "And what do you know of my grandmother's health?"

"She has always been close to my own grandmother," she reminded him. "Grandmama's eyes are not what they were. I often read her mail aloud." The lie was out before she could censor it. She would have done better to claim Lady Castleton had told her. He might know that the dowager's eyesight was unusually keen for her age.

But Charles had his own worries. Her remark barely registered as he visibly grimaced. This was another aspect of Lady Lanyard's recovery that he had not considered. She would have continued all her usual correspondence during the months between his visit and her death. He prayed she had maintained convention and not mentioned his supposed betrothal. It had not been officially announced. But what might she have said about Miss Sharpe? He was so wrapped up in horrifying possibilities that he forgot why he had intended to chide his cousin.

Melissa saw the grimace. Very interesting, she reflected as her own thoughts took wing. Charles was upset that she might know of that summer visit. Surely he was not suffering from a guilty conscience. The arrogant Lord Rathbone was not one to regret his actions. He was too far above mere mortals to care what they thought, so he must fear that his supposed betrothal was known. His consequence would suffer if people believed he had been jilted. But Lady Lanyard had told no one. Aside from questions of propriety, no suspicion had surfaced in London drawing rooms—not even from Lady Beatrice, who always knew everything.

They returned to the box in near silence. George took Melissa's arm and gave his attention to her for the remainder of the play and the farce that followed. Charles was so caught up in his new worries that he hardly noticed the rest of the evening.

Melissa was leaving Mademoiselle Jeanette's modiste shop the next morning when she nearly ran into another young lady who was about to enter.

"Clara!" she exclaimed in surprise. "When did you arrive?"

"Melissa! I had no idea you were in town," replied Miss Rosehill, taking in her friend's appearance. "It must be nearly two years since I've seen you. How long have you been in London?"

"Since early March."

"Really? I thought your brother was still at home."

"He is, of course. Surely you knew that I left Drayton last year. I have been living with my grandmother."

"I had forgotten. I spent the summer with an uncle and then went back to Mrs. Weatherbottom's School for Young Ladies without ever going home."

"I hear she is a terror," gasped Melissa.

"Absolutely. Papa finally let me leave last month."

"When did you arrive in town, then? I've not seen you."

"Last night. My parents refused to present me this Season, citing my age and their lack of funds. But Aunt Charlotte invited me to stay for a few weeks, so here I am."

Clara was seventeen, but had always seemed older. Her family lived not far from Drayton Manor, and the two girls had known each other all their lives, though they had never been bosom bows.

"I must return home," apologized Melissa, sidestepping a pair of haughty matrons who were glaring imperiously at finding the sidewalk partially blocked. "But get your aunt to call tomorrow. We will be at home. Castleton House on Berkeley Square."

"Certainly. It is good to find a friendly face. London is more than a little intimidating."

"But not for long."

Melissa pondered Clara's sudden appearance as she and Lady Castleton made their rounds that afternoon. The girl was both sweet and sensible, and would make someone a wonderful wife. Despite her comment about tight budgets, she had a good dowry. Her father had probably declined to bring her out to increase the chances that she would marry her first Season, thus sparing him the burden of a second sojourn in town. He always had been a nip-farthing. And that would account for Mrs. Weatherbottom, who ran a school in Lincoln that offered but one virtue—low tuition.

The Wharburton masquerade was held that night. Twenty years earlier, Lady Wharburton had started the tradition of holding a costume ball suitable for innocent maidens. None but the most proper were invited to insure that no one's reputation was threatened. This year she had outdone herself, rigging out her extensive ballroom as a forest glade. Trees in gigantic planters reached to the ceiling, their branches festooned with lanterns, mirrors cunningly expanding the effect. Banks of flowers, thickets of ferns, and even a babbling brook filled corners and alcoves. The doors to the terrace stood open to the night, with trees and shrubs arranged on either end of its flagstone surface furthering the illusion of the forest primeval.

Beneath this canopy surged a vast collection of disparate beings—Romans and Greeks; gods and goddesses; kings, queens, and other assorted rulers; Shakespearean characters; Cavaliers; French courtiers; Spanish grandees; Russian princes; pirates and rogues of every description; shepherdesses; gypsies; and ladies-in-waiting. Melissa settled her mask more firmly and smiled at Lady Castleton.

She had vetoed her grandmother's suggestion that she dress as Cleopatra, fearful that donning a black wig would trigger recognition as Harriet. Instead, she chose to be the fairy queen, Titania. Willis had arranged her golden hair into a nebulous halo that mimicked the billowing froth of gold netting comprising her costume.

"I never imagined anything like this," she murmured as they descended the stairs after greeting Lady Wharburton. A highwayman in a black domino grinned at her, his mask revealing beguiling aqua eyes.

"Stand and deliver!" he growled. "Your card, my lady." He then ruined the effect by adding, "please."

"So polite a marauder." She giggled, rapping him on the arm with her fan. "But you may have the country dance after supper, good sir."

"Surely you've a waltz to spare. Your cruelty overwhelms me, your majesty," he teased.

"As your arrogance does me," she riposted. "Country dance or nothing, Charles."

He grimaced, but complied.

The evening was almost magical. The pretense of anonymity added excitement, dissipating the usual *ennui*. Laughter bubbled continuously in the background, and even the most ponderous of partners seemed light on his feet.

Ampleigh whisked her into a spirited reel, keeping up a stream of chatter whenever he could, his usual shyness forgotten. He made a perfect Henry VIII, laughing over his portly physique that made the usual padding unnecessary.

George led her through the supper waltz, his closeness sending prickles marching across her skin. He was dressed as Lochinvar, and she wondered if he had decided to claim a cherished bride. The idea left her breathless. Hopefully she was falling in love with him at last. George certainly deserved it.

Supper was a lighthearted period spent laughing at Lord Heatherton's imitations of the luckless Mr. Bowles who, in trying to impress a young lady, had hired a horse too spirited for his meager skill and been thrown ignominiously into the Serpentine at the height of the fashionable hour.

Pretense usually caught up to one in the end, reflected a suddenly somber Melissa. She ought to reveal her own deceit before something happened to expose her, but that would be difficult to do without destroying herself. She had already added several lies to the account, both explicit and implied. And revealing her faults also risked harming Charles. No matter how much he deserved censure, she did not want to be responsible for calling it down on his head.

"Let us stretch our legs outside a moment," George suggested when they returned to the ballroom to find the musicians not yet ready to resume playing.

"That sounds delightful," she agreed, for the room was airless. Perhaps a turn on the terrace would restore her sagging spirits.

He led her to the railing, but properly declined to descend into the garden without adequate chaperonage. Charles had labeled him stuffy, though she had never considered him so. He could certainly not compare to Uncle Howard. On the other hand, he had never retained her hand too long or tried to kiss her—hardly the behavior of a besotted man. She wanted less restraint from a husband. But the thought proved premature. Smiling into her eyes, he led her along the terrace and into the trees, drawing her into his arms.

"You are beautiful tonight, my dear," he murmured before cutting off all comment. His lips were gentle, moving deliciously over her own. Melissa responded without thought, allowing her hands to creep around his neck as he pulled her closer. Her lips tingled where he touched, but neither of them was in danger of losing control. The increased noise from the ballroom drew them apart.

"We must return." He sighed, setting her reluctantly away.

"Yes," she agreed, unable to think of anything else to say.

Charles was waiting beside Lady Castleton, his social smile belied by the stormy anger seething behind slaty eyes.

"What were you thinking to go outside unattended?" he hissed as he led her to a set that was forming near the terrace.

"Odious beast!" she snapped. "How dare you? George is a gentleman. He would never harm me."

His fury increased. Forcing her hand onto his arm, he whisked her out the door and into the trees.

"Have you no sense of propriety, cousin?" he demanded harshly.

"Have you?" she replied stonily, her hands on her hips while she glared at him. "You have just committed the same dastardly crime."

"Do you expect to bring him up to scratch by compromising him?" he sneered, refusing to consider his unfairness or evaluate the cause of his anger. Rufton was so obviously planning to make an offer that betting at White's concerned when, not if, a betrothal would occur.

"You certainly have a low opinion of both myself and society, sir. There is nothing wrong with taking a turn about the terrace with a trustworthy companion. But I suppose you judge others by your own dishonorable history. Why Lady Wharburton included you on her guest list I do not know."

"Jade," he whispered, white to the lips. "With women like you around it is no wonder so many marriages are empty shells."

"As you know from experience," she tossed back, not bothering to censor her words in her anger. "How many wives have you seduced?"

"It is not my behavior we are discussing, but yours, Melissa," he growled, grabbing her shoulders. "A lady does not disappear outside with a gentleman unless she wishes to be thought fast."

"Fustian! And you know it. How can you sing such a different tune for others than you do for yourself?"

"I'll not have my family's honor destroyed by a headstrong chit!" He no longer cared if he made sense. He wanted to shake her. Or strangle her. Or ravish her. Emotion tossed him about until he hardly knew where he was.

"Family honor! You are not responsible for me, Lord Rathbone," she reminded him coldly. "You are so distantly related that nothing I do could possibly harm you, even were I a Jezebel. If my behavior is wanting, my grandmother will let me know soon enough. And there is little impropriety in spending two minutes with a gentleman who is seriously courting my hand. Now leave off being such an ass and return me to the ballroom."

Anger turned her eyes tawny. The cloud of netting cradled her, as a square of jeweler's velvet would cradle a precious stone. He teetered on the precipice, desire battling duty and paralyzing will. Desire won.

Groaning, he pulled her into his arms. His lips devoured hers, his tongue pushing behind them to taste her sweetness even as his hands swept her back and hips.

Melissa twisted away, slapping his face hard enough to leave the imprint of her hand on his cheek. "Cad!" she spat, eyes glaring in fury. "Dishonorable toad! You have just verified your reputation. How dare you kiss another when you are already betrothed?"

"What?" He shook his head in shock. What had happened? She had responded, as eager for the kiss as he. His brain seemed clogged with cotton wool, his body screaming to drag her closer, his fingers tingling with longing.

"You know very well that you are betrothed to Miss Sharpe and have been for some months. When is the wedding scheduled?"

"Where did you hear that?" he demanded. Lady Lanyard had told? Why? But that was a stupid question. It was another way to guarantee his compliance. And there was no point in denying it when he had no choice but to marry the chit. He shuddered.

"From your grandmother, of course. She was thrilled to discover that you were finally settling down, and so informed her cousin. Frankly, I pity the girl. You will not make a good husband."

"Come, come, Lady Melissa," Charles protested, trying to keep his voice teasing. "I am not yet married, Miss Sharpe will never know, and you can scarcely deny that you enjoyed that every bit as much as I did." He caressed her arm, sending shivers through them both.

"Of course," she agreed, even as she slapped his hand aside. "One can expect no less from a man of your experience. But a gentleman would never force himself on a lady. You are a libertine and a cad. Tales of debauchery surface wherever you go. The Willingford scandal echoed long after you were thrown out, you must know."

He gasped, opening his mouth to explain, but she cut him off.

"Did you think I would be ignorant? I've known them all my life. Their estate runs with my brother's. If you cannot control your base nature, I will cut you in public and bar Castleton House to your entry. Now are you going to take me to my grandmother, or must I return alone and advertise your perfidy?"

Furious, he unwillingly complied.

She was right, he had to agree as he brooded over a glass of brandy after seeing them home. He had overstepped the bounds of propriety by castigating her for spending five minutes outside with Rufton. The man had probably kissed her, but it mattered not. They were all but betrothed. His own behavior was far worse, his loss of control inexcusable. That kiss had burned deeply into his soul. She was the most passionate woman he had ever met. But even that did not fully explain his attraction. Perhaps it was her unavailability. His future was already determined: a lifetime shackled to an unprepossessing wife. Or maybe it was the challenge that her disdain offered to his competitive spirit. Either way, he looked bad.

Her diatribe haunted him. She knew about Lady Willingford. What a shameful mess that had been! All sense of honor had fled that week. He still did not understand why he had accepted the Willingford's invitation. Respectable parties where eligible misses were displayed were poison to his constitution, but that did not countenance his reaction. He had cuckolded a man under his own roof, an inexcusable act under any circumstances. That had not been a hunting party, designed for dalliance and peopled by light-skirts. And Carla had not even been his worst transgression. He had done the same to Knightsbridge, despite knowing that the man was his uncle's closest friend. If Knightsbridge had discovered the liaison, his grandmother would have learned of it and written him off for good. And he had very nearly been caught by one of Willingford's tenants. The most disgusting aspect was that he hadn't really enjoyed either of them.

That kiss also kept Melissa awake until nearly dawn. Her reaction had caught her completely off guard, drawing a response before her mind had time to think. But the excitement was strictly physical. She must remain strong in the future and never be alone with him. If it ever happened again, she would be lost. She had spoken truly during that last conversation with Beatrice. Charles was a very dangerous man who could easily seduce her. Her choice of costume had certainly been prophetic. She had found herself in the woods, lusting after an ass.

But she could not help comparing Charles's kiss to the one she had shared only minutes before with George. Poor George. He suffered badly in contrast. His kiss had been tender and sweet, and utterly dull. She had not considered it thus at the time, of course. Bea's voice echoed. *Once the emotions are engaged, you will no longer feel delight at another man's touch.* Poor George.

Charles had revealed a world of pleasure that she desperately wanted to enter. The awful truth must be faced. She had wanted him to continue, had wanted more than just a kiss. Her unladylike nature had nearly betrayed her. It was not the first time he had affected her thus. His embrace in the state apartment at Lanyard Manor had also aroused desire, though a pale imitation of her present state. *Don't allow anyone to touch you . . .* But she had, and now she was more confused than ever. Was this a physical thing that could be initiated by any man? *Touches are exciting . . .* Perhaps she was truly a wanton. But her mind refused to accept that theory. George had not raised a flicker, even when she prayed he would. And Heflin's attack had provoked only revulsion and terror. Her feelings must reflect Charles's skill as a rake.

If only Bea were here! She could have answered these questions. It was obvious that their previous discussion had not gone far enough. But Bea was gone, leaving her without understanding and with nowhere to turn. She certainly couldn't mention this to her grandmother, or even to Helena, no matter how open they claimed to be with each other. Helena had doubtless never entertained a wayward thought in her life. She was a proper miss, properly trained to assume a proper position as wife to a very proper husband. But none of that was true of Melissa Stapleton.

Conflicting messages swirled in her head. Lady Castleton swore that ladies did not have such feelings. Satisfying a man's needs, she said, was a duty a wife performed without complaint, and with a gentle husband it was not too unpleasant. Marriage to George would thus be perfect for his embrace had been tender. She could imagine nothing more than tenderness from him, but neither would he arouse her disgust. However, Charles did not fit that picture, for he evoked a shocking amount of excitement. Bea had claimed that such feelings were normal, whatever one's station in life. Perhaps society used the image of unpleasant duty to discourage girls from straying. But that seemed unreasonable. All ladies could not be liars. *Help me, Lord,* she prayed. *I am so confused. Is pleasure really wrong?*

But the truth would not solve her real problem. Charles might be damnably attractive and experienced enough to set her body aflame with a touch, but he was also irresponsible, unreliable, avaricious, lazy, and deceitful. She would never forgive him for gulling Lady Lanyard out of a fortune, and now she had a new grievance. He had just eliminated any hope of happiness with George. Lord Rufton embodied all the characteristics she wanted, and he would have made a wonderful husband. *Except in bed,* whispered a voice.

George called on her the next morning. She should have expected it, she admitted when she realized the purpose of his visit.

"My dear Melissa," he began, nervousness roughening his voice despite his efforts. The gold drawing room seemed cavernous with only the two of them in it. And cold. "You must know how much I have come to care for you, and I flatter myself that you return my regard. Please make me the happiest of men and accept my hand in marriage."

"George, I wish you had not done this." She sighed, praying her impressions were correct. The lack of a flowery speech was a good sign. "You are right that I care for you. Please, please remember that and take my words to heart. I am not the right wife for you, my dear friend. I am managing and have a sharp tongue. You would soon be unable to overlook that. And I do not believe that you truly love me, friends though we are. Think, George," she begged, laying a pleading hand on his arm as pain knifed across his face. "Think about Caroline and Thomas. Can you honestly say you feel like that about me?"

He bit his lip. "Well, not exactly—"

"Nor do I," she interrupted him. "I love you like a brother, George—better than a brother, considering the one I am cursed with. But it is not the same thing."

His shoulders slumped.

"You'll thank me someday," she promised, then pondered his expression. "Why are you so eager to wed?" she asked softly.

His eyes turned suspiciously bright. "It's my father," he

whispered, face crumpling. "He suffered an apoplexy at Easter and can no longer speak or even rise from his bed. He has long urged me to secure the succession. I cannot disappoint him."

"Oh, George." She drew his head onto her shoulder so he could hide his tears from her eyes. His arms came around her, one sob escaping before he regained control of himself. "I am so sorry, my dear. But you are intelligent enough to admit that a union that must last all your life should not be contracted just to ease his mind at the end."

"I know," he said. "But you are so lovely and so kind that I really believed we could make it work."

"See. You are nearly ready to thank me already." She smiled. "And perhaps I can help you yet. I have a friend who just arrived in town. She is seventeen, but I trust you will ignore that long enough to get to know her," she all but ordered when he flinched. "Had I not told you her age, you would never have guessed. Having come to know you, I sincerely believe that you and Clara would suit. If you call this afternoon, I will introduce you. You needn't worry that she will expect anything. I'll not warn her of your visit. You will simply be another new face. Nor will I tell her aught but that we are friends. We are still friends, I hope," she finished.

"Yes, Melissa. We are still friends. Perhaps even closer than before. You are right, of course. Without that spark that unites Caroline and Thomas, marriage must be a dull business. I have let urgency overset my usual caution and good sense. Thank you, my dear."

Hugging her close one more time, he straightened his cravat and bade her farewell. Melissa was left with the task of explaining to her grandmother why she had refused so eligible a gentleman.

Chapter Ten

Charles spent the next fortnight watching Melissa charm her way through society's bucks and beaux. She grew more desirable each day, setting his loins on fire if she so much as smiled in his direction. He tried to concentrate on the traits he hated—such as her continuing disdain for his character—but it did no good. Not even thoughts of the fortune he would forfeit if he gave up his quest for Harriet could calm his raging appetites. But he refused to give in. Once she was safely married, he would seduce her and get her out of his system.

But who was she to wed? Rufton's regard had shifted in recent days. He still hovered, dancing with Melissa twice at every ball and including her in theater and opera parties. But he was showing equal attention to Miss Clara Rosehill. Surprisingly, Melissa showed no irritation at this defection. In fact, she and Miss Rosehill appeared to be friends.

Her conduct puzzled Charles. She had been on the verge of accepting Rufton at the Wharburton masquerade, unless she had exaggerated the relationship as part of her tirade against his own misbehavior. He had often regretted losing control of himself that night, for it had severely hampered his chances of becoming her friend. Now he had no idea whether she had settled on someone else.

Lord Ampleigh still danced attendance, but there was no indication that he was serious. Likewise with Mr. Parkington, though Melissa herself was deflecting him. But Graffington was becoming a problem. The man's eyes gleamed whenever he looked at her, and Charles could imagine the lust stirring in that black heart. It made his own desire even harder to bear. Graffington had made no mistakes, hiding his vices and appearing to be all that was proper. But the delectable Melissa would be devastated by marriage to so heavyhanded a lecher.

He had tried to warn her, but she was either obtuse or deliberately ignoring him. His efforts produced another conversation overshadowed by his unthinking attack at the masquerade.

"Beware of Graffington," he advised her as they danced a quadrille one night. "He is not the pillar of rectitude that he pretends."

"He is sweet," she countered. "And delightfully humorous."

"It is an act," he repeated, glaring, though his face still displayed the correct social smile. He always lost his temper when he was with her, his usual charm and address blasted to shreds. He had never met a female who so consistently reduced him to a witless coxcomb.

"You sound jealous, my lord."

"Fustian! Me jealous of a black-hearted scoundrel? You have windmills in your head."

"I will make my own judgments," she glared back. "And I prefer to base them on character and behavior rather than on questionable hearsay from people with a history of pretense."

"What?"

"If you were not a consummate liar, my lord, you would have been forced into innumerable duels by now," she charged.

"He is so bad he has even been banned from the better brothels," Charles informed her in a low voice, ignoring her comment. Her eyes widened but the movement of the dance separated them before she could respond.

She stalked back to her grandmother's side at the end of the set and disappeared into the retiring room during the cotillion he had signed for later in the evening.

Charles hoped she would not encourage Graffington just to spite him, but he could not be sure. The situation was too critical to take a chance. And his delivery of the warning had been cow-handed. Instead of trying to force agreement, he should have challenged her ability to see past a social facade to the character lurking beneath. It might have given her something to think about. He did not care if she admitted her error as long as she distanced herself from a dangerous man. Despite the impossibility of pursuing her himself, he felt responsible for her. There was no other gentleman available to screen her suitors and weed out the undesirables. But he had handled the affair so clumsily that he had no option but to deflect Graffington himself.

The chance occurred several nights later at White's. He had been watching the faro table for a couple of hours, an amusement he had enjoyed since he had first come down from Oxford. At that time he had deliberately established himself as a student of human nature who chuckled over the foibles of others. It had given him a unique identity and an opportunity to mingle with his friends without risking his reputation. But in truth, he eschewed gaming because he could not afford to lose.

"Here's to the delectable Lady Melissa." Graffington drunkenly raised his glass when he again lost.

Charles grimaced, holding his tongue until he had managed to draw the man away from the crowd.

"It is not the thing to bandy a lady's name about in that fashion," he reminded him stonily.

"I'm going to marry the chit, so what difference does it make?" he slurred in response. "I'll answer for m'wife's honor."

"Come, come, Graffington. You cannot believe her family would approve your suit."

"Why not?"

"Let me be clear, my lord," stated Charles coldly. "The Castleton household is under my protection. I am aware of your reputation and aware of how you treat your women. Never would I place my cousin in your hands. Besides, you would certainly not suit."

"Never met a lass I didn't suit," he leered. "And her brother is her guardian. She is all I need in a wife—beautiful and well-dowered. Drayton would never listen to a word you say."

"Fustian! He may be indolent, but he cares for his sister."

"Hah!" snorted Graffington before lurching back to the tables.

Drayton really would hand her over to the first man who offered, Charles realized as he walked back to his derelict room. Especially if he received something in return. Lady Castleton must have increased whatever paltry dowry Melissa's father had left her. Thus Graffington would continue his pursuit unchecked. The man's finances were almost as bad as his own. There was no way Lady Castleton would reduce the dowry in Graffington's case. She would balk at the deceit. If word became public, Melissa's reputation would be badly damaged. Lying about a dowry was dishonorable.

Loathe as he was to stoop so low, he had no choice. A word here and a phrase there soon had all Mayfair buzzing about the evil Lord Graffington. His financial status was laid bare to the world. His reputation for violence became public knowledge, until even drawing rooms were buzzing with tales of how he had been barred from brothels. The clubs rang with estimates of how many girls had been injured during an evening with him. All the talk made the authorities wonder whether he was responsible for the recent deaths of several prostitutes. Haughty to the end, Graffington had no choice but to retire to his estate in hopes that the furor would eventually blow over.

Charles breathed a sigh of relief and turned his mind back to the problem of finding Harriet. But Melissa continued to invade his dreams. If only she didn't look so much like his grandmother's portrait! There was something about that picture that drew him, though he could never explain what. Certainly it was not lust, for he had never wished to meet the young lady on the wall. But it was Melissa's similarity that was plaguing him now. Otherwise, she would have been just another pretty girl.

Or would she? Restlessly he strode the streets, trying to force impressions and emotions into coherent thoughts. She was young and alive, in startling contrast to the picture. And there was her unpowdered hair, glowing in that unusual honey-gold. Perhaps that was the fascination. The contemporary clothing and vivid coloring added desire to an image that had previously piqued only curiosity. And her vibrancy was the antithesis of Harriet's black hair and sallow complexion. A sudden memory of Harriet's bitten fingernails flashed through his head and he shuddered.

Still he was caught up in looks, he berated himself. But Melissa stood out from the other pretty faces in London. He was not the only gentleman affected thus. She exuded an aura of . . . wantonness, he realized in shock. Innocent wantonness, a sensuality that attracted men like flies to honey, even more potent because she seemed genuinely unaware of it. So it was lust after all.

But there was more. Much more. He admired her views, even those she cited to his detriment. Judging people on character and accomplishment was an attractive idea. He had a hard time accepting the prevalent theory that title and breeding defined a man's worth. His gamester grandfather and inept father had done nothing praiseworthy in their lives. Neither the dissolute Lord Drayton nor the sadistic Lord Graffington deserved respect. Nor did he, for that matter. His cane sliced the leaves off a branch that overhung a garden wall, scattering ragged fragments across the walk and into the gutter.

That would change, of course. As soon as he found Harriet, he would rescue Swansea and improve the lives of his tenants.

He shivered. A vision of skeletal, sharp-tongued Harriet shimmered in sharp contrast to his cousin. Anger over his untenable position returned, now deflected toward Melissa. Why did she plague him when he was committed to finding Harriet? Yet how could he endure Harriet when his body and soul yearned for another?

In a blinding flash, he recognized his problem. He loved Melissa. And he could do nothing about it. Devil take it, what had he done to deserve this fate? He must forego the woman of his dreams to carry out the insane wishes of a dictatorial old lady. Tears threatened. He spent the rest of the night in his room, drinking himself into a stupor.

Melissa stared broodingly through her window as sheets of rain pounded the square. Rathbone had been right. Lord Graffington would have been a disaster as a husband. She had failed to discern his true character. He had seemed an ideal mate, speaking enthusiastically about his estate, respecting her ideas, demonstrating concern for other people. But it was all pretense. Under his charming social facade lurked an arrogant tyrant worse than Charles at his most officious.

Charles. In retrospect, she could not condone Lady Lanyard's dictums. Why had she chosen to test him in that way? Surely she had not expected him to beg for mercy. Even the most responsible man would hesitate to grovel. Had she wanted him to thumb his nose at the fortune he had been promised for so long? But she was too canny for that. Perhaps it had been a plot by Lord Lanyard. He might have traded on his mother's worries about her grandson's irresponsibility in an attempt to cut Charles out. Lord Lanyard's position had seemed sound, but Melissa was learning that many men were capable of deceit.

She sighed. This sidetracking merely avoided the question. Could she trust her own judgment? The world was more deceitful than she had ever imagined. Despite the emphasis on honor and truth, people even hid enjoyment behind careful social masks. 'Town bronze' did not mean social ease, as she had always thought. It referred to the armor casing that hid all emotion from the world. But it also hid truth so effectively that even the most canny observer was often fooled. All of society could be hiding monstrous faults. The fact that Charles had hidden his financial woes for years was obviously not unusual. Graffington had done the same, as had others. She had best listen if Charles offered advice on suitors again, for information was often discussed in the clubs that did not surface in drawing rooms. Even her cousin's debauched past had its uses. How else had he discovered that Graffington was being blackballed by the better brothels?

The rain increased, falling harder than ever and blocking her view of Gunter's across the square. There would be no promenade today. And just as well. She needed to discourage Mr. Parkington. He was a nice enough gentleman, but not someone she could love.

She had sung that refrain before, she recalled, laughing without mirth. In George's case, events had worked out even better than she had hoped. Clara was starry-eyed. There was little doubt that she was deeply in love, and George seemed the same. Melissa saw the glances they exchanged, and was glad, though it hurt just a little to watch. Not that she was jealous, for she would never have formed that kind of attachment to him. But she was envious. If only she could discover such a partner for herself.

Lady Hartford approved of the match. "I hope he did not hurt you by turning his attentions elsewhere," she probed one afternoon when the two found themselves alone in the corner of Lady Debenham's relentlessly Egyptian drawing room. By choosing a cluster of the most uncomfortable chairs ever designed by man, they assured that no one would join them.

"Certainly not," Melissa murmured, then gave in to temptation. "He offered for me some time ago. I refused him. His father's illness had pushed him into rushing his fences. I introduced him to Clara the next day, and he has since thanked me for saving him from himself."

"Ah." Caroline relaxed. "I had not realized how desperate his father's condition was until yesterday. Poor George. They are very close. It will be hard on him when the end arrives."

Melissa had absently agreed, again wishing she knew someone who could offer her the love that she needed. *Charles*, whispered a voice.

"Fustian!" she now exclaimed aloud. Despite her disapproval of Lady Lanyard's test, his behavior had been despicable. There was no way to respect a man so base that he would use trickery to acquire a fortune just so he could continue his indolent lifestyle. And he was still lolling about town when, by his own admission, Swansea needed his attention. The fortnight he had planned to stay had already lengthened to nearly a month.

Lady Lanyard had wanted Charles to demonstrate responsibility and to achieve something noteworthy with his life, but all the time, he had been deceiving her. Nor had he been truthful when he implied that he would use the money to improve his estate. He had spoken of problems the day he returned to town, but beyond releasing his steward, he had made no mention of solutions. At least he was being unusually circumspect in his liaisons. No rumor identified his current partner. In fact, his restraint was odd enough to have caused comment. She snorted as inelegantly as Harriet ever had. He had probably used some of his ill-gotten gains to set up a high-flyer instead of preying on society's matrons.

But despite this recital of his faults, her treacherous mind dredged up memories of his kisses. She blushed, turning away from the window and accidentally brushing the draperies with her bosom, sending excitement all the way to her toes. *Wanton,* she accused herself. It was shameful to feel this way. Why did Charles affect her so strongly? His teasing attentions were very annoying, for she suspected he was deliberately trying to seduce her. He had denied debauching innocents, but with his history of deceit, there was no reason to believe him. After that attack on the terrace, she could not trust him to be alone with her. It was almost as bad as the weeks when Lord Heflin was visiting Drayton Manor.

Thinking about Charles was a waste of time. She would never consider him as a mate, despite his noticeable effect on her wayward body. But that was nothing more than curiosity aroused by her talk with Beatrice, and the forbidden titillation exerted by any of society's rakes—witness Lord Thornhill! Shaking her head, she picked up a book and forced her eyes to read.

But try as she might, wanton thoughts kept returning. She was talking to Helena at the Brookfield ball when her eyes locked onto Charles's. From halfway across the room, she could see the desire that blazed in those aqua depths. Without volition, her body tightened, her mind conjuring pictures of his long, slender fingers caressing her, of his powerful arms crushing her into his muscular being.

Horrified, she tore her gaze away, praying that her color had not heightened. Shame washed over her. Why had she alone been cursed by unseemly desires, for other girls certainly did not feel this way. Her eyes scanned the ballroom. Take the elegant Lady Barbara, or the flighty Miss Wanstat, or the pea-brained Lady Mary. Their imaginations did not run amok. There must be something wrong with her. Beatrice should not have awakened her awareness. This continued obsession with her body made her feel a freak. Or perhaps the Drayton dissipation had affected her after all. She showed as much penchant for lechery as the most debauched male.

Charles suddenly realized that he had not inhaled in nearly a minute. Black spots swirled before his eyes. Forcing a deep breath, he directed his feet outside, where he could think. The electrifying bolt that had passed when Melissa's gaze locked on his had nearly knocked him unconscious. Her aura of sensuality was growing, affecting him to the point of insanity. And she felt it as well. That was what had paralyzed him—the awareness in her eyes. Not that she deliberately employed her body against him. Other emotions also swirled there—confusion, longing, terror. But she perceived his desire, responded to his admiration, and was learning to recognize passion.

The last thing he wanted was to hurt her. He was committed to Harriet, so could not help Melissa discover her passionate nature. His body protested, but he held firm. He must wean himself from Melissa's company and try to find Harriet. He would honor the commitments he had already made for escorting his cousins, but accept no new ones. Regret gnawed at his heart, but he refused to relent. Even the musical tinkle of her laugh that triggered shudders of disgust at the memory of Harriet's vulgar bray could not sway him from his course.

But a night at the theater that included Melissa nearly shattered his control. She was wearing a low-cut green silk gown that accentuated the gold in her hair and eyes. A ribbon sash fastened just under her breasts, drawing his eyes to their generous swell and evoking sweat on his brow. Even the long, shapely legs visible where her skirts clung could not draw his eyes from her bosom. His fingers tingled with the need to cup and caress them—and more. He was amazed at the blatantly erotic thoughts surging through his mind. Even worse was the embarrassment of having to position himself in the back of the box. Skin-tight pantaloons had definite disadvantages.

He tried to solve his problem by spending the night with a willing widow, but that only made things worse. It was appalling to discover too late that he had little interest in her practiced ministrations. He barely managed to conclude the evening without disgracing himself. Nor did the experience alleviate his desire for Melissa.

He paced his tiny room, irritation growing at the lack of space. Would he ever find Harriet? The new phrasing of the old question caught him off guard. The chances of locating her were very slim. Months of effort had led precisely nowhere, making him wonder if she was a ghost. How could anyone disappear so completely? But if Harriet was unavailable, then so was the fortune.

Giving up on his room, he strode in the direction of Green Park. What would he do if he had to live in his present state of poverty? The idea was daunting. No more London. No more well-cut jackets from Weston. No more quality horses. No more access to society's bedrooms. But that last did not bother him. He no longer wanted access—except to Melissa's.

Swansea was in terrible shape. But it was located in the heart of Kent, in one of the most productive areas of the country. With work, yields should improve. He had studied enough books on estate management to know what had to be done. And he knew almost to the shilling what it would cost. Melissa's dowry would cover the most urgent problems. The prospect was actually intriguing. Rescuing so run-down an inheritance would provide satisfaction. And Melissa could help, for it was the sort of thing she enjoyed. The future suddenly looked bright.

Decision made, he smiled at the milkmaids tending the flock of dairy cows at the end of the park, splurged on a cup of fresh milk, and headed home to change.

Melissa glanced warily around the gold drawing room, surprised to find neither Willis nor Lady Castleton present. There was only Charles. He filled the space, reaching into every corner, displacing the air to make breathing difficult. She had never known the room to be so warm.

"I will summon my grandmother," she stated.

"She knows I am here," he countered. "She has granted me a few minutes alone with you."

"Why?" Fear rose in her eyes, stopping him in his tracks.

"Don't look like that, Melissa," he begged. "You must know I would never hurt you."

"Do I?"

"Of course you do. I love you, my dear, and want nothing so much as to make you my wife."

She felt her eyes widen as thoughts raged unproductively through her head. Her heart sang with joy at the words, but reason retained control. What kind of game was he playing now? Never had she had more reason to distrust him. *Do not confuse physical pleasure with love,* warned Bea again. *Do you feel as strongly about the non-physical relationship?* Despite the sensations Charles could arouse, she could not tie herself to a selfish and unscrupulous man. His weaknesses mirrored what she was trying to escape. Her father had merely existed for most of his life, too lazy to make anything of his estate, too incompetent to enlist the aid of able employees. Her brother was both weak and dissipated. Charles had demonstrated plenty of dissipation in his short life; he could so easily turn into another Toby.

Charles watched the conflicting emotions race across her face, his tension growing as the seconds passed with no response. "I have been too blunt for you, haven't I, my dear? I should have uttered some flowery speech to allow you time to consider. But I fear that all the fancy words have flown. I can think of nothing to say."

A new fear surfaced as his face assumed the same cajoling expression that he had used to coerce her at that inn. She had not revealed her identity, relieved that his ignorance made it unnecessary. But if she consented to marriage, he would inevitably find out. How would he react to her deceit? Not that she had deliberately set out to trick him, but she had lied more than once since that first fatal silence, including the claim that Lady Lanyard had revealed his supposed betrothal.

"My lord," she stated icily. "How can you possibly betrothe yourself to me when you are already betrothed to another?"

Charles had forgotten that Melissa thought him tied to Harriet. Cursing himself for accepting the path of least resistance at her first mention of that ignoble scheme, he racked his brain for an explanation that would not reveal his perfidy.

"That betrothal was never official," he began slowly, watching her face for any sign of reaction. "My grandmother wanted me to marry before her death, and arranged a match with the daughter of a friend. We barely knew each other before attending a house party at Lanyard Manor last summer. She was still too young to make any public announcement, being barely seventeen at the time. Grandmama accepted the delay and died happy, knowing that I was comfortably set up. But Harriet has since met someone she truly cares about. Since nothing had been officially announced, I agreed to forget the whole thing so she could accept his hand. There was never any attachment beyond comfortable friendship, certainly nothing of the love I feel for you."

What a glib tongue he has, she seethed. *I can never believe a word he says.* She hardened her voice. "I doubt you feel love, my lord, for you cannot know me very well. You have created an image out of some perceived similarity between me and your grandmother. But it is not real. Infatuation will quickly fade, and you will be thankful you are not saddled with me. We should never suit, for we are as chalk and cheese. Now if you will excuse me, I must ready myself for afternoon calls." Rising, she exited before he could voice further arguments. She barely made it to her room before bursting into tears.

Chapter Eleven

Charles agonized through the night. Unable to sleep, he paced his minuscule room. Why had she turned him down? He could swear that she was attracted. Even beyond the physical spark that lit whenever they were together, there was a deeper link that connected them, illustrated by that knowing look they had exchanged at the Brookfield ball. He could not have felt it so strongly unless there was an answering chord in her.

Harriet. Cursing himself for the fool he had been, he reached for the brandy decanter and poured himself a generous glass. What devil had prompted him to embark on such a half-witted deception? Nothing had gone right since. In a moment of drunken misery, he had succumbed to a single ignoble impulse that he would regret for the rest of his life. His grandmother had tied her fortune up so that he could never inherit it. Even worse, the woman he loved had spent their entire acquaintance thinking that he was promised to another.

Of course! Again he had been utterly stupid. After years of studying his fellow man and laughing over idiotic actions taken with no thought to the obvious consequences, he had failed to apply the lessons to himself. Talk about rushing his fences! From the first moment they had met, Melissa had considered him no more than a potential friend. He had been so caught up in pursuing Harriet he had hardly noticed. After he had confirmed his betrothal, Melissa could never think of him as a suitor. He should have belied the story from the beginning. That option being closed by his own base insanity, he should have at least announced an end to the engagement before commencing a courtship. That was the problem with lies—he kept forgetting the fiction.

His life had turned into a nightmarish farce. By the time he discovered he could not live without Melissa, he had already admitted to a betrothal with Harriet. He shuddered at the tale he had employed to erase that unwanted connection. It was preposterous, making him look like a weak fool. But he could hardly correct the record now. Admitting to nearly a year of deliberate falsehoods would be even worse.

So he must apologize for his unseemly haste. But suppose he had mistaken her objection. *We are as chalk and cheese.* Why would she believe they were incompatible? Aside from their undeniable physical attraction, they shared several interests. She was a superb rider with a keen eye for horseflesh. She loved art, though his knowledge was deeper. He could appreciate her desire to help others; it was one of the things he loved about her. She had studied estate management, and probably knew more about it than he did. Perhaps that was her objection. She might view his ignorance as proof that he lacked seriousness. After all, she did not know how precarious his financial situation remained.

He tossed and turned for the remainder of the night, finally deciding to ask her. Convincing her to marry him had become the most important goal in his life but it was impossible to plan a courtship without knowing what hurdles he faced. He could not afford any more mistakes. And he certainly could not afford any more lies.

Melissa was surprised when Charles called. She had spent her own sleepless night. A proposal of marriage was the last thing she had expected. His declaration of love continued to reverberate through her ears, though it could not be true. She doubted he even knew what love was, for he was too self-centered to understand selflessness. Infatuation she could believe. And lust. But that was a poor basis for marriage.

Unfortunately, she could no longer deny her own truth. She loved him. But there was too much that she disliked about him to consider marriage, and not just for her sake. He would never be happy with her. She would force him to take personal charge of his estate and join campaigns to assist the needy. He would have to give up raking, for she would make his life a living hell if he so much as looked at another woman. No man could accept such sweeping changes in his life, and she would accept no less. They would not suit. Unfortunately, Beatrice had never warned her that love did not always conform to reason. If she had known, perhaps she could have prevented this deplorable situation.

"Would you accompany me to the park?" he asked once the greetings were over.

She frowned. He was acting the perfect gentleman caller, but she distrusted him. Yet she would be safe in his curricle. "Very well, my lord. It is a lovely morning."

She had relaxed by the time they reached Hyde Park. He kept the conversation general, as if their last meeting had never occurred. But he signaled his groom to depart at the gates.

"What is the meaning of this?" she demanded.

"I need to talk to you and do not want an audience." He smiled, but his eyes remained serious. "You have nothing to fear. I will not hurt you, and there can be little impropriety in driving with your cousin and acting head of the family."

"Fustian. A third cousin does not have such privileges," she scoffed. "And I cannot trust a man of your reputation."

"Please, Melissa," he begged. "Don't rake me over the coals. I must understand why you turned me down, for my own peace of mind, if nothing else."

She scowled at him, but his usual arrogance was missing. Several of Jake's pet phrases stampeded through her mind. So the beast was going to try charm . . . Was his infatuation stronger than she had thought, or was this a case of bruised pride? She feared being alone with him, even in the public arena of Hyde Park. An undeniable streak of wantonness lurked just beneath her surface that she had not yet learned to control. She must curtail this discussion as soon as possible by making him understand that his suit was hopeless. Brutal truth would make a good start.

"You are too much like my father and brother," she stated baldly. "They were weak, dissipating their lives in frivolity and vice, while caring nothing for their families or estates. Father was lazy. To give him his due, he never indulged in reckless gaming, having enough sense to understand that he could not afford even small losses. But he never raised a finger to improve his position, either by adopting modern agricultural methods that might have increased his income, or by encouraging cottage industries that would have expanded his rents. What little cash he could lay his hands on went for horses, his one big extravagance. Woe be unto anyone who tried to deflect stable funds into useless fripperies like food and clothing for his growing children!"

Charles blanched at the picture she was sketching, but she gave him no opportunity to respond.

"My brother inherited all Father's weaknesses and none of his strengths," she continued flatly. "He has no understanding of his responsibilities, and no interest in learning. His great vice is gaming, in which he is urged on by his so-called friends. His character is woefully lacking, leading him to follow any suggestion put to him."

"How did you become so different?" he asked when she paused.

Melissa grimaced. "You should know that the females descended from Lady Tanders are a strong lot, dedicated to self-reliance and improving the world. From what I have heard, your grandmother was such a one. So is mine, as was my mother. I will not wed a man whose goals are different from my own. Nor will I consider a weakling. From my own observations, I can only conclude that you inherited nothing but the Rathbone indolence. Your sole accomplishments are those misdeeds that built your deplorable reputation. Your estate sits idle and wasted while you squander your days lazing about town. Name one thing that you have done to help your fellow man or even to maintain your own inheritance."

"You wrong me," he protested. "I have spent the last several months on my estate, evaluating its problems and trying to address them."

"Why? Because you finally inherited a fortune? Many changes could have been made without spending a groat. Why did you do nothing earlier? The reason is obvious. You care only for yourself and the pleasure of the moment."

"My financial position has not changed." He frowned, one hand touching hers as if to soften her anger.

She snatched her hand aside, appalled at how the light caress burned her flesh, despite the double layer of gloves that lay between them. Fear of succumbing to his wiles joined anger at his faults and his refusal to admit them. Her temper shattered, blinding her to the import of her words.

"That is your largest fault," she snapped, her usually velvet voice assuming a strident harshness. "You are a lying, scheming cheat whose word counts for nothing. Never would I ally myself with a deceiver."

"What are you talking about?" Fear of what her words might portend masked the vaguely familiar tones.

"You, sir. 'Financial position has not changed,'" she quoted him bitterly. "You have been on the rocks most of your life, my lord, though you have gone to great lengths to hide it. That, sir, is deceit. But that is the least of your crimes. What about the despicable scheme you hatched with your supposed intended? How could you dishonor a young girl so badly as to fake a betrothal—which you continued doing until yesterday? You have sunk as low as a man can get, Lord Rathbone. Contempt is too mild a term to describe what I feel for you."

"I can explain, Melissa—"

"Do you expect me to believe a word you say?" She turned amazed eyes on him, eyes that radiated scorn despite a shine of tears. "I will never wed a man I cannot respect. You, sir, are ruled by your passions, something no woman can respect. There is little reason to believe you would honor your marriage vows, since you have spent most of your life seducing others away from theirs. You even tried to seduce poor Harriet's aunt when she was under the protection of your grandmother's roof. But the list of faults always terminates in your avarice. You took advantage of a young girl's innocence to trick her into a continuing deception for your own benefit. I can never respect a man who would go to such lengths to gain a fortune. Deceit is intolerable."

"Melissa—" he protested again.

"No, my lord. The topic is closed. You will take me home now. Forget this insane notion and leave me in peace."

She folded her hands in her lap and refused to say another word until he helped her down at Castleton House. Against his wishes, he complied with her request, biting off the protests and explanations that wanted so badly to come out.

Was she right? he asked himself a hundred times. Why could he not have fallen in love with a lady who accepted society's evaluation of a man's worth? Why must he desire one who demanded more than a title and estate? He snorted. The questions contained their own answer. He had always found society chits boring.

He wasn't the fribble she thought him, though his public image fit that label all too well. There was no way she could know his myriad interests. Society ridiculed intellectual pursuits, so he kept his studies quiet, but he read extensively and was interested in the inventions that were appearing with greater frequency. There was a scheme afoot to build a new kind of roadway that would accommodate Trevithick's steam engine. He had seen the first Catch-Me-Who-Can when it appeared near Euston Road some years before, and had been intrigued by its potential ever since. It could not be operated on existing roads, of course, for it needed a line of steel rails, but the possibilities were enormous for developing a system of transportation that would carry goods faster than canal boats. Yet he had never made these interests public. They smacked of business. Society disdained anyone smelling of the shop.

Changing her opinion would be difficult. Her objections were far worse than he had expected, and they rose from deep-seated fears of her own. The men in her family had not given her a very high opinion of their sex, and his own reputation could hardly counter it. It would have been easier if he had taken his seat in Parliament, but he had never gotten around to it. He sighed. She was right in some of her charges. He had not accomplished much, though the intentions were there. He had never meant to fritter away his life in dissipation like some did. But he was entitled to a few years of frivolity before settling down. Society agreed. Surely he could make her understand that his past was only youthful exuberance. But how?

He must start with his rakish reputation, convincing her that those days were behind him. It was hardly an acceptable topic of conversation, but he had to try. Fidelity was important to her. Yet it would be difficult, for she would never believe claims that none of his liaisons had interested him beyond their bedroom encounters. Even there, they rapidly bored him. And how was he so certain that Melissa was different? It would be her first objection. He did not know, but he could not imagine tiring of her. Nor could he imagine enjoying another woman now that he knew her. It was a frightening thought. Without Melissa, the future looked bleak. Her passion had called to him from the moment they had met. Never had he encountered so strong a force. *Except that last day with Harriet,* whispered a voice.

Harriet. Lady Lanyard must have emptied the budget in her letter to Lady Castleton. No wonder Melissa considered him deceitful. She must have spotted every lie at the moment of utterance. He wanted to crawl under the bed and hide. But that explained that infamous clause in the will. His hand slammed against the mantle in disgust. What incredible stupidity he had displayed! His grandmother had been just as canny as ever and had discovered the deceit. Harriet had been too far removed from his usual tastes to pass her scrutiny. Why couldn't it have been Melissa at that inn? He had always cultivated beauty, and he despised schoolroom chits. It would have been better to refuse to cave in to her dictates. He had forgotten her lectures on self-reliance. But she had reaped her revenge, writing her will to coerce him into life with a homely commoner. And it was no more than he deserved.

Something had been fretting the edges of his mind and finally burst into the open. How did Melissa know that he had tried to seduce Mrs. Sharpe? It was not a topic his grandmother would include in a letter to her cousin, regardless of her own feelings. And she would have been furious. She could not have known of the attempt and remained silent. More than once she had castigated him for affairs that had come to her attention. Had she heard of this incident, she would have burned his ears to cinders with condemnation, and he would never have had a chance of inheriting. It was a consequence he had ignored at the time, for he had been too caught up in his own burning needs to care. Melissa was right again. He had often been ruled by his passions, frequently to his detriment. Self-control interfered with pleasure. But how had she learned of his offer?

A continuing deception. Harriet's role was not continuing. The girl had dropped all pretense when she left Lanyard Manor. Of course, she must fib about what she had been doing for those two weeks.

The truth slammed home so quickly it felt like a body blow. Melissa knew more than even Lady Lanyard had. And there was only one way she could have learned it. She must know Harriet. Or she might have met Beatrice, which amounted to the same thing. Dear God! After giving up all hope of finding the girl, the lady to whom he had just proposed marriage held the crucial clue. And Harriet must be higher up the social scale than he had imagined. She might know Lincolnshire because she had been a guest at Drayton Manor, perhaps even being a distant cousin on the Stapleton side.

His legs collapsed, and he dropped into a chair. Tremors shook his hands. Melissa had turned him down quite decisively. Harriet was the key to inheriting a fortune. What, in God's name, was he to do?

The topic was closed, Melissa reminded herself as tears stung the backs of her eyes. There were too many negatives to ever consider it. Her heart tightened in protest, but she pointedly ignored it. She could not allow a wayward heart and wanton nature to lead her into a situation that must prove disastrous. She could not accept either indolence or infidelity. But even worse was the ultimate effect of her own deceit. Charles would never forgive her, nor would he accept a shackle to Harriet, whom he had held in contempt from the beginning.

She turned her attention to dressing for Lady Webberly's ball. Throwing her heart into enjoying other gentlemen's company was the quickest way to get over her unsuitable infatuation. It seemed to work. She laughed with George, flirted with half a dozen admirers, and danced with a dozen charming men. If her gaiety was a trifle forced, no one noticed, least of all herself. She kept her mind focused on pleasure, a task made easier because Charles was not among the guests.

Lord Hartford was escorting her to Lady Castleton after a spirited reel that had reduced them both to laughter, when Melissa spotted a late arrival. Her newly honed social skills kept the smile on her face and the teasing in her voice, but her heart dropped through the floor. Lord Heflin paused on the stairs, a triumphant sneer twisting his mouth.

Revulsion stabbed her from head to toe. She had almost forgotten her fear of the man. He had been absent from town all Season. She had relaxed upon discovering that he was not welcomed at marriage-mart entertainments. So what was he doing at a marriage-mart ball? Others were asking the same question. Several matrons collected their innocent daughters and left for more congenial gatherings.

"Shocking!" murmured Mrs. Scott, furiously fanning herself.

"I don't care if he is her brother," declared Lady Cranford, glaring daggers at their hostess, who was bustling across the ballroom, face reflecting horror. "She had no business inviting him."

Heflin's predatory eyes scanned the room, pausing periodically when he spotted a particularly delectable miss.

"Half-brother," corrected Lady Beatrice, London's premier gossip, avidly storing every detail in her traplike mind. All knew she would disseminate specifics of society's reaction during tomorrow's calls. "And at least ten years younger than Lady Webberly. Judging from her face, he arrived without an invitation. I wonder why. He cannot have been in town more than two hours." Her eyes gleamed with speculation.

Melissa shivered as Heflin's piercing gaze raked her before moving on. Did he recognize her? What would he do? He was a vindictive man who never forgave a slight. She had injured both him and his pride.

"What happened to his leg?" gasped Lady Debenham as Heflin moved down the stairs. He noticeably limped and leaned heavily on a cane.

"An accident perhaps?" offered Lady Cranford.

"That is why he has avoided town so long," decided Lady Beatrice. "He despises showing weakness."

"Then why appear before it is healed?" asked Mrs. Scott.

Lady Beatrice glared, as if at a slug. "Obviously, the condition is permanent," she snapped. "I must discover how it occurred. I had heard of no accident." She sounded aggrieved.

Melissa shivered. Had she done that? The second stab had bitten deeply into the leg that was now lame.

She continued dancing and chatting, her social facade hiding her trepidation. But her mind raced in circles. Danger lurked. His limp was pronounced, his other grievances equally serious. He approached one of her partners, their glances confirming that they were discussing her.

Terror engulfed her after that. Heflin's eyes followed her constantly. Even from across the room, she could see their gleam, could detect in that gaze the lust and excitement of a hunter. He would make her pay for her temerity. And the price would be steep. She finally pleaded a headache and begged her grandmother for an early night.

Lady Castleton called Melissa into her room early the next morning. "What is between you and Lord Heflin?" she demanded sharply.

"Nothing, Grandmama," she denied. "He is one of Toby's friends, as I mentioned last summer. You know why I left."

"He is downstairs, demanding to see you," stated Lady Castleton. "When he was informed that you are not at home, he replied that, as your betrothed, he cannot be kept from the house."

Melissa gasped. "I thought Toby swore that no arrangement had been made!"

Picking up a letter, Lady Castleton held it out. "So I thought also, but look at this."

Melissa read, her hands shaking so badly she could scarcely see the words.

I don't know how these stories arise, Toby had written. *The silly chit overreacted . . . if you wish to keep her, I would be grateful.*

"Dear Lord," she choked, tears starting in her eyes. "That is just how he responds when he wishes to deny doing something. He never openly disagrees with anyone and is an expert at making you think he supports you when he is really straddling the fence."

"Are you telling the truth, Melissa?"

"Of course. I overheard them discussing a possible betrothal. Beatrice and I left that night, leaving a note for Toby that repudiated any arranged marriage and stated that Heflin was a base cad. Why?"

"Lord Heflin states that he not only has your brother's agreement to this supposed betrothal, but that you welcomed his suit, and the settlements are all arranged."

"So he is a liar as well as a lecherous rogue," she spat, pacing furiously about the room. "I have not spoken to the man since I escaped his attempt to ravish me by stabbing him."

"You never mentioned that before," she complained, but her face twitched in amusement.

"It was an act of desperation, Grandmama, and not one I am proud of. I suspect it underlies his current claim, for it likely caused his limp. He will seek revenge. But if Toby signed settlement papers, what are we to do?" Fear pierced the words.

"First, we must see how serious the situation is," stated Lady Castleton, rising regally to her feet. "Come, Melissa."

Lord Heflin haltingly paced the drawing room. His eyes gleamed at the sight of Lady Melissa. Her simple morning dress of sprigged muslin made her appear a delectable morsel.

"My lord," began Lady Castleton firmly when she had taken a chair. "My granddaughter denies any arrangement with you, and I believe her. There is no betrothal and never will be."

He drew himself up in haughty fury. "The arrangements are complete," he swore. "The wedding is scheduled for the first of next month. If she tries to cry off, she will become a pariah."

"When were these supposed arrangements made?" Lady Castleton countered. "There has been no question of marriage since she has been under my care. Lord Drayton made no mention of it when he consigned her to me nearly a year ago."

"We signed the settlements before she left Drayton Manor," he stated.

"Nonsense!" spat Melissa, unable to hide her loathing.

"There was never a question of marriage, as you well know. I would not wed you were you the last man on earth."

"Show us these supposed settlement papers, my lord," demanded Lady Castleton.

"I will bring them this afternoon," he promised, but they both saw the flash of surprise that suffused his eyes. He had obviously not expected opposition. Few ladies dared contradict a gentleman, and fewer would believe a green chit's word over a lord's, regardless of his reputation.

"If such things exist, you may take them to my solicitor," ordered her ladyship, naming the man. "Good day, sir."

Barnes appeared in the doorway with Lord Heflin's hat and cane. He glared, but departed.

"What now?" sighed Melissa, knowing that this represented but the opening skirmish of what could prove a long and nasty war.

"Do you think Tobias signed papers?" asked Lady Castleton.

"I doubt it. He hates being caught in a squabble, for it is impossible to take both sides at the same time. He probably promised Heflin that he could have me in exchange for forgiving his vowels. But he would have received my note repudiating everything before it could go further. If Heflin raised the question of settlements, Toby would have put off any discussion until I had formally accepted his hand, probably making some excuse for my sudden absence. With the negotiations hanging, he could break up the house party without meeting his debts, delaying the reckoning until my return."

"If Heflin pushes, he would sign, though."

"That's a fair assessment. But why would Heflin be interested? I was hardly worth looking at last summer. In fact, he said something about getting me with child and locking me away in the country."

Lady Castleton frowned in thought. "You say you stabbed him, injuring him badly enough to cause his limp?"

"Yes, though I am guessing about the latter. He was certainly mobile enough to be in Toby's study several hours later. Perhaps the wound festered. Or the limp may have some other cause." She paused, but decided that complete candor was necessary. "There was more than that to irritate him." She related his escalating attentions, concluding with full details of how she had escaped. Lady Castleton's chuckle quickly died into a frown.

"You have wounded his pride, my dear," she sighed. "First, by not succumbing to his advances, and then by striking so harsh a blow to his person. I have heard tales of his ferocity when crossed. He is not a man to shrug off slights."

Melissa shivered. "So what can I do?"

"Tobias is a problem that must be addressed. If he is as weak as you say, Heflin can coerce him into signing anything. As your legal guardian, he can indeed force you into marriage. We must block that possibility. I will immediately send Saunders to Drayton Manor with orders to bring Tobias back to town. We will make sure that he does not sacrifice your interests to his own."

"Thank you, Grandmama," whispered Melissa, tears suddenly streaming down her face.

"What is the meaning of the stories making the rounds?" demanded Charles as soon as Melissa entered the drawing room that afternoon.

"What are you talking about?"

"Lord Heflin is claiming that he is betrothed to you, and has been for nearly a year." Anger blazed from his eyes.

"Dear Lord!" Her legs collapsed, depositing her onto a couch with less than her usual grace.

"Are you implying that he lies?"

"Of course, he is lying!" She glared at him.

"Why would he spread such slander?"

"It is a long story." She sighed. "He is a friend of my brother's. Toby owes him a great deal of money. He offered me to Lord Heflin in exchange for forgiving his debts, but I refused to cooperate. It was then that I left home to live with my grandmother. Toby informed us that nothing had come of the idea. I had not spoken to Heflin again until this morning, when he paid us a visit, claiming a betrothal and threatening me with all manner of public ridicule if I did not agree."

"The nerve of the man!" spat Charles. No wonder Melissa had such a low opinion of gentlemen, he mourned, for Drayton was even worse than he had thought. And no wonder she decried weakness so loudly. What had she suffered from so dissolute a brother? "When did this take place?"

"The beginning of last summer. Toby hosted a party attended by several of his friends. I could not stand the company and left."

"Was Matt Crawford one of them?" he asked in sudden suspicion.

"Yes. Why?"

"Nothing."

Since returning to town, he had been trying to uncover the identity of the Captain Sharp who had fleeced his friend, but success had eluded him. Matt had refused to name the cad, and no one else he talked to had attended Drayton's gathering. So Melissa knew something else he had wanted to learn. He had never considered asking her, assuming that she had departed long before the party got under way. Heflin must be guilty. There could not have been two cheats at one small party. Since Drayton owed Heflin a fortune, it had to be him. It was up to Charles to see that the scoundrel paid for his slanderous tales. The motivation was now doubled. Heflin had injured both his best friend and the woman he loved.

"I suppose my only option is to retire to the country," said Melissa with a sigh. "I can hardly stay in town after this."

"Nonsense." He caught her gaze with his own. He could feel the connection crackle between them, could see in her eyes that she felt it too. But this was not the time to pursue it. "Few people believe his tales, Melissa. His reputation is so bad that no reputable family would accept a suit. I did not come here to castigate you for encouraging the scoundrel, but to warn you. Only knowledge of his stories will allow you to refute them."

"I will deny everything," she swore viciously. "And Grandmama has already sent for Toby. With a little pressure, he will swear that no overtures took place."

Chapter Twelve

The next week was so tense that Melissa nearly jumped out of her skin at every sound, barely managing to hide her strain and appear normal. Toby had not yet arrived, and as the days passed, she began to fear that he really had signed settlements. Heflin could gain admittance to no other reputable entertainments. Fortunately, continuous rain canceled the daily promenade in Hyde Park, where he might have confronted her, but she could never venture forth without the fear of seeing him. Lady Castleton made sure that at least two sturdy footmen always accompanied them, and Charles danced attendance every evening, but their efforts did little to ease her mind.

She had denied Heflin's claims, shaking her head over his wine-induced delusions. After the first day, Heflin remained suspiciously quiet. The *on-dit* was replaced with fresher scandal, but Melissa knew she had not heard the last of it.

Lord Ampleigh grew warmer once George's eyes turned to Clara. Melissa sighed as she refused an invitation to a lecture on telescopes, citing other plans. Something must be done about him. She did not want to refuse another offer. It would become public, for Geoffrey was not polished enough to hide his feelings. Her credit would suffer if she turned him down, and his confidence would never recover.

She excused herself to the retiring room one evening when she spotted Lord Ampleigh making his determined way to her side during a waltz she had kept free. An antechamber was empty, so she slipped inside and locked the door. There must be a way to discourage him. As she paced about in agitation, voices from the next room rose in argument. Noting that the connecting door was ajar, she went to close it and froze.

"You must not acquire a reputation as a bluestocking, Mary," snapped an angry voice. "It would ruin you! Asking

Mr. Hempbury if he has visited the observatory in Greenwich is dangerously improper."

"But you promised, Mama!" wailed the unfortunate Mary. "You promised faithfully that if I consented to a Season and behaved myself, you would arrange for me to visit there."

Melissa's eyes widened as the argument intensified. Tiptoeing closer, she applied an eye to the crack, amazed to see Lady Donnington and her pretty daughter, Lady Mary, glaring daggers at each other. The girl was a pattern card of featherheaded propriety, amassing a sizable court of fawning cubs who shared hardly a brain among them. To discover that she was both a bluestocking and a budding astronomer was the answer to a prayer. And best of all, Lady Mary seemed demure, just the sort of female Geoffrey needed.

"Can you give me a hand?" she murmured to Helena following supper.

Helena nodded and received permission from her mother. "What is the matter?" she asked in surprise when they headed away from the exit instead of going to the retiring room to fix a tear.

"Lord Ampleigh is becoming a problem," admitted Melissa. "His attentions are growing too pointed. Though he is a dear friend, I could never consider wedding him. But his confidence is so fragile, I do not wish to turn him down. You are going to help me deflect him."

"You want me to cast sheep's eyes at him?" choked Helena.

Melissa giggled. "Of course not. That would just set him up for a different kind of pain. No, I found the perfect girl for him, but you must convince her to be herself."

"Who?"

"Lady Mary Dunn."

"You cannot be serious!" exclaimed Helena. "She is the most insipid, pea-brained ninny I know."

"She certainly plays the part well. That toad-eating mother of hers apparently forced her to town for the Season, then convinced her that displaying either intelligence or emotion would condemn her to spinsterhood if not to outright ostracism."

"You mean she didn't want a Season?" demanded Helena.

"She prefers her studies."

Her eyes bulged. "How do you know all this?"

"I overheard an argument between mother and daughter a little while ago. It seems the girl is an astronomer."

Helena nearly laughed. "So that is what caught your attention. Ampleigh has bent my ear more than once on the subject. But where do I come in?"

"You must help me convince Lady Mary that her mother's ideas are too rigid. You have such a reputation for propriety, she must believe you. Then we will introduce her to Ampleigh and hope for the best. Despite his unprepossessing appearance, she cannot help but like him better than those coxcombs that are flitting around her now."

They arrived at the alcove where Lady Donnington was gossiping with several friends. Helena deftly disposed of Mr. Dawkins, while Melissa drew Lady Mary aside.

"I understand you are interested in learning," Melissa murmured. Fear and surprise lit Mary's eyes.

"Your mother is narrow-minded," she continued. "Many ladies now admit to serious interests, though few flaunt them."

"Yes, indeed," corroborated Helena. "Consider Lady Hartford. Or Lady Hartleigh. You may not have heard about it, but bluestockings were all the rage following Madame de Staël's visit three years ago."

"But Mama says I will be ruined if my interests become known," protested Mary.

"That may have been true at one time," agreed Melissa. "And some of the less intellectual people still believe it, but those whose opinions will matter to you do not care. You must think of the future. If you attract a husband by hiding your true self, what will he think of you when the truth comes out, as it surely must?"

"And how would you enjoy life shackled to someone like Mr. Dawkins?" added Helena.

Mary's eyes widened.

"Exactly," nodded Melissa. "It is your life, not your mother's. Am I correct in thinking you enjoy astronomy?"

She nodded. "Do you also study it?"

"To be honest, no," stated Melissa. "My own interests run to estate management, not that I expect to ever practice it. But after watching my father and brother ruin theirs, I am determined to wed a man who understands his business."

Mary turned hopeful eyes to Helena.

"Me neither," she admitted succinctly. "I prefer good works, especially setting up schools for tenants and villagers."

Mary's shoulders had visibly slumped.

"Not to worry, Lady Mary," smiled Melissa. "We know a

gentleman who adores astronomy. He often visits the Royal Observatory."

"Really?"

"Don't expect a god," warned Helena as Mary's face lit as if touched by a beacon from heaven.

"Very true," agreed Melissa. "He is knowledgeable, but not much to look at. I'll introduce you if you promise to be nice. I wouldn't have him hurt for the world. He is sensitive about his appearance, apologetic about his interests, not overly graceful, and very shy."

"I don't mind," swore Mary. "Handsome gentlemen intimidate me. I am not very good socially."

That explained her vacant stare when surrounded by suitors, realized Melissa. And her timing was perfect. The next set was a waltz, and Ampleigh was already approaching.

"You are just the person I wanted to see," Melissa began, before Ampleigh had a chance to ask her to dance. "Have you met Lady Mary?"

"I've not had the pleasure," he admitted unenthusiastically.

"How remiss of her mother! Lady Mary, may I present Lord Ampleigh. My lord, Lady Mary Dunn, daughter of Lord Donnington. You are just in time to resolve an impasse. Lady Mary is a student of astronomy, and has been asking me about the Royal Observatory, but I cannot recall your descriptions with any precision. Can you help?"

"Delighted." This time he sounded sincere.

"Perhaps you could talk while executing this waltz," suggested Helena. "That way her mother will not be upset."

The suggestion was quickly taken up.

"Do you think they will suit?" asked Melissa as they returned to Lady Castleton's side. She and Lady Stokely were still deep in conversation.

"I don't see why not." Helena nodded to the floor, where the couple twirled round the room in animated discussion.

When Melissa spotted them together again during the next waltz, she smiled and heaved a sigh of relief. Their eyes were locked in blatant adoration.

Charles relaxed in the reading room at White's, idly perusing the paper while most of his mind grappled with the problem of Lord Heflin. Something about that situation didn't ring true. He could not imagine even a man of Heflin's venality going to such lengths to acquire a wife who despised him.

Even were he planning to lock her away after getting an heir, he could not imagine it. Those debts must be enormous. But that did not make sense, either. Why would Heflin fleece the boy? Everybody knew that Drayton never came to town because he was destitute. It had been true for at least thirty years. Heflin had attended school with the current earl, so he must know the truth. Charles could only conclude the man had been after Melissa all along. She was a delectable package, and Heflin might have conceived an obsession for her. He would have been in a position to watch her grow and develop.

"Mind if I join you, Rathbone?" Charles looked up to find that Heflin had already taken the chair nearest his own.

"I'm afraid I cannot stay. I've an appointment with my tailor," he lied, folding the paper and preparing to rise.

"I won't keep you," stated Heflin snidely. "But you will stay away from my betrothed in future. She will no longer need your escort."

"Peddle your delusions elsewhere," snapped Charles. "My cousins are under my protection and will remain so."

Heflin's face darkened with fury. "I'll not tolerate a libertine near my promised bride."

"Enough," scowled Charles, rising to leave. "She is not and never will be your betrothed. Even Drayton is not that lost to honor."

"I'll make you sorry you were ever born if you continue," warned Heflin softly.

"Likewise," he glared.

Determination lit Charles's face as he strode back to his room. Heflin had abandoned honor. It was time to make a concerted effort to expose him. At Lady Cunningham's ball that night, he sought out Matt and four other friends. A brief meeting in the library inaugurated his campaign. He related Heflin's crimes, starting with the cheating of Matt and Drayton. Once he explained the threat against Melissa, Matt willingly backed him up. At least one of them would watch Heflin at all times until they caught him. Meanwhile, Charles and Matt would protect Melissa.

It sounded good, but Charles could not rid himself of worry. As long as Heflin was in England, Melissa was in danger.

Another battle had raged in his head for days, and he now turned his thoughts to resolving it. His love for Melissa was stronger than ever, something he had been forced to acknowledge when Heflin's claims surfaced. He did not want to live without her and would do everything possible to protect her from harm. Yet temptation continued. Even Melissa might not compensate for a life of near-poverty. Could his love survive years of hardship? It was not a question calculated to improve his self-image. He had never felt this way about another woman, but the fact remained that he invariably grew bored with even the best of his liaisons.

Money would guarantee a continuation of the style of life he had pretended to for so many years. Swansea would return to prosperity. He had learned enough about his inheritance to badly want that. It was not fair to force his tenants and staff to live and work in nearly medieval conditions. He had been evading his responsibility to them, but would not do so again.

A prosperous estate and comfortable living would come at some far future date through hard work, frugality, sacrifice, and luck. Or they could be achieved immediately by marrying Harriet. Could he spend his life shackled to the chit? It was true that he had felt an unexpected surge of desire for her, and her social standing might be closer to his own than he had previously considered. That would explain her lack of awe over his title. A decent wardrobe might help her appearance, but nothing would improve her character. She had loudly proclaimed her disapproval of him. Her mannerisms were better suited to a stable than a drawing room. That strident voice grated on his ears, and her braying laugh would be disturbing even in a man. Against that he could place only an expertise with horses. Her faults and continued criticism would send him off in search of a congenial mistress before much time had passed. Was that what he wanted?

You would never honor your marriage vows . . . You have spent your life seducing others away from theirs. Melissa was right. It had never bothered him to cuckold other gentlemen, even friends on occasion, for most of them were doing the same to others. Marriage was a contract that enhanced a man's fortune and assured his succession, but an unwritten understanding gave both partners a wide degree of freedom, provided they were discreet. That unspoken agreement bound him to shelter a wife, no matter who else he bedded, and demanded that she provide an heir before dallying with others. Harriet would be welcome to follow that path.

But could he accept infidelity from Melissa with any complacency? The glass he was holding shattered. He would kill any man who touched her, and probably wring her neck as well. He had come close to doing both when Heflin's claims first surfaced. There was an emotional component to their relationship that made nonsense of society's standards. And it wasn't just lust. He would never willingly share her, to be sure. But beyond that, he could not tolerate anyone hurting her, including himself. That was what had stopped his tongue that day in the park, and what prevented him from compromising her. He could not force her to accept him.

He considered the married couples he knew, unconsciously dividing them into two groups. One contained gentlemen like Oaksford, Sanders, and Henderson, who freely bedded others. Oaksford could hardly be blamed, as he had been compromised by a conniving chit looking for a title. He banished her once he had an heir and hadn't seen her in years. But the others had all wed in the usual way and enjoyed conventional marriages.

Contrasting those were couples like the Hartfords, Wrexhams, and Blackthorns. Even though several of the gentlemen had once been blatant libertines, all continued to dote on their wives even after years of marriage. And their ladies were equally devoted.

It must be love that spelled the difference. And that was encouraging, for he certainly loved Melissa. He frowned. If she loved him, keeping a mistress would hurt her, something he could never do. Distressing her would hurt him as well. The cost of the pleasure would be too high. Pleasure? His eyes widened. He did not want intimacy with others. The idea of bedding Harriet curdled his stomach.

He spent a sleepless night arguing himself around in circles. Every time he thought he had made up his mind, something pushed him back on the fence. Money or love? Comfort or happiness? City ease or country labor? Harriet or Melissa? Finally, at dawn, he laid the last doubts to rest.

"Good morning, Charles," said Melissa as she joined him in the drawing room. "You are out unusually early today."

"I need to talk to you," he admitted.

"What about?" she asked nervously, unsure what he wanted. Aside from his obvious lack of sleep, there was something different about him. Perhaps a hint of vulnerability. "Has Heflin again besmirched my name?"

"No. Except for ordering me to avoid you, he is remaining oddly silent, though I suspect he is plotting a new strategy.

Perhaps he has sent someone to coerce a written agreement from your brother."

"He will fail in that. Grandmama's secretary left immediately. I expect Toby to arrive any time."

"Good."

She claimed the chair nearest the fireplace and motioned him to another, but instead he prowled restlessly about the room. She watched him pace, his leashed power reminiscent of a caged lion. Just now he did not resemble a dissipated wastrel. Had Heflin really threatened him? If Charles suffered an injury she would never forgive herself. Another minute passed before he turned troubled eyes onto her.

"I need to discuss my behavior last summer." She gasped. "You included it among your reasons for refusing my suit. The words have haunted me ever since."

"What are you talking about?" she asked suspiciously, fearing that he had discovered she was Harriet. Her incautious words had plagued her ever since she lost control of her wits that day. But that was typical of her exchanges with him. He always managed to reduce her brain to mush so that she revealed more than was seemly of their ignoble past. She was sick of the endless lying.

"I still hope to convince you to marry me, my dear," he began. "But I cannot do so without revealing my less honorable actions. There can be no secrets between us if we hope to achieve happiness."

Melissa bit her lip. He sounded serious, intelligent, and responsible. Maybe this was her opportunity to set the record straight about her own deceitful behavior—unless he was feigning to coerce her into something she would regret. He had lied that night at the inn.

He did not note her expression as he resumed his pacing, describing in a low voice the infamous letter he had received and its demands for marriage. "I do not know how she believed I could accomplish that on such short notice. There was no indication that her faculties were impaired, and she had always been a canny one. I left immediately for her estate, praying that Uncle Andrew had misinterpreted her intentions. I hoped I could at least convince her to tie the inheritance to a future marriage."

He glanced imploringly at Melissa. She nodded, but refrained from speech.

"A storm stranded me at a country inn, where anger and fear

prompted me to drink much more than usual. In that condition, I made the acquaintance of a fellow traveler, a young lady in distress because the house to which she was going was closed for a fortnight, and she had no place to stay. In a mad moment of weakness, I offered her shelter if she would pose as my betrothed."

Melissa gasped, her eyes glaring into his. Was he now claiming it was an impulse?

"I know it was wrong, Melissa," he admitted, pain showing in his voice. "If I had been sober, I would never have succumbed to such a hare-brained idea. But I was not. And I have paid dearly for that imposture. There was no betrothal. I lied when you raised the subject. Harriet deplored the deceit, and often castigated me for my greed. I believe you may know that yourself."

She gasped again, this time in trepidation. Did he know? Had she made an utter cake of herself by discussing Harriet as though she were real? Fear, uncertainty, and embarrassment froze her tongue, so she again offered no response.

"You know more than Lady Lanyard could possibly have written to Lady Castleton," he continued. "You must have learned about it from Harriet. My behavior was despicable in many ways. I suspect that I was acting under a temporary madness, brought on by the sudden withdrawal of what I had always considered an inviolable promise. If nothing else, I owe Harriet an apology. Do you know her? Can you give me her direction? Did she take any harm from my actions? She never would have agreed to so dastardly a course if there had been any alternative. I coerced her rather badly."

"Why should she wish to hear from you, my lord?" Melissa asked, so relieved that he had not discovered the truth that she automatically kept up her own charade. "You used her to achieve your own goals. She has nothing to gain from further acquaintance, and everything to lose. Contacting her risks exposing you both."

Charles smiled. "You do know her."

"Enough to know that she wishes no further discourse with you. She has no love for trickery, and even less for greed," she snapped.

"Then she should enjoy my dilemma." He grimaced. "I am well paid for my moment of insanity. My grandmother left me her fortune as promised, but only if I marry Harriet before next

Christmas. If I do not, the money will be split among several charities."

Melissa nearly choked. There was no way she could ever admit her imposture after this. *My financial position has not changed.* He had spoken the absolute truth that day. She clasped her hands in her lap to still their trembling and tried to keep her voice steady.

"I am surprised that you linger in town, then. Why have you not sought her out already?"

"I tried." Pain twisted his face. "She refused to give me her direction. I spent months trying to trace her, without success. It is as if they were ghosts who vanished back into the otherworld."

She shivered at his words. He was closer than he knew.

"She was familiar with Lincolnshire, so I scoured that area as well. Now I know she must have been visiting you."

He dropped into a chair facing hers. His aqua eyes caught her gaze, holding it in a stare that tumbled shivers down her spine. Beguiling eyes, as she had noted before, capable of driving away reason.

"And then I met you and fell in love," he continued softly. "The inheritance means nothing to me now, dearest Melissa. I want only you. But guilt assails me over Harriet. I must beg her pardon and make sure that she is all right. If my actions have brought her any suffering, I will never forgive myself."

"She suffers not," stated Melissa. "But you delude yourself. How can you not offer for her once you have met again? You will grow to hate yourself for whistling down a fortune."

"Never!" His shaking head also denied the charge. "And I have no interest in meeting her. But I must satisfy my conscience about her safety, and apologize for forcing her into so sordid a scheme."

"I cannot help but wonder," she replied with a frown, fighting to keep from drowning in his gaze, "if Lady Lanyard had not called your bluff, would you feel guilty now, my lord?"

"I do not know," he admitted honestly. "I would hope so."

"How did you think to convince her to wed you, when you admit she disapproved of you?"

"Again, I do not know. It was best that I could not trace her earlier. We would not have suited, for she was not at all what I would have wanted in a wife. Now there is no question of it, for I am in love with you."

His words steadied her and strengthened her will. It was as

she had feared. He was in love with Lady Lanyard's portrait rather than herself. He knew that Harriet would not suit. Yet the only difference between Harriet and Melissa was in appearance and a handful of social graces. Her heart protested but she ignored it. Her own attraction was primarily for his admittedly handsome exterior.

"I will not disclose her whereabouts," she vowed. "But I will send a message if you wish."

"Send my apologies, and assure her that if she has need of support, especially in regards to my misbehavior, she need only ask."

"Very well, my lord."

"Will you stop this infernal 'my lording'?" he snapped. "My name is Charles. Use it."

"I cannot, my lord," she refused gently. "It would imply too much closeness." His new disclosures made marriage impossible.

"Damnation, Melissa, I love you," he protested. "I want you for my wife. And despite your words, I suspect you love me."

"Enough, my lord. I admit to an attraction. You are a handsome man, as you well know, but that is merely physical. As is your own infatuation. You are enamored of a walking image of your grandmother's portrait. But that is no basis for marriage. The shell can change, and often does, but the true test of worth is what's inside. Character and deeds are what count, and based on that, you are a sad specimen. I will not wed without respect, and I cannot respect you, as I have mentioned before. Even this self-professed moment of madness that led you to deceive your grandmother was no more than greed and a desire to continue your idle pleasures unchecked. I'll not go through life like my mother. She struggled for eighteen years before Papa killed her in an act of irresponsible drunkenness. Toby has gamed away every penny he inherited, and more. His response was to try to sell me to Heflin, who needs a brood mare to supply future generations of dissipated libertines. I want more from life than that."

"You wrong me, Melissa. I can offer more," he pleaded. "I love you. I could never do anything to hurt you or to denigrate you. And you are far more than just a beautiful face. I have known many beautiful women, and loved none of them. It is the character beyond the shell that calls to me. I am not offering you an easy life. We would not be awash in money, but there would be goals to pursue and accomplishments to enjoy.

The prospect is daunting, but it is also exciting. With you at my side, anything is possible. I need you, my love. Will you please accept my hand?"

Could she trust him? she wondered as she took a turn about the room, her face creased in thought. He spoke words that she wanted to hear, committed himself to projects that she would love to share. But she suspected that he recognized Harriet and was hiding that knowledge to circumvent her objections, for she had already admitted wanting a man of serious pursuits, and he knew she despised fortune hunters. But she was not as gullible as he thought. The truth was obvious. He could not possibly believe that Harriet, who abhorred deceit, would have related so sordid an episode to another. His proposal was just another ploy to get his hands on Lady Lanyard's money. He hadn't changed. Even his pathetic recital of supposed guilt was nothing but a play on her emotions.

Discovering the truth would have been all too easy for him. Her own stupidity in revealing facts only Harriet would know would have started the process. Despite her changed appearance and intensive training in mannerisms and movement, she still forgot on occasion. Anger summoned Harriet's strident tones. Shock prompted broad gestures she had learned from Jake. Memories of that afternoon in the Lanyard gallery returned. He had mumbled deprecation for his grandmother's ideals and philosophies, yet she shared those ideals along with that lady's looks. He had just finished praising several of them in the course of his proposal. No man could change so much in so short a time.

But part of her fought against this reasoning. There was no evidence that he knew her deceit. Perhaps she was being too particular in her search for a husband. Was it possible to find a man who embodied all the characteristics she wanted? George had satisfied most, being intelligent, responsible, frugal, honest, and dedicated to his estates. What he lacked was passion. Charles called him stuffy and she supposed he was. Perhaps it was an inevitable companion to the other traits she admired. Must she accept risky behavior to find the passion her soul craved? Yet she did not want to live on the edge of disaster. Only deep-rooted mutual love might make that kind of life possible.

The news about the will was poetic justice. He had failed Lady Lanyard's character test, so the lady had reaped her revenge. The cream of the jest, of course, was that the girl was a figment of the imagination, and thus could never become his wife. Ironically, if Charles had continued his original course, he would have passed and probably received at least some of the fortune immediately.

It was time to make a decision. She had to be honest and admit that she loved him. But happiness was impossible unless he returned her fervor. Without that, she would despise herself for accepting a man whose character displayed so many traits she abhorred. Her love would turn to bitterness, and she would dwindle to a harpy who would make his life miserable. It was unlikely that he loved her in the way she needed. She could not expect whatever lust burned between them to last, for no lady had ever retained his regard for long. Alas. She turned to face him.

"Words. Nothing but words. It is easy to mouth them, but deeds are what matters. I am sorry, my lord, but you already have my answer. We would not suit. Your interests and proclivities are not what I desire in a husband."

"Have you considered what accepting me would mean to you?" he answered. "Lord Heflin's claims must hurt you."

"I will not embark on a betrothal merely to thwart so low a creature," she snapped, thankful that he had again demonstrated his unsuitability, for her heart was already protesting her decision. "You demean me by even suggesting such a thing."

"Forgive me, my dear," he begged. "I spoke without thought. It hurts to see you maligned by so base a creature."

"Enough, my lord. I do not wish to discuss this again. If you continue to press, we shall have to bar the doors against you. I would not wish for such a rift. It would inevitably become public."

He had rushed his fences again, admitted Charles as he walked home. Despite understanding her objections, he had forged ahead too soon. He must banish all impatience. This was not a time for open battle, or even for siege. He must first demonstrate that her impressions were wrong. She had little reason to rely on men, given the Drayton history. In light of her knowledge, his own continued deceit would have cast her view of him into stone. She was right. Words could not undo such an image. That would require deeds, and deeds would take time.

And so he embarked on a course of education, treating her as a friend and cousin but refraining from anything personal.

He discussed his serious interests with her, asking advice when she demonstrated superior knowledge, and offering insights when his was greater. The goal was to let her see his innermost core, so that she could accept that his past behavior was not the shallow waste that was reported.

They spoke of Swansea and its problems. She seemed surprised at the emotion he revealed, whether frustration, fear, or love of its beauty. Another topic they explored was his interest in railroads, and his burning desire to involve himself with their future. Melissa was not repelled by the subject; she asked well-considered questions and displayed curiosity. Nor did she think this fascination was misplaced.

"Why don't you pursue it, Charles?" she asked when he described an investment group that was looking for backers. "You know so much."

"I suspect that the plans are too grandiose to return a profit any time soon." He shrugged. "Besides, it takes money to make money, and I have none to spare. Perhaps by the time a more reasonable plan surfaces, I will be in a better position. Or I may never feel secure enough to take the risk. My father frequently demonstrated deplorable business sense, and I always fear I may have inherited it."

"In this case, I doubt it," she replied. "You seem well versed in all potential pitfalls."

Her words brought a glow to his heart. But despite a growing closeness, he could sense no change in her antagonism to marriage. His frustrations mounted until he began to wonder if there was some other, unnamed, objection to his suit.

Chapter Thirteen

"**W**hy does Lord Heflin insist you are betrothed to him?" asked Lady Hartford at the Riverton ball.

"Is he still trying to ruin me?" returned Melissa, fear visible in her eyes. "I hoped he had given up by now."

"Thomas heard him at Boodle's last night." She had maneuvered them into an alcove where they could talk without being overheard.

"Dear heaven, what am I to do?" Melissa moaned, tears glistening in her eyes despite her determined smile. It would never do to appear upset in public. "He is an evil man."

"Granted. But why is he after you?"

"My brother owes him money," she explained grimly. "Heflin offered to forgive the debt if I would marry him. Toby refused. This may be revenge, or perhaps he believes that I will change my mind."

"Don't ever change your mind," urged Lady Hartford. "Some libertines can be reformed—and they make wonderful husbands, as I well know—but he is not of their number."

"I won't. But there is no denying that his claims are hurting me. Despite his reputation, society wonders if I am guilty of equivocation. *Where there is smoke, there must be fire*," she quoted miserably. Even George's apparent defection was being cited as proof that more underlay Heflin's claims than she was admitting. Several members of her court had transferred their attentions in recent days. Not that she would have accepted them, but it made her look bad.

"Perhaps Thomas knows something that will encourage Heflin to leave town," mused Lady Hartford.

"I doubt it. He is not a man to retreat from public opinion."

Where would it end? she wondered as Lady Hartford took her leave. Her only hope lay in Toby, though there was yet no sign of him. She was beginning to worry that his dissipation might be so pronounced that even coercion would not work.

They had never been close, and she had not seen him in ten months. His only communication had been that slippery response to the letter Saunders had carried to Drayton Manor. Her ladship had penned a blistering condemnation of his character and morals, calling the wrath of God down on his head for endangering his sister. Melissa had not seen his reply until the day Heflin visited Castleton House. Had Heflin actually forced agreement to a betrothal? Fear of facing a *fait accompli* might keep Toby away.

She shivered. But things could not have progressed that far. Heflin had never produced a contract. When he had left Drayton, everyone believed Melissa was on her way to America. It was unlikely that he would have heard differently until he arrived in town. But her come-out had caused enough of a splash to resurrect his pique. Girls who injured him could not be allowed to enjoy the approval of society.

But this was a ball and she could not spend the evening worrying. Abstractions and frowns would further erode her image. She tossed a dazzling smile at her first partner, and joined him for a country dance.

"You are in looks tonight, my dear," murmured Charles as they executed a quadrille three sets later.

"I cannot believe it," she countered. At least she did not have to pretend with him. He was becoming a close friend. "Heflin is repeating his claims, and there seems no way to stop him. Continued speculation is eroding my reputation."

He sighed, squeezing her hand in commiseration as he led her through the pattern. "I know, though it will rebound when this is over. I heard him last night. Not only is he reviving the tale, but he is doing it more determinedly than before. When is your brother due?"

"Who knows? Grandmama sent her secretary to fetch him a fortnight ago, and I expected him within a week."

"Might he have refused to support you? I would wager Heflin thinks so. His recent reticence may have been a waiting period to see what Drayton would do."

Her expression lightened as she considered the question. It was the same one she had asked herself, but Charles's touch freed her from fear and melancholy. "If so, Saunders would have returned by now. The same is true if Toby admitted that settlements had been signed. Perhaps he is not at Drayton Manor. That could explain the delay."

He smiled as they moved into the next figure, distracted for a moment by her grace. "Where might he have gone?"

She was having trouble thinking. His smile raised uncomfortable heat. She had refused to waltz with him, and now suspected she should ban quadrilles and cotillions as well. Vanquishing her fear allowed other emotions to intrude. "I don't know. The friends I am familiar with are all in town."

His eyes glittered at her reaction, but he pushed all personal thoughts from his mind. If he hoped to win her hand, he must go slowly. Turning the conversation to pottery, he discussed his plans to expand a small kiln near Swansea to provide work for some of his tenants. She had made the suggestion several days earlier.

Despite the defection of much of her court, Melissa did not lack for partners. Only one mentioned Heflin's claims, and she repeated what she had told Lady Hartford. George led her out after supper. He was still the only gentleman she dared waltz with.

"You may wish me happy, Melissa," he grinned, pulling her into a momentary hug. "Clara accepted my suit."

"Congratulations," she said through a wide smile. "I am thrilled for you."

"I owe you more than I can ever repay," he continued. "You were right about everything, my dear. I now know what Thomas has been experiencing all these years."

"You truly love her, then?"

"Oh, yes. Words cannot describe it."

She saw the stars in his eyes, and knew he spoke the truth. "I wish you all the best, George. In everything." She quickly banished a spurt of envy. "How is your father?"

He sobered. "A little better, but he will never be himself again. The doctor does not expect him to live past the end of the year."

"It is difficult to lose a parent," she admitted, tightening her hand on his shoulder in sympathy. "Particularly one to whom you are close. Let Clara help you deal with the pain. It can only bring you closer."

"Thank you, Melissa. You are wise."

"When is the wedding?"

"We have not set the date, but I expect it will be at the end of the Season. Neither of us wants to wait."

"Shall I wish Clara happy?" she asked as the dance swirled to a close. "Or did you anticipate the announcement?"

"She knows I am telling you. You introduced us, after all."

"Then I will congratulate her. You've no idea how delighted I am for you, my dear friend."

"I think I do," he countered softly. "And I pray you will find equal happiness for yourself."

She found Clara and led her into an empty anteroom.

"George told me of your betrothal, Clara. Congratulations."

"He is the most wonderful man!" she exclaimed, her face glowing with happiness. "I cannot believe that he actually loves me!"

Melissa gave her an exuberant hug. "He will make you a good husband. And you are the perfect wife for him. Take good care of him, for I count him a friend."

"You do not feel slighted?" Clara asked hesitantly. "I heard that he had been courting you before I arrived in town."

"I suppose that is how it looked to society," hedged Melissa. "But George has never been more than a friend. He loves you, and I am happy that he has found someone worthy of him, though I always suspected you would suit. That is why I introduced you."

The words set Clara's fears to rest, and they spent several minutes discussing wedding plans before Clara returned to the ball. Melissa remained in the anteroom. Her temples throbbed with a worsening headache, and not just from the increasing tension of Heflin's campaign. Despite her genuine pleasure in her friends' joy, the announcement cast a pall on her spirits. *Pray you will find equal happiness.* It was not possible. She had fallen in love with a fortune hunter. She could only hope that the attachment was a temporary infatuation. Sadly, her initial impression of his character was not wholly true. He had revealed serious interests and fascinating dreams. Whether he would pursue them was still unknown, for talk was cheap and he had shown no inclination to do anything in the past. *But most projects require money—*

"Well, well, what have we here?" an oily voice gloated. She jerked her head around in terror. Lord Heflin blocked the doorway. How had he gotten in? Lady Riverton would never invite him.

"Excuse me, my lord, but this set is ending, and I am engaged for the next," she said coolly, giving him a chance to behave. But he refused to budge, and she dared not push her way out of the room.

"Ah, my blushing bride," he sneered, locking the door and

limping toward her. He was dressed all in black, emphasizing his satanic appearance.

"I am not and never will be your bride," she declared, forcing terror aside to examine her options. Screaming would attract attention, but if anyone found them alone, she would have no choice but to wed him. She had no weapon. The locked door made his intentions ominous.

"You are wrong, Melissa," he declared icily. "You will wed me. It is the only way I can recoup anything from that disastrous house party. Drayton is no gentleman. He played where he could not pay, lying for years about his wealthy but nip-farthing father. The slight retribution I extracted is insufficient. You must rectify matters."

She retreated behind a couch. "I am not responsible for my brother's debts." Hefting a vase in her hand, she threw it, but it smashed harmlessly against the wall when he ducked.

"Come, come, my dear, there is no need for hysterics," he scoffed. "Your guardian offered you in lieu of money, in a legally binding contract. But you need not despair. Life with me can be pleasing."

"Conceited ass. You are too selfish to please anyone," she snapped, circling to keep the couch between them.

"This discussion is pointless, Melissa," he declared, his brow twisting into a scowl. His voice turned deadly. "Nor is your brother the only debtor. You owe me for past slights. And you owe me for this cursed leg. I always collect my debts. The larger the account, the more you will pay." He feinted, then lunged the other way, but she eluded him, again placing the couch between them.

"Damn you!" she shouted, lobbing a candlestick that glanced off the side of his head. "Leave me alone. When will it sink into your obtuse brain that I am not interested?"

"What you want is irrelevant. You can start paying right now, jade," he snarled. "You'll discover that marrying me is your only option. No one else will touch you when I'm done." He leaped over the couch, his hand catching her hair as she jumped aside.

But his leg buckled as he landed, knocking him violently to the floor. She went down with him, already twisting to smash a fist into his temple that loosened a stream of lurid curses.

The connecting door to the next anteroom crashed open, and Charles surged through. Muttering vicious imprecations, he dragged Heflin to his feet, planted a quick series of blows to his head and stomach, then landed one on his jaw that again sent Heflin sprawling. Flinging the limp body into the next chamber, Charles turned to Melissa.

"Are you all right?" he asked anxiously, kneeling beside her, fear and anger still blazing in his face.

She burst into tears.

"Shh . . . It's over . . . Relax," he crooned, pulling her head onto his shoulder. Terror at Heflin's obsession shuddered through her, but Charles's soothing voice continued, his palms stroking gently over her back. Gradually the blackness receded and the shaking stopped.

At last she lifted red eyes to his. He had seated himself on the couch and now held her in his lap. "How did you get here?"

"I was in the next room and heard something crash against the wall." Fortunately, his friends had already left. They had been plotting new strategies to drive Heflin from town. "When I realized that someone was fighting off advances, I opened the connecting door to investigate. How did you come to be alone with that reprobate?"

One last shudder wracked her. "Miss Rosehill and I came in here to talk. When she returned to the ballroom, I stayed behind to ease a headache, but Heflin barged in moments later. Why was he here? Surely Lady Riverton did not invite him." She straightened, accepting his proffered handkerchief.

Charles was frowning. "A good point. She would never include a man of his stamp in her gatherings. I must talk to the footmen."

"No, Charles," she pleaded, eyes again blazing with terror. "If this comes out, it will ruin me!"

"You cannot think me that low, Melissa," he objected. "I can certainly complain about finding the fellow in the hall, and ask how it came about. That will alert other hostesses to be more careful."

"I am sorry," she apologized. "My thinking is still fuzzy."

Rising, she set about the daunting task of restoring her appearance, grimacing at her mirrored image. Ruined hair. Red eyes and cheeks. Her dress pulled off one shoulder.

"This is hopeless," she wailed in despair. "I may as well send for Grandmama and go home."

"Nonsense," he rejoined, appearing behind her in the mirror. "A few quiet minutes will take care of your eyes. Let's see what we can do with this hair." And before she knew what he was about, he had gently set her hands aside and was expertly repinning her locks.

"You have done this often," she charged five minutes later when he had restored her coiffure to its former glory.

"Be grateful that I have." The teasing voice further relaxed her. "You must return to the company. I do not know if Heflin is still around but he is certain to make claims." He turned serious. "You must be able to account for your time away from the ballroom. Did you tell Miss Rosehill about your headache?"

"Yes."

"Will she agree that I was in the hall when she left?"

"Possibly."

"Excellent. I will escort you to the retiring room and wait outside while you mention your headache, then take you back to the ballroom. That should cover your absence." He turned her to face him, and repositioned the shoulder of her gown. Excitement flared as his fingers stroked her creamy skin.

Melissa cursed her traitorous body. She tried to glare at him, but her eyes would not cooperate.

"Don't look at me like that," he choked, but it was already too late. His hands slid down her back as his lips descended, banishing all thought. Groaning, he pulled her closer until her exquisite breasts pressed against his chest, their hard nubs stabbing into him despite the fabric that separated them.

An answering moan rose from Melissa. She opened her mouth to his, reveling in his dancing tongue. If his earlier kisses had been exciting, this was pure heaven. Her hand reached up to thread his hair. *Repeated touch overwhelms reason.* Shock at her wantonness broke through the pleasure and she abruptly pushed him aside.

"Let go, you lecherous cretin," she sputtered furiously. "For all your fair words, you are no better than Lord Heflin."

Charles was gasping for breath, desire making nonsense of her speech, but the slap she delivered to his cheek finally penetrated his senses. He grimaced.

"You cannot claim you did not enjoy that," he protested.

"You are experienced enough to turn any lady's legs to jelly. And you know it!" She glared.

"Forgive me, Melissa," he begged. "I lost my head for a moment. My only excuse is that I love you."

"If you truly loved me, you would not treat me like one of your light-skirts," she charged. In truth, she was angry at herself rather than at him, but she could not afford to ease the tension lest she again succumb to her vulgar nature. A glance in the mirror confirmed that her hair was still perfect. He obviously had much experience making love to society ladies during balls.

"Please forgive me," he begged again.

"You will escort me to the retiring room," she ordered coldly. "You will use your acting skills to play the part of a supportive relative, but I do not wish to see you outside of that role again."

"Very well, cousin." Charles's heart froze at her cold tone. Surely she would relent. This was no more than an emotional outburst brought on by her harrowing evening. But he could not be sure. She had never been conventional; that was one of her attractions. But it meant he could never judge her by his experience with others.

He stayed nearby for the remainder of the evening. She carried it off well, for any shadows in her eyes were explained by her headache. He took the precaution of seeing them back to Castleton House, but there was no sign of Heflin.

Shame had already replaced anger and fear. She had been right to castigate him. After rescuing her from the uninvited advances of a selfish libertine, what did he do? He took the fellow's place. Such stupidity was appalling. One impulsive moment had wiped out all his careful stratagems. It would take a long time to live down this disgrace.

Melissa lay awake long into the night, the emotions of the evening disallowing sleep. Heflin's threats terrified her. He had moved beyond the unprincipled libertine who had tried to seduce his host's sister. Though there had been no choice at the time, her method of discouraging him had been a mistake. His score against her was growing: She had refused his advances, her inexperience preventing her from spurning him gently; she had injured both his pride and his body, leaving a lasting reminder of her attack; his claims prompted society to heap scorn on him and scoff at his words. And now there was Charles's assault. *I always collect my debts.*

But overriding her terror was something even worse. Charles's embrace was like nothing she had ever dreamed. How could she live without fulfillment of that promise? If only she could be sure he truly loved her. Memory of his caresses forced her to throw aside the coverlet.

Beatrice had been wrong. Allowing young ladies to learn about the power their bodies could exert was dangerous. It removed caution and focused nebulous feelings into concrete pictures that were impossible to ignore. And Lady Castleton had been wrong as well. Relative or not, allowing a libertine like Charles to escort them was flirting with disaster.

But that insidious voice again intruded. Perhaps Charles's claims were true. He was not as selfish as she had initially believed. He had pushed his way into that antechamber to rescue a lady from unwanted advances *before he knew the identity of either the victim or the rogue.*

Chapter Fourteen

Melissa was dressing for dinner when she was summoned to her grandmother's sitting room.

"Toby!" she exclaimed. He was hardly a sight for sore eyes. His face was creased in worry lines, its puffiness and sallow complexion informing the world that his drinking was worse than ever. Fading bruises further discolored one cheek. But his eyes were surprisingly clear.

The travesty of a smile appeared as he examined his sister. "Melissa?" he whispered uncertainly. "Is that really you?"

"You needn't act so shocked," she replied tartly. "What happened to your face?" *Slight retribution . . .*

He grimaced. "Heflin set a pair of thugs on me a couple of weeks ago, threatening to finish the job if I failed to pay him. What is going on?"

"Did Saunders tell you nothing?" asked Lady Castleton.

"Only that Heflin was trying to destroy Missy's reputation."

"Did you promise him my hand in exchange for forgiving your debts?" demanded Melissa, contempt clear in her voice.

His eyes slid away from the contact. "He offered for you."

"I am well aware of his offer. I overheard it. That is what drove me from Drayton, if you recall. What did you say?"

Silence stretched.

"We must know the exact truth, Tobias," injected Lady Castleton sternly. "He claims that you signed settlements for such a union."

"I signed nothing," swore Tobias, sitting up straighter as the others visibly relaxed. "He offered for Missy, and I gave him permission to address her. Well, what else could I do?" he demanded when she glared at him. "He holds too many of my vowels for me to annoy him."

"Did you promise that she would accept him?" pressed his grandmother. "We must know how serious this is. Unfortunately, you are the girl's guardian, and she is still under age."

"I made no promises," he swore.

"He is determined that Melissa should marry him," continued her ladyship. "Has he any grievances beyond what I already know?"

"There is no possibility of paying my vowels," muttered Toby. "He knows that. Attaching Missy would at least give him something. I was surprised at the time, for she was not much to look at. I must say, you've improved." He shook his head after another lengthy perusal of his sister. Her peach gown made her hair and eyes seem even lighter.

"He was furious with me at the time," admitted Melissa. "You know how I rebuffed him. Beatrice had also driven him off."

"He never mentioned that," groused Toby. "What did you do to him?"

She sighed. "When he tried to ravish me, I used my knee to effect and stabbed him twice with a pair of scissors. He still limps."

Toby flinched. Lady Castleton frowned. "And your cousin also rebuffed him?"

"Yes. The last time, she smashed a pitcher over his head."

"Oh, dear," sighed her ladyship. "Pride and revenge. A deadly combination. He must despise your entire family."

"Is there no hope, then?" asked Melissa.

"Don't be a simpleton," Lady Castleton snapped. "Toby's repudiation of any agreement will be enough to scotch this rumor. But that will hardly be the end of it. He will try something else. The first thing to do is to divide his targets. Beatrice is beyond his reach. But we cannot allow him to attack one of you through the other. It is imperative that we divorce your hand from Toby's debts." She whipped out a paper and handed it to Lord Drayton. "This is an assignment of Melissa's guardianship. Sign it. It relieves you of all responsibility by naming me her sole guardian."

Melissa's eyes opened in surprise. Toby looked uncertain.

"Sign it, Tobias. If you care for her, it is the only way to protect her. And it will also help you. He knows you are destitute. Few men waste time beating a dead horse."

He signed.

"Good. I suspect his attack was meant to intimidate you into supporting his claim. That avenue is now closed. If you have no say in her future, he must work through me."

"But he can still force your hand," pointed out Melissa. "He tried the other night, trapping me alone in an antechamber."

"How did you escape?" asked Toby.

"Charles rescued me that time, but there is no guarantee that such luck would favor me in the future. And it provides him a further complaint. I smashed the side of his head, and I'm afraid Charles roughed him up as well."

"Who is Charles?"

"A distant cousin who has been squiring us about."

"Charles can take care of himself. But you are right about the dangers you run," admitted Lady Castleton. "Even were you to wed another, he might still try to ravish you. The man is the devil incarnate."

"So we need to get rid of him permanently," mused Melissa. What a daunting proposition! He was immoral and unethical, but he had broken no laws. Few liked him, but only the marriage-mart rounds were closed. If her disclosures made society choose to ostracize him, it would only add to his grievances. He would still pose a threat, perhaps an even worse one. Somehow they needed to exile him from England, but few actions could force a lord to flee the country. "How much do you owe him?" she asked Toby.

He reddened. "That is none of your business!"

"Answer the question, Tobias," snapped Lady Castleton. Her eyes glared into his, impaling him like a butterfly on a pin.

"Fifty thousand," he muttered.

Melissa gasped, but bit off a sharp retort. She could not afford to anger him until he had refuted Heflin's claims.

"How came you to lose so much?" demanded his grandmother.

"At first it was only small sums," he protested, "but as the days passed they grew. The luck should have changed, but it didn't. I've never seen such a rum run. It would have changed, I am convinced, but after Missy left, the party broke up."

"Don't you dare blame me for your own stupidity," she snapped. "Every gamester in history has followed that same twisted logic. Are you sure he wasn't cheating?"

"Gentlemen never cheat!"

"Toby, you fool, Heflin is no gentleman. I don't care what his breeding is. Any man who would force a lady and set thugs on an opponent would certainly not cavil at sharping cards."

His face blanched. "He will call in the debt immediately if you push him."

"And you would land in prison," his sister finished for him. "You should have thought of that earlier. There is no chance you can pay him. Your only hope is to prove him a cheat. Then you will owe him nothing." She could see regret at signing the transfer already swimming in his eyes. He was terrified of her intentions, but he no longer held the means to control her actions.

"We must first quash these rumors," stated Lady Castleton. "You will accompany us this evening, Tobias. I will raise the subject of Heflin's claims soon after we reach the ballroom. You will deny that any arrangement was made, admitting that he requested permission to pay his addresses, but that you refused. Is that clear? You refused his suit based on his reputation as a libertine. He has never been a contender for her hand. You will also announce that Melissa's guardianship passed into my hands upon your father's death."

"He will kill me," he protested.

"Tobias!" she snapped, straightening into an iron-willed avenger who dominated the room. "You will protect your sister!"

"But—"

"Heflin will not harm you if you follow my instructions to the letter. You will not visit the clubs. You will not leave this house unaccompanied. You will remain sober at all times. We will find the evidence to prove fraud. Once he has been forced to leave the country, you may do as you please."

His face clearly showed indecision.

"Are you going to protect Melissa, or must I send you home?" demanded Lady Castleton. "Heflin's thugs will easily find you there."

"I will do as you say," he sighed at last.

"Repeat your story," she ordered.

He parroted her statements.

"Excellent. Go change into evening dress." He left.

"What took him so long to get here?" asked Melissa.

Lady Castleton grimaced. "That boy is heading for a bad end. Saunders discovered him sprawled unconscious in the library. It took two days to sober him up enough to talk sensibly, and two more to browbeat him into helping you. They stayed at Drayton for another week to allow his injuries to heal, although he still suffers from broken ribs. Saunders also had to augment his wardrobe. He can do you little good if he cannot appear in public."

"I do not trust him, Grandmama."

"He will do for the moment. Wresting your guardianship from his hands was the most important thing. Even if he refuses to renounce Heflin, he can no longer pose a threat. But I suspect that we can force a public admission that no betrothal was arranged."

"And then he can leave. He can be nought but an embarrassment if he stays. His drinking must have worsened. Never has he looked so bad."

"We will hold him to a healthy regimen. Fear of another attack will keep him in the house. The staff has already been told that he is to take no wine, not even at meals. I cannot afford to have him drunk. Good food should improve his constitution. What he does later is up to him. If he is smart, he will continue, but I've little faith in that."

The evening progressed as planned. Though Toby's appearance surprised much of society, his statements were accepted without question. Melissa was again surrounded by an enormous court. Toby managed to stay sober, eschewing the wine available for the gentlemen.

"How did you talk him into coming to town?" asked Charles as they twirled down the line of a country dance.

"Grandmama can be very forceful when necessary. And Toby has always bent with every breeze. I only hope he does not embarrass me before he leaves."

"What will Heflin do now?"

"I do not know. Toby is terrified. Heflin had already set men on him for not paying his vowels. Grandmama forced him to sign over my guardianship before he realized all the implications. He already rues that. This will not stop Heflin from wreaking revenge on either of us." She shivered. "We must force him into fleeing the country, but that means proving that he cheats."

"How do you know about that? I have been looking for evidence for weeks," admitted Charles. "But so far I've come up empty."

Surprise jerked Melissa's eyes up to his. She suppressed the yearning that erupted as their gazes clashed. He was searching too? He must have started before he learned that Heflin wished her harm. "Why?"

"He fleeced a friend of mine last summer."

"Mr. Crawford, I suppose. Have you discovered anything?"

"Not yet, but I will talk to your brother. Perhaps he can offer a clue."

Melissa abandoned the subject, but she could not get it out of her mind. Here was more evidence of Charles exerting himself in an unselfish way, for he had no personal stake in exposing a Captain Sharp. Concern for others—helping a friend; rescuing a maiden in distress. A warm glow settled in her heart.

"What is the meaning of the tale I heard last night?" demanded Lord Heflin as he limped across the morning room.

"What tale was that?" replied Toby uncertainly.

Heflin stooped over Drayton, determination glaring from his eyes. "There is a story making the rounds that you deny promising me your sister." Dangerous undercurrents vibrated through his voice.

Toby cast wild eyes around the room, freezing when Lady Castleton appeared in the doorway. Her glare was even more potent than Heflin's. He remembered the transfer of guardianship.

"You know I denied your suit," he answered thinly.

"Good morning, my lord." Lady Castleton swept regally into the room. Heflin stepped back in surprise, allowing Toby to skitter away. She took a seat between them, and motioned both to sit.

"You cannot have forgotten our talk," swore Heflin, ignoring her greeting to address Toby.

"Lord Heflin," snapped her ladyship. "You forget your manners. We have tolerated more than enough of your dastardly insinuations. Both my granddaughter and my grandson have denied your claims. I will not listen to another word on the subject."

"You cannot squirm out of it with lies, Drayton," Heflin growled. "I will tell the world exactly what you said and why."

"You may say whatever you like," declared Lady Castleton. "But few will believe you, and ruining each other cannot affect Lady Melissa. Tobias is not her guardian. Now enough of this farce—" But Heflin was no longer listening.

"You swore—." He turned furious eyes to Toby, springing to his feet as if to attack, but Lady Castleton cut him off.

"Enough!" she barked, rising to her full height in haughty fury and blocking his path. "Your behavior is offensive, sir. I will not have a brawl in my drawing room. Depart at once, and do not return."

Barnes appeared in the doorway, Heflin's hat and cane in his hands. Two footmen stood just behind him. Impotent rage glared from Heflin's face, but he bowed stiffly and departed.

"You will remain in the house," she ordered Toby. "Use the time to recall everything you can about those card games. Melissa is right. We must find evidence of cheating."

The following week, Toby and Melissa attended George's party at Vauxhall Gardens, arranged in celebration of his betrothal to Clara.

Melissa was enthralled by the fairyland appearance of the gardens, with their thousands of lights and multiple attractions. A puppet theater entertained laughing crowds, far enough removed from the concert plaza to make the dialogue audible. A rope dancer plied her arts near the pavilions. The group listened to the concert and admired the cascade before adjourning to the supper boxes. George looked ready to burst with pride as he accepted congratulations, making the usual jokes about leg-shackles and mousetraps seem silly in light of his glowing happiness.

"How are you enjoying your brother's visit?" asked Charles softly. He slid a plate containing wafer-thin slices of ham and beef in front of her and offered lemonade.

"We get along all right when he is not drinking." She frowned as Toby helped himself to another glass of rack punch.

"Perhaps I should show him the Hermit's Walk," Charles suggested, forgoing his need to talk to her. He was still trying to live down his actions at the Riverton ball. "We can discuss those card games. Maybe he can give me a clue to how Heflin does it."

She nodded in approval, smiling as he deftly detached Toby from the group and led him away. Matt claimed the vacant place at her side and joined in the humorous discussion she was conducting with the Hartfords.

"The fireworks will begin soon," announced George some time later. Everyone rose to head for the knoll that offered the best view.

Matt offered Melissa his arm. "Have you ever seen fireworks?"

"Never. Are they as spectacular as I have been told?"

"Better." He entertained her with descriptions of other shows he had watched, including the special ones two years earlier that had celebrated the victory at Waterloo. In the jostling crowd they became separated from the rest of their group.

"Not to worry," he shrugged. "We will all return to the box afterward."

And she did not worry, for Mr. Crawford was always the perfect gentleman. If anything, he treated her better than he did others, perhaps because he was still embarrassed over the previous summer. They had never mentioned it, but she had seen the discomfort in his eyes.

Melissa squealed with delight as rockets burst in dazzling displays of colored fire. Catherine wheels brought gasps of pleasure from the gathered crowd. Matt's comments on the history of fireworks, and his descriptions of how the shells were loaded, led to an animated discussion when the show was over. He had an avid interest in pyrotechnics and had visited many specialists. Melissa suddenly realized that most of the crowd had dispersed.

"This is fascinating, Matt, but we had best be getting back." She sighed. "My grandmother will worry if I am too long absent."

"Of course." He helped her to her feet, placing her hand on his arm. They retraced their steps to the main concourse.

"Toby is looking better than I expected," Matt commented, drawing her to one side as a group of inebriated gentlemen and squealing females chased one another recklessly along. "Has he turned over a new leaf?"

"Time will tell. Grandmama refuses to allow him anything to drink while he stays in her house. Whether he continues that course on his own, I would not dare to guess." She shrugged.

He shook his head, angling away from the entrance to the infamous Dark Walk. "He has set himself on a ruinous course. It is painful to watch, as you must know. But it wasn't always that way. He was a good lad when he arrived at school, though he had a tendency to recklessness. And he was quite the best horseman—." His voice abruptly ceased as rough hands jerked him aside, a fist smashing into his jaw. It was over in a moment, his unconscious form slumped on the ground.

Melissa tried to scream, but the attacker covered her mouth and dragged her along the darkened path. Not until they had rounded two corners did he turn her to face him and remove his hand.

She screamed.

"It will do you no good, my dear," sneered Heflin. "No one pays attention to such sounds here. They are much too common."

His arms pulled her closer, his mouth already descending to her own. She twisted her head aside and screamed again.

"You are adding to your debts," he growled, grabbing her buttocks to grind her against him. Her fear was already increasing his lust.

"Cad!" She spat in his eye, and tried to push him away.

Smacking her cheek, he twisted her arms behind her and pinned her against a tree. His freed hand wrenched her face up to his. Revulsion engulfed her as he forced his tongue into her mouth. She bit him.

"Bitch!" he growled, ripping her dress to her waist.

Nausea welled. This bestial attack had nothing to do with love. There was no pleasure to be found in so violent a confrontation. Darkness threatened even as she continued the hopeless fight, stomping sharply on his foot and freeing one hand to claw deeply into his face. He jerked his head back, hissing in fury.

Before she could draw breath to scream again, someone pushed through the adjacent shrubbery and attacked. She hardly took in the brawl that followed, for she had collapsed to the ground in hysteria, one hand feebly trying to pull her gaping gown together.

Charles endured Toby's inane chatter for more than an hour. It rapidly became clear that the fellow was too stupid to have suspected cheating, and had been too drunk to remember any of the games. How could so hulking a toad have so exquisite a sister? He was leading the way back to Rufton's box when they chanced across a group of bucks, some of whom knew Drayton. They were harmless fellows, Charles decided, excusing himself.

But the box was empty, as the fireworks display was starting. It was useless to look for one group in the darkness of the grassy knoll, so he sighed and settled in to wait. An hour later he was taut with worry. Melissa and Matt had not returned.

It was ridiculous, he fumed at himself. There was no one

with whom she would be safer. Matt had vowed to help him
protect her. But he could not ignore his fear. No one was responsible when drunk, and Matt had the lowest tolerance for
wine he had ever encountered. He headed for the viewing
area.

It was empty. Were they wandering the side paths? He
ducked down the first trail, nearly running its length before
doubling back on the next. A distant scream pierced his ears.
Despite all logic, he knew it was Melissa. He thrust through
shrubs to the next walk as she screamed again. He had the direction now and could picture exactly where she was—on the
second turn of the Dark Walk.

Charles knew Vauxhall very well. He had conducted numerous liaisons with well-bred ladies in its quieter corners, and he
knew the Dark Walk like the back of his hand. Racing along
the adjacent trail until he was opposite the second corner, he
pushed his way through the surrounding shrubbery. A half-un-
conscious Melissa was pinned against a tree. Red fury nearly
blinded him. He attacked.

A loud thud pulled Melissa out of her haze and she looked
up. Charles stood over a prostrate Heflin, whose jaw sagged
beneath a nose that bled profusely. He prodded his adversary,
but Heflin did not move.

"Are you all right, Melissa?" he asked, kneeling beside her,
his breath coming in gasps.

"I th-think so," she sobbed, allowing him to pull her up.

"Let's get away from here." He led her through the darkness
until they came to a shelter. Moonlight filtered through sparser
trees.

"Dear Lord," she shuddered. The light revealed her di-
sheveled appearance. "I can't go back like this."

He frowned. She was a mess. Her torn dress gaped. Her hair
was down on one side, and a growing bruise already discolored her cheek. He fought down renewed fury. "Lady Castleton will be ready to leave," he assured her. "If you wrap my
cloak around you, you can escape notice. It is chilly enough to
excuse borrowing it."

"Right," she agreed, her teeth chattering—though Charles
suspected from reaction rather than from the cold. Her hands
fumbled with her gown, unable to obey even simple commands.

"Let me help you," he offered, swirling his cloak over her

shoulders. He automatically reached down to better arrange her dress. And that was a mistake. His thumb could not resist brushing her breast, drawing a gasp that fueled his own passion. She was the most responsive lady he had ever known.

"Melissa," he groaned, drawing her tightly into his arms.

The emotional chaos of the evening had driven reason into hiding. Her only thought was that she was safe. So very safe. And cherished. His love enveloped her even more warmly than his cloak. She lifted her face, opening her mouth to his kiss.

Without thinking, he maneuvered her into the shelter, his hand teasing her exposed breast. Her moans spurred him on as he sank onto a bench, pulling her onto his lap and lowering his lips to her nipple.

"Dear Lord, Charles," she gasped, arching into his touch. Every caress ignited new fires. She abandoned thought. Nothing mattered but that she loved him.

"Melissa," he panted, returning eventually to her lips. A distant shout penetrated his fading conscience, reminding him where he was. And with whom. He managed to muffle his curses into gibberish. How was he to prove himself responsible if he could not keep his hands off of her?

She protested as he stood and set her on her feet.

"Forgive me, my dear," he begged, hastily draping his cloak completely around her to hide that delectable body from sight. "I am sorry to have led you astray again. But you can hardly claim indifference. Please, Melissa? Please? I love you. I want you. I need you. Please marry me."

She shook herself to clear her head.

"This is not the time, Charles," she begged. "Too much has happened tonight. I cannot think straight." *If he had not stopped, the decision would be made*, whispered that voice. The thought widened her eyes. He could have won right now, but he was allowing her to make her own decision. And she had to respect him for it.

"Very well, my love."

"Where did you leave Toby?" she asked once he had skillfully repinned her hair and straightened his cravat. By resolute concentration, she had restored her breathing to normal and reclaimed her composure. He had been visibly fighting for his own control.

"He should be fine. We met a group of gentlemen he knew

from school. All are unexceptionable, so I left him with them. He should already have returned to the box."

She took his proffered arm. "Let's make this quick."

"And you must stay in the shadows, love." Anger flicked through his voice. "That swine bruised your cheek."

But Toby was not at the box.

"I will find him and bring him home," he promised Lady Castleton. It took him more than an hour. Toby's unconscious body was shoved under the shrubbery alongside the Dark Walk.

Chapter Fifteen

Melissa received Charles in the drawing room almost innocently early the next morning. She had gotten little sleep, for the evening's events had kept her pacing much of the night.

Heflin was no longer an irritation. His assault had put to rest any hope that he would leave her alone. Even accepting Charles would not remove that threat. He no longer cared for public opinion, or even civilized behavior, wanting only to destroy her.

But Charles made a formidable foe, proving to be surprisingly competent and showing himself to be intelligent, capable, and purposeful. Nor was he the selfish toad she had labeled him. Whatever had delayed him from improving Swansea, he appeared to be committed to it now. His plans for the future were practical and promising. Perhaps losing the fortune he had so long counted on had forced him to take charge of his life, to utilize his talents. He had risen to the challenge, becoming a better man because of it. Lady Lanyard would approve if she could see him in his new persona. There was much of the iron-willed Lady Tanders in him after all.

Melissa had learned many things about society since her arrival in London. The world of the *haut ton* taught indolence to its children. The most important parts of a girl's education were manners and the art of flirting so that she could attach a husband in her first Season who would provide for all of her needs, allowing her to spend her life on gossip and entertaining. Gentlemen did not wed until some ten years later, but in the meantime, they were encouraged to idle about town, drinking, gaming, wenching, and sparring. Frivolity was king, while serious pursuits earned young men the contempt of their peers. Anything involving productive work was anathema to a real gentleman.

In that context Charles was an admirable man. He was never

mentioned in tales of heavy drinking, excessive gaming, or juvenile pranks. Even his well-established reputation as a rake seemed consigned to the past. She recalled Lady Hartford's comment about reformed libertines and shivered. Charles was different from his peers, and that difference must arise from his own character. It could not have been learned, for there had been no one to teach him.

"You are up early, Charles," she commented now. He looked as tired as she.

"There are several things we need to discuss," he said seriously, his face creased into a frown, though his eyes lit at sight of her. He deliberately remained by the fireplace.

"What?" She thrust her awareness of him aside and sat on the couch.

"Your brother was badly beaten last night," he began baldly. "He is staying elsewhere for the moment. I did not dare bring him here."

"Why? We would not shrink from caring for him."

"I know that, love." He smiled wanly. "But I do not want anyone to know where he is. He was unconscious when I found him, very near where you were attacked. He only regained his senses at dawn and remembers little." Charles had been up all night, frantic that Drayton might die. Though logic refuted the idea, he felt responsible for the beating. Lady Castleton had declared that Toby should never be left alone.

"Does he know who did it?"

"Heflin. Toby and his friends watched the fireworks together before Toby headed back to the box. I suspect Heflin had been stalking him, for as soon as your brother was alone, he pulled him into the Dark Walk and nearly killed him."

"It would be easy." Melissa sighed. "He does nothing but drink, and is in deplorable condition. But why do you look guilty, Charles? This wasn't your fault. In fact, if you had not found him, things could have been worse."

"I was supposed to be looking after him," he reminded her.

His assumption of responsibility raised a warm glow in her heart. She was only beginning to know this side of him. Now that she no longer filtered his actions through suspicion, she liked what she saw.

"Nonsense, Charles. You are not my brother's keeper. Toby is six-and-twenty, plenty old enough to order his own life. If he chooses to behave rashly, he must accept the consequences. He knew Heflin would be upset by his repudiation of that fictional betrothal, and he knew he could not afford to wander off alone."

"That was part of it. But I suspect this had more to do with the considerable debt that your brother owes."

"Heflin won by cheating. This was a combination of frustration and revenge."

"Matt knows he cheated but we cannot figure out how. I must expose him to protect others." His restless energy disallowed remaining propped against the fireplace. He was pacing the room as he spoke.

"Is Matt all right? Heflin attacked him as well as me. With everything else that happened, I forgot him." She blushed.

Charles grinned, eyes twinkling in shared memory, but he quickly sobered. "He has a bruised jaw, but nothing serious. He is chagrined that he was bested so easily. Toby is staying in his rooms for now. But enough of that. It is time to speak of us, Melissa." He stopped just out of reach and gazed longingly at her.

"Can you so easily give up your dreams of wealth?" she asked. It was the last barrier.

"The only thing I want from Harriet is forgiveness for dragging her through so improper a deceit. I pray her reputation was not damaged by her assistance."

"She is fine and harbors no ill feelings."

"That removes a weight from my heart," he admitted. "I love you to distraction, Melissa. But before you give me your answer, you must know the full reality of my situation. We've talked of it in bits and pieces, but you must understand the entire picture." He paced nervously about the room. "Swansea was a prosperous estate fifty years ago. Its problems started with my grandfather, who had a penchant for deep gaming and abominable luck. In order to finance his losses he began to skimp on upkeep. By the end of his life, he had raised rents beyond what the tenants could pay. Many left, their farms sinking into disrepair as no new tenants could be found. The remaining ones could barely scrape sustenance out of the land after paying such exorbitant sums. Some of them eventually gave up as well."

"Poor people," murmured Melissa. "Where did they go?"

"Two families left for the colonies as indentured servants. One found a new situation on another estate. The rest disappeared into London's slums." He grimaced. "My father abhorred his parent's profligacy, vowing to return the estate to its former preeminence, but he had little head for agriculture and no inclination for work. He tried to recoup his fortunes through investment, but his judgment was unsound and everything he tried lost money. Yet, like my gamester grandfather, he was always convinced that the luck would turn, that the next venture would succeed beyond his wildest dreams. In truth, they were just alike, both addicted to a ruinous activity."

"And you are not?" she asked.

"One might conclude so until recently," he admitted sheepishly. "Though I must plead for compassion. It is true I did nothing to improve the situation, but I had been told almost from birth that a fortune would be mine on my grandmother's death. I expected to sweep home and correct all problems as soon as she died. I had already lowered the rents, though that meant I could barely scrape by in town. I've been making ends meet by selling off the family art collection."

Melissa's brows raised in surprise, but she said nothing. The fact that he would part with something he loved came as a shock.

"In retrospect, I made a big mistake. I should at least have taken stock of the situation when I inherited. A different steward and procedural changes could have helped, even without any new investment. But I was young and caught up in a young man's life in town. I did not expect my grandmother to live much longer."

He sighed. "In truth, I wanted all or nothing, choosing to avoid the frustration of seeing problems that I could not correct. Now it is different. Fate has denied me the means, and I suspect that was for the best. Finishing the job any time soon is impossible, so I must content myself with addressing those deficiencies that can be improved, and accept living with the rest. It will be a long fight, Melissa, but I am convinced that I can ultimately succeed, because the course I have set is hard work and reinvesting all profits into the estate."

"How bad is it?"

"My father put even less into upkeep than my grandfather had," he admitted ruefully. "Worse, he made no attempt to improve methods or incorporate any of the new discoveries. The steward was lazy and hidebound, content to let things go the way they had always gone."

"Who is running the estate now?" she asked curiously.

"I did not replace him, assuming his duties myself. My best

tenant is seeing to affairs while I remain in town. Once I return, I do not expect to leave again. There will be no money."

"I see. So you are offering me a penurious life in the country with little hope of socializing." She kept her face carefully neutral, not revealing that such a life was what she preferred.

"Yes. But at least it will have purpose to it. And there is one other admission I must make, my love. Though I need you desperately in a personal way and cannot envision life without you, I also need your dowry. I have tried to find a way to put it in trust for your own use, but I cannot see how. There are things that must be done immediately if there is to be any hope of success. The tenant cottages require repair or replacement. The manor must have a new roof if it is to survive. The abandoned farms need to be cleared and planted. And I must invest in some of the new machines."

"You seem to have covered the essentials. What about cottage industries?"

"I have not had time to look beyond the obvious. We have already discussed the pottery. Cottage weavers cannot compete with the mills these days."

"There might be other things," she suggested. "Cheese making, basket weaving, bees, leather goods . . ."

"You are more knowledgeable than I in that area," he commented, settling onto her couch.

"I spent much time in my uncle's library this past winter. He has an extensive collection of books on estate management and craft industries."

"Will you marry me then, my love?" he asked, stroking the back of her hand with his fingers.

She paused a moment in thought. What he really needed was his grandmother's fortune, of course. And she could provide it. Or could she? How could she prove that she was Harriet Sharpe? It would not take much to convince Charles, for she could easily recount their arguments. But that would hardly convince solicitors and courts. She had changed so much that no one at Lanyard Manor would recognize her, and Beatrice was unavailable.

And how could she explain her own continuing deceit? She should have confessed the moment Charles appeared in London, but she had not, fearing that he would expose her to society. By the time she understood that he would never have harmed her, she had learned of the will. By now the deceit was too entrenched to change. Thus the means to rescue his estate was forever denied them. But he did not know that.

"Charles, I fear that you will grow frustrated under such straitened circumstances. You will come to hate yourself for not pursuing Harriet, and hate me for deflecting your course. I could not live under such conditions."

"I will not," he denied sharply. "I love you too much to ever wish for another. Having experienced that joy, the idea of a marriage of convenience turns me cold. I know things will be frustrating, but I have felt the exhilaration of personal achievement these past months, and it more than makes up for the sacrifices we must make. Let Grandmama's fortune go to the charities she designated."

She smiled, watching as hope exploded across his face. "Then I will marry you, Charles."

"Thank God," he breathed, drawing her into his arms. From the first touch of lips, she could feel his joy, feel the matching chords in her own heart. This was so right. So perfect. And she understood at last why Beatrice had taken widowhood so hard. Having lived with this, who could adjust to loneliness? His kiss deepened, building shocking heat and longing in the secret recesses of her body. She was half-lying on the couch, Charles stretched out beside her. Irresistibly curious, her hand trailed lower to touch the bulge straining at his pantaloons. Shock convulsed him.

"Don't, Melissa," he begged, drawing back and raising her hand to his lips. "I'll lose control and ravish you here and now. I cannot dishonor you so. Besides, your grandmother would be furious. She will be in here any minute."

"Of course," she agreed as reason returned and she steadied her breathing. She gently stroked down the line of his jaw, sending another tremor ripping him from head to toe.

"The wedding had better be soon," he muttered, "or I'll die of frustration."

"As will I," she admitted. "I am hopelessly wanton around you."

He grinned. "We'll post banns immediately. I think I can hold out for three weeks."

But can I? wondered Melissa.

Charles scanned the reading room at White's, relaxing as his eyes found Matt Crawford. The message had stressed urgency.

Matt poured wine. He had chosen a pair of chairs far removed from anyone else. The crowd was thin, offering even more privacy.

"Why the summons?" asked Charles quietly. "Is Drayton all right?"

"He is fine. I think we have Heflin." Matt's face remained calm, but his eyes glowed. "He played piquet with young Dawkins two nights ago, adhering to his usual practice of requesting a new deck from the house. After they finished—Dawkins lost four hundred pounds—I found a new deck wedged into the chair seat. Damned careless of him, but his attention was distracted by a contretemps just as the game broke up—Devereaux and Willingford over Willingford's wife."

"I heard about that. It is amazing that Devereaux has not faced more problems." He was a libertine who had worked his way through most of Mayfair's bedrooms in a twenty-year career. Along the way he had learned to read character very well. It was odd that he had missed tagging Willingford as the furiously possessive sort. Charles recalled his own encounter with the gentleman and shuddered. "But finding a deck of cards in a chair proves nothing."

"I know, but it started me thinking. The problem has always been proof, for he invariably starts with a fresh deck, and examining the cards afterward reveals no nicks, scratches, or marks of any kind. Last night I played with him myself, but this time I came prepared. When his attention wavered after the third hand, I replaced the deck we were using with a new deck I had brought with me, then excused myself with a crack about his skill still being too much for me. It was late and we both left, so I doubt he knows yet. His deck was definitely marked, though so subtly it takes a keen eye to notice, especially in dim light. He must have eyes like a hawk. I took it to the steward this morning. There should be an announcement any minute."

Charles whistled softly. "Good work, Matt. What will he do now?"

"I don't know, but there are too many people who have lost to him lately for him to stay. I suspect empty coffers brought him here. He is too sensitive about his limp for any other explanation."

Charles agreed. If the man had known in advance that Melissa was in town, he would have arrived at the beginning of the Season.

Heflin arrived, a frown creasing his face. The steward approached, choosing to speak to him in the middle of the reading room. Somehow, others sensed that a drama was about to take place, for the gaming and dining rooms were already emptying as gentlemen jostled for position.

"You have been charged with cheating, sir," intoned the steward, pulling the cards from his pocket. "I have examined the deck you used with Mr. Crawford last night, one which was not obtained in this house, sir. The cards are marked."

Gasps echoed around the room. Heflin's face had paled.

"Nonsense!" he exploded. "If something is wrong with the cards, then Crawford is responsible." But the glares directed at him by every man present froze further protests on his tongue.

"It would be interesting to hear your explanation of why Mr. Crawford was the loser," declared the steward, "but there is little point. Your membership in this establishment is terminated, Lord Heflin. You will not darken these doors again." Two burly footmen had appeared to usher him out. Heflin glared, but when it became obvious that they were prepared to use force, he turned and strode away.

By evening the news was all over town, and the other clubs had also rescinded his membership. By morning he had fled to France, for those whom he had fleeced were already dunning him to return their losses.

Chapter Sixteen

Toby returned to Castleton House as soon as Heflin left town. Melissa was appalled by his injuries.

"It is nothing," he disclaimed, and indeed he was no longer bedridden. But his face was still a mass of bruises that prevented him from fully opening his eyes. A sling supported a broken arm, and he walked with a limp.

"Why did he do it?" she asked.

He shrugged. "You were right about him, Missy. He was evil. This was in retaliation for not paying my vowels."

"But he won by cheating!"

"Do you think he cared about that?" Toby demanded incredulously. "If anything, it gave him an extra grievance. He wasted a full month milking a dead cow, and turned up lame besides. But at least he is gone, and I am under no obligation to pay." Satisfaction brought a supercilious smirk to his face. "And you are well set. Rathbone seems wealthy enough."

She caught the gleam in his eye and sighed. "Forget it, Toby. He is as poor as we are. We will retire to his estate."

"Have you no brains?" he demanded sharply. "You could have your pick of wealthy gentlemen. Why throw yourself away on a pauper?"

"You will have no hold on any gentleman I wed, so what do you care?" she countered. "You are no longer my guardian. Remember? I have more important criteria for choosing a spouse than wealth. And you still have Drayton Manor. With a little effort, you could turn it around. You are sitting on a gold mine, Toby. Stay away from wine and work on improving the estate, and your income will soar. Stay away from the gaming tables, and you'll keep the new wealth. You could be the first earl in a century to be a success."

"Enough! I don't need you to tell me how to run my life," he growled, limping toward the door. "And you are as dishonest as Heflin. You tricked me into signing away my rights, cheating me out of settlements that should have been mine. You've got what you wanted. Now leave me alone. You shan't be welcomed at Drayton again." Slamming the door, he shouted for Barnes, demanding that a carriage be readied.

Melissa shook her head, blinking away tears. Despite everything, he was her brother. Hope proclaimed that he would relent when he had calmed down, but reason knew otherwise. He was selfish, caring only for what she could bring him, and all the while he was racing down a path of self-destruction. Even without the debt to Heflin, Toby was on the verge of ruin. Saunders had verified that the estate was mortgaged to the hilt. Without the immediate remedy of hard work and reinvestment, it would never produce the income to retire those debts. If he did not kill himself through some wine-induced folly, he would soon land in debtor's prison. It seemed likely that the title would come to an ignominious end with the seventh earl.

Could anyone have deflected him from his ruinous course? Their grandfather had been a high stickler who disdained any form of manual labor. His chief interest was hunting, but an accident when Melissa was four damaged his hip so that he could no longer sit a horse. Thereafter, he spent winesoaked days reliving his most exciting runs in rambling monologues. What a charming example of coping with adversity to lay before an impressionable eleven-year-old boy.

But surely their mother could have countered it!

Her head shook. It was true that Lady Drayton believed in self-reliance and accomplishment, but her husband did not. Like the fifth earl, he was an indolent man who eschewed toiling for his bread and cared only for hunting. If his steward failed to produce what he considered a respectable income, the man was fired. Melissa could recall thirteen stewards before her father's death. Lady Drayton was appalled, but he accepted no interference in his affairs. She chose to live in her own world rather than fight his edicts, burying her frustrations, except for lengthy monologues poured over her daughter.

And that was something else Melissa had forgotten. Despite sharing the same parents, she and Toby had been raised very differently. Once he left the nursery, Toby rarely spent time with Lady Drayton. Instead, he lived in the stables with his grandfather and father, absorbing their interests and their views on his role in life. At age fourteen, he was packed off to school, where he made friends with people like Heflin. It was no wonder he had turned out as he had.

Charles arrived an hour later.

"Good morning, love." In deference to Willis, he contented himself with kissing her fingers instead of drawing her into his arms.

"You are here early," she smiled back.

"The jewelers finally finished cleaning the Rathbone ring. I am sorry it has taken so long. Every viscountess since the first has worn it, but none could possibly compare with you, love. I cannot shower you with jewels as you deserve, but my soul accompanies this ring and is now in your keeping." He slid it onto her finger.

"Thank you, Charles. And mine goes with you." She raised her eyes to catch his gaze, brushing his cheek with her other hand.

"Know that I love you, now and forever," he murmured, crushing her close and kissing her until both shook. A cough from Willis intruded and he pulled back.

"My solicitor is to meet this afternoon with your grandmother's man of business to arrange the settlements. He requests that we see him briefly before then."

"Why?" The bride was never involved in legal proceedings.

"I haven't a clue. Will you be here?"

"Of course."

"In the meantime, may I take you driving?"

"I would like that, Charles. Is Harper with you?"

"He is out front with my curricle." As usual, her smile set his limbs trembling. *Only two more weeks,* he reminded himself.

"That will be all, Willis," she ordered. "Tell Lady Castleton we will return shortly."

He eschewed the usual parks this day, instead turning north for Hampstead Heath, wanting nothing more than to be alone. He was tired of stopping every few minutes to exchange pointless gossip with friends and acquaintances.

The air was clear and pure, heavenly after the smoke and soot of London. The early June sunshine sparkled on grass, wildflowers, and the occasional streamlets that tumbled down verdant hillsides. Birds sang lustily from trees and shrubs, swelling their hearts with gladness. Charles drove one-handed, the other draped around Melissa's shoulders, his fingers caressing her arm.

"How well do you drive?" he asked when they were out on the heath. They had been deliberately conversing on impersonal topics since leaving Berkeley Square.

"Uncle Howard lets me take out his chestnuts."

He handed the ribbons into her care, freeing his other hand to brush lightly against her breast.

"Not now," she objected with a laugh. "Do you wish me to make a cake of myself by overturning us?"

Sighing, he returned his hands to his own lap. She was an excellent whip, he realized as his attention turned to her driving. His grays were spirited and still fresh. Though well into their bits, Melissa maintained perfect control, holding them to a brisk trot. Two squirrels chased across the road, but she corrected their shy almost before they reacted. Something nibbled at the edges of his memory, but it disappeared when her spicy perfume assailed his nostrils.

"Let us walk awhile," he suggested as they approached a wooded stream. "Where did you learn to drive so well?"

She laughed without mirth. "My father's passion was horses, you might recall. The stable was the last thing he let go as the money disappeared. His head groom was the finest I've ever encountered, and he taught me to ride and to drive. It broke his heart when the horses went. Papa kept him on with some tale of a temporary setback, though Jake knew quite well what was what. They died two days apart."

"You were blessed with a good teacher," he stated. "Rarely have I seen anyone with your skill."

Leaving Harper to hold the horses, he turned upstream, his fingers entwined with hers. Sunlight filtered in bright shafts and curtains through the trees. A lark warbled somewhere across the water.

"Glorious day!" she exulted, dropping his hand and twirling around, her face raised to a shaft of sunshine. He reached out to grab her, but she darted out of reach to pick a cluster of primroses growing on a bank, threading them into his buttonhole, where they glowed against the green of his jacket.

"Thank you, love," he smiled, hugging her. "They almost match your hair."

"You're being silly." She giggled. "They are much lighter."

"And nowhere near as rich." He loosened his grip so they could continue upstream. But he could not relinquish all touch.

Thereafter, they strolled with arms about each other's waists, the warmth and excitement of the contact wrapping them in a cosy shell. The path turned away from the stream, but they continued onward, wandering idly through the copse until the trees opened into a flower-strewn dell.

"Beautiful," she breathed.

Sun intensified the perfume of a lilac bush, bathing them in its heady scent. Several bees droned somnolently as they went about their business. Thick grass formed an emerald carpet, unusually vivid with its dots of pink, white, and yellow flowers. The brook murmured and chattered over rounded stones. It was a magical place, a fantasy world of their very own.

"Yes, you are," he agreed, swallowing awkwardly. Her eyes sparkled, her face glowed, and her tongue ran across those irresistible lips. His mouth followed.

Her arms twined about his neck, her hands drawing his head down as he deepened the kiss. He paid homage to her eyes, her ears, her throat. Excitement quickened as the passion they shared stirred to life. She pushed his jacket aside to caress his shoulders and back.

Folding it into a pillow, he lowered her into the soft grass. The back of her gown opened easily, baring her breasts to his lips.

"Yes, Charles, yes," she moaned as he drew a nipple into his mouth, suckling until she writhed beneath him.

He was lost in the wonder of her soft skin and instant response to every touch. The world receded to a dim corner of his mind. Nothing was real but the woman in his arms. Cool fingers left fiery trails across his chest, and he realized that she had untied his cravat and unfastened his shirt. Discarding them, he bent his head to another kiss, reveling in the difference love brought to an activity he thought he understood.

Melissa's head was swirling, the excitement he could always raise lifting her to heights she had never imagined. The silky hair on his chest produced new surges of desire as it brushed across her breasts. More. She needed more. She needed to discover what had so often disturbed her dreams. Her love expanded, swelling her heart until it threatened to tear her apart.

"Charles!" she cried, her words cut off as he plunged his tongue into her mouth.

Charles was teetering on the brink of dishonor. *You must stop*, a voice urged. He had already pushed this too far. *You are a gentleman. Return home,* ordered his conscience. *Patience. Only two more weeks . . .* But he was starving. He needed a little more, just one more kiss . . .

She reached down to trace the bulge that pressed against her thigh, and he was lost.

"I want you now," he choked, his tongue lapping eagerly at her breast.

"Yes, Charles, please. Oh, please," she begged, convention forgotten, nothing mattering but that he was here and could relieve her burning pain.

A quick thrust claimed her, and he reveled in her sweetness, in an excitement he had never before experienced. She was perfect, made just for him, and he was whirled away in an agony of exhilaration.

Her gasp was gone in a moment. No dream could compare to the reality of his touch. Her eyes bore into his as they reached the crest, seeing clear to his soul and laying bare her own. Then the world exploded, tumbling both into oblivion.

When Charles and his solicitor arrived, the look he bestowed brought a blush to Melissa's cheeks. How had she allowed herself to lose control? How had he? *Repeated touch overwhelms reason . . .* The morning drive had taken a turn that neither had expected. He had apologized, of course, but neither could honestly admit to shame. The next two weeks stretched interminably. Unless they were constantly attended, they were bound to succumb again. She had never imagined such ecstasy.

But his arrival also raised a spurt of fear. She recognized his solicitor—the same man who had attended Lady Lanyard.

"Why are we here?" asked Charles once they retired to the library.

"As you know, I was solicitor and financial adviser to your late grandmother, Lady Lanyard, as well as to yourself," the ponderous voice began. "She left a codicil to her will that was to remain secret for nine months, or until such time as you announced a betrothal. In the second event, it was to be opened and read with both of you present."

Melissa exchanged a puzzled glance with Charles, noting that his breathing had quickened, as had hers. Perhaps Lady Lanyard had not cut him off after all. Nine months. She had ordered that he wed Harriet within twelve months. What would she say in nine? Lady Lanyard had a devious mind that might have conceived another test. Would she offer some new disposition based upon his behavior in the interim? Perhaps the labor he had lavished on Swansea would earn him an inheritance after all. She prayed.

"If I might continue," stated the solicitor, drawing their eyes back to him. He broke the seal and read.

I have long believed that my grandson, Charles Henry Montrose, eleventh Viscount Rathbone, has the potential to become a responsible and productive contributor to the world, but so far he has fallen into all of society's traps, exhibiting only selfishness and sloth. My son has reported numerous cases of unsound judgment, unethical behavior, and irresponsible living. I cannot allow my first husband's hard-earned wealth to be dissipated on idle pleasure. Marriage to the right woman could steady him and give his life some purpose, but my life draws to a close, and he shows no sign of settling down.

To determine the extent of his selfishness, my son suggested informing Charles that his inheritance was contingent upon marriage. Charles succumbed to temptation, willing to stoop even to dishonorable deceit to obtain my fortune.

Charles blanched. Melissa gasped. The solicitor's dry monotone continued unchecked.

However, whether by blind luck or good judgment, he produced a girl who will make him an excellent wife. To that end, I composed my last will and testament. That cannot be my final word on the subject, though. There is every possibility that he either cannot or will not pursue the marriage he claimed to be contemplating. I therefore address this codicil to other contingencies.

All dispositions set forth in my last will and testament are to remain in effect, excepting that amount designated for my grandson, Charles Montrose.

In the event that he does not wed within twelve months of my death, the money will be divided among my designated charities.

In the event that he marries someone other than Harriet Sharpe, my solicitor, Mr. Andrews, will determine his reasons. If he weds to obtain a large dowry, he will re-

ceive one quarter of my estate. If the union arises from
mutual regard, he will receive one half, the remainder
going to the above charities.

Charles heaved a sigh of relief, a broad smile breaking out
on his face as the words registered. Half was all he really
needed. Even a quarter was enough to set Swansea to rights
with money to spare. He exchanged a sparkling glance with
Melissa.

The solicitor droned on. *"In the event he marries Harriet
Sharpe, also known as Lady Melissa Stapleton, he will receive
the entire amount."*

Mr. Andrews continued to read, but no one was listening.
Charles turned furious eyes on Melissa, whose face had
blanched.

"Excuse us," he growled, grabbing her arm and jerking her
across the hall to the morning room.

"You lying, deceitful harpy!" he stormed, slamming the
door behind him and thrusting her brutally aside.

"Me!" she exploded in return. "You've done nothing else
since first we met."

"You lied before I ever raised the issue," he charged. "Miss
Harriet Sharpe! And who the hell was your supposed aunt?"

"You don't understand—"

But he cut her off, fury engulfing him until he could barely
think. "You devised this whole trick in revenge, didn't you?
You would have let me starve rather than reveal yourself. How
you must have gloated over my discomfort. Did you plan it together? All those private talks. Sweet little Harriet, doing her
best to help me retain what was mine. Sweet little Harriet, who
is nothing but a scheming, vindictive jade!"

"All you care about is money, isn't it?" Melissa countered,
glaring in white-faced fury. "All your sweet words mean nothing. You are wrong right down the line, but what do you care?
Babbling on about work and accomplishment just to disarm
me when all you wanted from the beginning was a fortune so
you could continue your indolent way of life."

"Wrong, am I!" he glared. "I should have listened to your
protests in that damnable inn. You planned this from the start.
When did you tell her? The first day? The second?" He
smashed his fist onto a table, knocking a lamp to the floor and
smashing it.

"Arrogant toad! I told her nothing. Lady Lanyard had your

measure from the beginning. I could see it in her eyes that first afternoon. She was furious that her own flesh and blood could stoop so low!" His words barely registered. The suspicion was back. Had he known who she was? Tears clouded her eyes, a lump pressing into her throat until she could hardly breathe.

Charles's face was livid, his hands clenched into shaking fists. "Lies! Always lies! Who can believe a word you say? Claiming you despise deceit when you were already embarked on one and readily agreed to another. Continuing them long after they served any purpose. I saw no such signs. And neither did you."

"You were too sick to see anything, and too stupid to understand it if you had," she charged. "Your only thought was how to keep from vomiting all over her."

"Whatever happened last summer has no bearing today, Miss Harriet Sharpe," he countered furiously. "How do you explain condemning me to a life of poverty, when a single word would have released me? Do you hate me so much? What have I done to earn such spite?"

"Don't you dare blame me!" she hissed through gritted teeth. "If you were not so selfish a schemer, this would never have happened. You alone are at fault. You make a fine play at innocence, my lord, but I know you now. You will say anything that furthers your own interests. I never really believed that you could fail to recognize me, and now I am proved right. It's been an act from the start. You care nothing for me. I am merely the means to line your pockets. That's all I've ever been to you. Well you can forget it. I despise fortune hunters. And I despise you." Twisting the Rathbone ring from her finger, she threw it in his face, escaping in a swirl of skirts and barely making it to her room before tears engulfed her.

Charles remained in the morning room, frozen by shock. What had happened? It was long before he could move.

Chapter Seventeen

Charles stalked furiously into his room, slamming the door so hard the brandy decanter fell off the adjacent table. Damn the wench! She had been playing him for a fool from the start, tricking him completely. But why? Surely she could not hate him enough that she must revenge herself this way.

Had he misjudged her? Was she nothing but a fortune hunter out to snare a rich husband? She had steadfastly refused to marry him until he revealed Lady Lanyard's will. The timing of her acceptance now seemed deucedly suspicious. He revealed that marrying him would reap a fortune. She had spent a lifetime living in poverty. And so she overcame all objections and agreed to a betrothal. He shivered.

No! A fist smashed into the wall. It was not possible. And that was an exaggeration, anyway. She had turned him down that day. It had been weeks before she accepted him. If she wanted the money, she would have revealed herself earlier. But perhaps she had feared his reaction, planning to wait until it was too late for him to renege. Yet he still could not believe it. After years of studying human nature, his judgment was better than that. Money was not her goal in life. But that left only the conclusion that she hated him for plunging her into so dishonorable a deception—and it had been dishonorable. He groaned.

But that didn't make sense either. She couldn't hate him. Memory of her body arched into his kiss tightened his groin. She could not have responded that way if she hated him, so it must have been revenge. He would pay for that scheme. How long would she have let him suffer before she revealed the truth? Until just before the money went to charity? A lifetime? Perhaps his original charge was true. Lady Lanyard had known of his ploy, had known Harriet's true identity. She had written her will to tie him to a chimera, raising his hopes when there was no chance of success. As further retaliation, she had directed him to seek out Melissa. They could have plotted the ultimate punishment: Make him fall in love before casting him brutally aside.

No! He groaned again. It could not be. Whatever Lady Lanyard's motives, he could not believe that Melissa was that venal. And who would expect Harriet to grow into so stunning a woman? It would not fadge. And so he was back to her deceit.

He paced angrily about the tiny room, smacking his fists on walls and tables as wave after wave of fury swept him. She had lied from the moment they met, claiming a false name and inventing a false background. And she had help. The woman who had posed as her aunt had also lied. And who was that maid? It certainly wasn't Willis.

Embarrassment increased his fury. In retrospect, it seemed incredible that he had not seen through her deception earlier. There had always been a strong sense of familiarity about her, starting with her appearance, like seeing his grandmother's portrait come alive. And that was more true than he had ever admitted. Chagrined, he poured a glass of port and stared at himself in the mirror.

Was he stupid, or merely credulous? He had been bewitched since the first day he had seen her. A wave of longing broke over him, and he downed the wine in a desperate swallow. He had ignored every niggling thought, passing off even blatant coincidences. Did he really believe that she was the embodiment of that painted image that had fascinated him for so long, that she actually held his soul in her keeping? Fustian! But he had to admit that he had been so caught up in her appearance and his own growing passion that he had never considered any of those odd thoughts clamoring for attention. Even the original wording of the will should have tipped him off. *Known to me as Harriet Sharpe.* It was a screaming clue that she was someone else.

There was so much that he had never questioned. She knew more of Lanyard Manor than was possible unless she was Harriet. He snorted in disgust. Some student of human nature he was! Harriet would never have revealed that scheme, even to a bosom bow. She had been against it from the first, bemoaning what it could do to her reputation. Then there were Melissa's riding and driving skills. He had more than once compared her to Harriet, though admitting Melissa was better. In fact, she was as good as Harriet would have been after several months around quality horses. And that explained Harper's comments after they had returned to Berkeley Square that morning.

"Damn, but she's a good driver," Charles had said.

Harper nodded in his ponderously thoughtful way. "T'lassy's always been a bonny good whip, t'ain't she?"

The groom had recognized her. *He* had not been misled by golden curls and amber eyes. *His* attention had not been riveted by long legs and a bountiful bosom. Sitting up behind, he had watched her hands and the way she handled a whip, and had instantly known who she was.

Was Charles Montrose really such a shallow man? Did he become so engrossed in minutiae that he never looked at the whole? Melissa claimed he was ruled by his appetites, and he had to admit she was right. There was no other explanation for his utter lack of intelligent thinking. He poured another glass of port, wishing he had not spilled all the brandy.

There were other similarities he should have spotted. The wastrel brother, the pet name Missy, Harriet's inconsistencies. Her knowledge of the Willingford party came from neighborhood gossip—it had been a Drayton tenant who found him that day. No wonder she was able to back up his story so effectively. She had lived all her life in Lincolnshire. And her social aplomb—she was not a sixteen-year-old farm girl, but an eighteen-year-old aristocrat.

He should have known weeks ago. Melissa's criticisms of his character and reputation echoed Harriet's, and both Harriet and Melissa had turned down Heflin. He recalled Harriet's description of how she had done so, and shuddered. No wonder the man hated her so much. He could never allow the ignominy of it to pass unpunished.

The walls were closing in, suffocating him until spots danced before his eyes. In desperation, he left to stalk the streets, alternately cursing her and choking back tears. It wasn't fair! His suffering was too much for one small indiscretion. The penalty was a thousand times worse than the crime. But thinking grew harder as the hours passed. Images swirled through his mind—Harriet curled on a bed in uncompromising disapproval while he coaxed her aunt into helping him; Melissa passionately pulling him closer, her innocent wantonness driving him to heights he had never before experienced; Lady Lanyard displaying that cat-in-the-creampot smile when he bade her farewell to join Harriet; Melissa pinned against a tree while Heflin ripped her gown; Swansea suffering from decades of neglect and mismanagement.

And new doubts surfaced. Melissa was not a vindictive person. Despite his passionate longing he did not merely want her as a bed partner. He admired her intelligence and genuine concern for those less fortunate. She had a firm grasp of reality and such sound judgment that he could follow her suggestions without fear of emulating his father's flawed decisions. There must be something he had overlooked, some explanation for this debacle of deceit.

A night of fevered restlessness calmed his anger and forced him to face facts. Despite everything, he loved her. He no longer gave a damn about the money, or his grandmother's plots, or even her possible need for revenge. They must discuss the situation rationally and dispassionately, then put it behind them and get on with their lives.

He arrived at Castleton House almost indecently early, ready to listen calmly to whatever she had to say.

"The ladies are not at home," intoned Barnes, blocking the door to keep him on the step.

"When will they be back?" he asked.

"I am sorry, my lord, but the ladies will not be home to you again."

His hands clenched with the effort to control himself. Every muscle wanted to shove Barnes aside and accost Melissa in her room. The nerve of the wench! Was this part of her revenge? Had her anger still not cooled into reason? Or had she been serious? *I despise you! I despise you! I despise you . . .*

"Tell her I have called," he rasped at last, handing the butler his card. "If she wishes to see me, she knows where I am." Turning on his heel, he strode down the street, fury and pain again lashing his mind.

A week followed of almost continuous drunkenness. He avoided all entertainments, knowing he could not see her without a confrontation that would best be held in private. Not until he lashed out with deadly fists, laying Matt out on the street for commenting on his public debauchery, did he begin to pull himself together.

"I'm sorry." He sighed, helping Matt to his feet.

"You needn't tell me what happened," he protested, rubbing the jaw that had barely recovered from Heflin's blow. "But at least do your grieving in private. A gentleman does not wear his heart on his sleeve. Every drawing room in Mayfair is buzzing with speculation."

"I suppose I may as well go back to Swansea," Charles said. But that was admitting defeat. His pride despised the idea. "I keep hoping she will relent and at least talk to me."

"Didn't you know she was gone?" Matt asked in surprise. "They returned to Devon four days ago."

Charles shuddered, leaning weakly against a post as his knees gave out. Gone? Her hatred must run deeper than he had thought. But why? That was the eternal question. Why? He suddenly realized that he had never been able to explain her initial deception. Harriet existed before he met her. His first impression at the inn that night had been of a girl running away from home.

"Matt," he began uncertainly. "There must be more to this problem than I understand. It may have roots in Drayton's house party. Will you tell me about it?"

Matt paled at the question, leading his friend up to his rooms while he considered how to respond. The agony in Charles's eyes was hard to endure. "All right," he finally agreed. "Though that is not a time I care to remember."

"Who was there?"

"Drayton, of course. The other two were Heflin and Dobson. It was a month of drinking and gaming, with Heflin as the big winner."

"I know that. He cheated both you and Drayton out of a fortune. What about Dobson?"

"I think he broke even."

"And Melissa was alone with the four of you?"

"No. She had a cousin chaperoning her, a Mrs. Stokes. We didn't see them much. Lady Melissa disapproved of the whole affair. Heflin and Dobson were both making plays for the cousin."

"Good-looking woman?"

"Yes. Middle thirties. Shapely. Widowed American, but straight-laced as they come."

"Was that her cousin Beatrice?" Charles asked.

"Right."

So there was a relationship there. He recalled how straight-laced the lady was. Guilt flared over his own attempt to seduce the woman. Damn! Melissa knew about that, too. And Willingford. And his play for the lower-class Harriet. No wonder she ranted on about his character.

"What sent Melissa fleeing to her grandmother's?"

"I don't know." But guilt flashed across his face.

"Matt, I must know. You didn't try to force her, did you?"

"Certainly not!" he blustered, then abruptly sagged in dejection. "If it were only something that simple. I spent my time playing the supercilious prig who criticized everything she did. I probably made her life hell. She wasn't well versed in lady-like behavior in those days, and Toby wouldn't lift a finger to help her. Her clothes were abominable, her mannerisms were common, and her language belonged in the stable. I even ragged her for biting her nails, though my own behavior was largely to blame. I suppose I was venting my frustrations on her. The more I lost, the snootier I acted. But that's not the worst of it. My greatest sin was getting so foxed one night that I cascaded all over her."

"Oh, God," Charles groaned. Harriet had claimed to despise gentlemen. Could he blame her?

"You know I've never had a head for wine," pleaded Matt. "I was so embarrassed that I quit drinking. I never want to go through that again. It was hard enough having to face her in London this year, but she never said a word, acting as if it hadn't happened. Her magnanimity is a thousand times better than I deserved. I could not have blamed her for spreading the tale and ruining me."

"What about the others?"

"Dobson was too busy seducing the servants to pay any attention to Melissa. She wasn't much to look at. You'd never believe it to see her now, but she could have passed for a London waif. Heflin was making a play for her, though—warm remarks, brushing against her, following her with his eyes—you know the routine. She avoided him whenever possible. After the incident with me, she and her cousin took to spending the evenings in their rooms. We only saw them at dinner."

"Heflin is not the type to let that stand in his way," frowned Charles.

"No, he is not. I don't know what happened, but the day before she left, he turned up limping. Badly. Spent much of the day in his room."

Charles was stunned. Melissa was responsible for Heflin's limp? That stab must have been worse than he thought. She would have known what his reaction must be. No wonder she and Beatrice had left. And that explained Heflin's attempt to force a betrothal. She had claimed he sought revenge, and she

was right. Heflin wanted to wrest payment every day of her
life for her temerity.

So where did that leave him? He did not know. He still had
no idea why she had concealed her identify from him.

He left for Swansea the next morning. With Melissa gone,
there was no reason to remain in town. He was making a spec-
tacle of himself, and it was too expensive. Unless he could talk
her into resuming their betrothal, he was destitute.

Was that why he wanted her back? he asked himself several
times over the next few days. He reviewed all the arguments
he had conducted with himself during the past months. The answer remained the same. He wanted her. Without her, he was
an empty shell. Life had no meaning.

A week after his return he wrote her a letter. She returned it
unopened. Pain again attacked him. He tried again. And again.
If she wanted to be stubborn, he would be equally stubborn. In
the meantime, he threw himself into estate work. If nothing
else, it kept his mind occupied during the day and left him exhausted enough to sleep at night. And he sketched her a dozen
ways. A hundred. But he was never able to capture that elusive
spirit that haunted his dreams.

Melissa handed Charles's latest letter back to the footman,
closed her bedroom door, and burst into tears. She had cried
for six weeks.

What was she to do? She could not wed a man whose pri-
mary concern was money. Yet life without Charles was daunting. It was the eternal dilemma. She had not realized how
much she loved him until he was gone. Nor did she realize
how much she needed him. She had known at Lanyard Manor
that he was a dangerous man. He spoke to something within
her that she had not wished to recognize. That fear underlay
much of her resistance to him. And she had been right to be
afraid. What he spoke to was a vulgar emotion that proper
ladies were not supposed to feel. But it was too late. He had
awakened wanton desire that remained unfulfilled and now refused to crawl back into hiding and leave her in peace. She had
not managed a single night's rest since that disastrous
argument.

Her mind raged in turmoil, questions haunting her. Did he
love her? She could not relinquish his calling card, with its declaration scrawled on the back. It stayed with her always, its
message now blurred from constant handling. She had again

judged him wrongly. In recalling that disastrous argument, it seemed that he had not known until that very moment that she was Harriet. But his charges continued to echo. *Condemning him to a life of poverty . . . deceitfully denying him a fortune . . . letting him starve . . .* There had been no attempt to understand her or to discuss anything rationally. He had shouted blame, prosecuting, judging, and condemning without allowing her a single word in defense. And the crime was cheating him out of a fortune.

How had she been trapped in this coil? Each step had seemed so reasonable. Most of the lies were small—insignificant explanations that got lost within larger discussions. Many were automatic responses offered in self-preservation. Others were mere silences that allowed misstatements to stand uncorrected. Yet every tiny deceit had wrapped her in a thicker blanket of dishonesty that now threatened to smother her. Scott was right. *Oh, what a tangled web we weave . . .*

The beginning was so simple—using an assumed name when she fled from Toby's plotting. She still did not see how she could have done otherwise. Heflin's injuries were far worse than she had thought, and his thirst for revenge was stronger. Toby had tried to trace her, giving up only after Heflin left.

But that deceit led to the larger one—agreeing to help Charles. Again there had been no choice. They had no place to go and no money. Yet she would never have accepted his offer if she had not already been using an assumed name. It endangered her reputation. But it had seemed easy. Who would connect Harriet with Melissa?

Then there was hiding her identity when Charles first appeared in London. In retrospect, she should have admitted the truth then. It would have saved her from further deceit. But he would have immediately claimed her hand so he could inherit the money.

There were other lies, of course, all growing from her failure to identify herself. Every time she accidentally revealed something that had happened during that stay at Lanyard Manor, she had to lie about how she learned the information. Every new lie made it harder to admit the truth. By the time she discovered that Charles had not inherited Lady Lanyard's fortune, it was too late to admit that she was Harriet. And so she had continued the charade, finally accepting his hand when he convinced her that the money was irrelevant.

Until that last argument. Every charge revolved around money. It was not just important, it was vital. It was central to his existence. The question returned—had he known her identity before proposing? His acting had always been excellent. She had forgotten his skill at feigning affection, even for Harriet, whom he despised. His rage could have been another pretense meant to punish her for her own deceit, the courtship nothing but another ploy.

Furious and disillusioned, she had barred the door against him and spent a sleepless night tormenting herself with questions. If nothing else, the exercise held the memories of his lovemaking at bay. She had always trusted reason above emotion, but emotion was waging a strong campaign.

Barnes reported Charles's call, describing his appearance as tortured and handing her his card. On the back was scrawled *I love you*. She spent hours in bitter sobbing, the sodden card clutched tightly in one hand.

"I wish to return home immediately," she told her grandmother that night. There was no way she could face the *ton*. Seeing Charles in public would destroy her. Reason could not possibly hold sway face to face. There was no doubt that he would seek her out, for she was the key to his inheritance.

Lady Castleton stared at Melissa's puffy eyes. Whatever had happened would not be resolved any time soon. Her granddaughter had inherited the Tanders stubborn pride. "Very well," she agreed. "But I had hoped you could be happy with Charles. My cousin, Lady Lanyard, believed that you were the perfect wife for him, and her judgment was usually sound."

"Thank you, Grandmama," she replied, ignoring the comment about Charles. But she could not get it out of her mind. *Perfect wife, perfect wife . . .*

Her last meeting with Lady Lanyard echoed through her mind in stark clarity, but with disturbing new insights. Melissa now realized that her ladyship had already known Harriet's true identity, and she suddenly understood how. Except for the dress and hair, the eighteen-year-old Lady Lanyard had looked much like Harriet. If Melissa had known of the family relationship, she could have better disguised her appearance, and fabricated every part of her story, but she had not. Once the suspicion was raised, it would not take much effort to match the facts Harriet had revealed with Lady Melissa Stapleton's life.

Now those final words reverberated through her head with

new meaning. *See that Charles does something useful with his life . . . You will know where his interests and abilities lie . . . Take care of him . . .* And she had agreed. Oh, she had worded her response so that she would be under no obligation to see him again, but the situation had changed. Was she reneging on an oath by abandoning him now? There had been little reason for an informed Lady Lanyard to expect them to meet again. She must have guessed that Harriet/Melissa would never seek him out. So why extract the promise?

But, of course! That was the purpose of the codicil. The other provisions were nought but obfuscation. Its *raison d'être* was to tell Charles where to find Harriet. It was to be opened in nine months, giving him three months to woo her, and giving Melissa time to grow into a copy of Lady Lanyard. What a wretchedly devious lady! She must have known of his infatuation with the portrait, but to assure his interest, she had attached the fortune to Melissa's person, expecting his charm and address to easily win her hand once he put forth the effort. *Perfect wife . . .*

But it was too late. He had shown all too clearly where his priorities lay. Even if she could trust his love, she could never crawl back to beg his forgiveness. Her own behavior deserved contempt. And so she and her grandmother returned to Devon.

Lady Castleton continued to be supportive. She did not press for an explanation, accepting the broken betrothal and already talking of returning to London the next Season. By then, the gossip would have died and Melissa would be an even bigger success. Melissa agreed, but without enthusiasm. The prospect sounded appalling. She did not want another Season. She wanted Charles . . .

She returned again to his lust for a fortune. Was it inherently evil? Charles had a responsibility to his tenants and employees. All landowners did. There were some who controlled the lives of thousands of dependents. And that required money—for upkeep, wages, modernization, local industries. She could hardly condemn him for spending some on himself, for living in town like other lords. She had seen no evidence of waste in his life. Granted, he had nothing to throw away, but that hadn't stopped many another. She did not like to believe he would suddenly turn profligate after so many years of care.

So money itself was not the problem. But she could not eliminate the possibility that his courtship was all pretense. If he had lied about loving her just to reap a fortune, life would soon become a living hell. She would rather live without him than face the scorn he had directed at her in the beginning.

Determinedly drying her eyes, she crossed to the window. It was time her wayward body accepted reality. She would never see Charles again. She couldn't.

Bright summer sunshine turned the lawn to an emerald carpet, as roses blazed red and white in contrast. One year ago today, a fierce storm had stranded a terrified young innocent in a country inn. Forcing aside the memories, she directed her thoughts to the future.

What was she to do? Uncle Howard was disgruntled at her return and was growing testier by the day. Broken betrothals did not exist in his world. She was a disgrace, someone to be hidden away when people came to call. And the situation was even worse than he knew, for she had finally admitted to herself that she was with child. She had denied it for as long as possible, making excuse after excuse—her system was upset from the emotional beating she had taken; traveling home from London had thrown her off schedule; the hectic pace of the Season had wearied her—but she could no longer avoid the truth. Her hand slid across her still-flat stomach. A child was growing inside. Charles's child.

What had possessed her to indulge in intimacy before marriage? It ran contrary to all convention, to all morality, to everything she had ever believed in. Yet she had not only allowed it, she had actually encouraged it. Scarlet stained her from head to toe. Even fear and embarrassment could not banish the memories, raising again the constant yearning to be back in his arms. And she could never blame him. It had not been seduction. She had offered no word of protest, instead begging for more and doing things that he had already warned her would make him lose control.

What was she to do? Again her fingers verified that no one could yet guess. Her grandmother would be shocked to discover how wanton Melissa had proven. Uncle Howard would ban her from his estate. A broken betrothal was nothing compared to bearing a bastard child. Even Lady Castleton's patience would not extend that far. Melissa had demanded they judge her on deeds, so she could only accept their verdict.

Lady Lanyard would have understood, she knew in a flash of insight. She had warned against this very thing. And the self-confident Harriet had sworn that such a fall from grace would never happen. Perhaps her ladyship had learned the hard way, succumbing to blandishment during the months she awaited marriage to an elderly stranger.

But she was digressing. This was one problem that would not resolve itself. She must find a refuge before her condition became known.

She could not go to Charles. If he thought her deceitful for trying to withhold his inheritance, what would he think if she consented to marriage just to give her child a name? Their mutual recrimination would inject a festering canker into their relationship that must eventually destroy them. Never would they recapture the passion they had shared. She would rather be ostracized than endure a life of strained distrust with one she loved so dearly.

But she must leave. As she watched the roses nodding in the summer breeze, the answer appeared. There was one place she could go that was logical enough to prevent suspicion, and far enough removed to conceal her child. She examined the plan from all sides, then nodded and sought out Lady Castleton.

"I cannot endure this another minute," she announced baldly.

"What, Melissa?"

"Idleness is driving me crazy," she declared. "I must find something to occupy my time. I will never be able to put this behind me if I do nothing but brood."

"Did you have a particular activity in mind?" she asked.

"Actually, I did. I thought a visit to my cousin might help. She has often spoken of America. Her home is in Baltimore, which is quite civilized. A few months in her company would drive away these blue devils, and I could return for the Season relaxed and refreshed."

Her grandmother surprised her by agreeing to everything, even her offer to make the arrangements when she went into Exeter to purchase traveling clothes. She would try to sail within the month.

Lady Castleton frowned long after Melissa left the room. She did not know what had happened, but it was more than time those two patched up their differences. That Melissa loved Charles was obvious. Nothing else would drive her from the country. And it was equally obvious that he cared for her. His daily letters continued, despite every snub. They were ideal for each other, but Melissa was mired in stubborn pride.

She reread the last missive she had received from Lady Lanyard. Abigail spoke of her fears for Charles's future, her impressions of Melissa, and her wish that they marry to rejoin two branches of Lady Tanders's family. How Abigail had arrived at her conclusions was unclear, but the weeks in London had confirmed her cousin's shrewd judgment. It was now up to her to see that the wedding took place.

But Melissa could never be bullied into receiving him. Her pride would not allow it. She must be tricked. Nodding her head, Lady Castleton laid her own plans.

Chapter Eighteen

Melissa examined her cramped cabin and grimaced. This was a private, first-class accommodation? Two months in such a confined space already seemed daunting. A narrow bunk, a tiny washstand, a single chair, her traveling trunk. Most of her luggage would remain in the hold until she arrived in Baltimore.

A wave of weariness washed over her, and she sighed. She really ought to go up on deck for one last look at England, but she was too tired. Her efforts to appear normal, despite the morning sickness and exhaustion of her condition, had worn her to the bone. Thank God, she could finally abandon pretense and be herself.

"Go find your own quarters," she ordered Willis. "I will rest a while."

"Yes, milady."

Willis was the only one who knew everything. Melissa had lied to Lady Castleton right through their farewells, babbling about what they would do during the coming Season, speculating on who from her court would be back. Lies. She was sick of lies. She determinedly blinked away her sudden tears. There would be no second Season. She was not going to America to visit Beatrice. She was moving there for life.

Her heart twisted again over the decision, but she had no choice. To return, she must give up this child, but that was impossible. It was all of Charles she would ever have. Even visiting England would never work. She could not risk seeing him. The pain of a confrontation would kill her. Once she was gone, he would accept defeat and follow the time-honored method of repairing his fortunes. His charm would win him an heiress. And if he accomplished the deed quickly, he would recoup a quarter of Lady Lanyard's wealth. If he convinced Edwards he loved the chit, he might even get half. She

did not want to hear about it. She didn't even want to think
about it.

She had made her own travel arrangements, booking as the
widow, Mrs. Sharpe. It would protect her child from the
stigma of bastardy and would allow her to claim a connection
to Beatrice, whose mother was born a Sharpe. It was the last
lie, but a necessary one.

Charles's face again hovered before her own. His every
touch returned to haunt her. Unquenchable tears flowed, and
she wept long and hard, finally falling into exhausted slum-
ber.

Charles had been at Swansea for two months. The number
of critical chores was daunting, but he didn't care. It was all
that kept him from Bedlam. Images of Melissa tormented him
day and night. He no longer cared why she had deceived him.
He wanted only to hold her in his arms and love her. But the
prospects grew dimmer each day. Fifty returned letters sat on
his desk, taunting him every time he entered his study. What
had he done to deserve this?

You were selfish, whispered a voice. *And arrogant.* And it
was true. Even the way he had humbled himself to convince
her to wed him was selfish. He had analyzed her objections,
then adopted positions to counter them. Despite his words, he
had not always believed in what he was saying. The irony was
that he now did. He had become so intimately involved in
Swansea that he was wholeheartedly following his own pre-
scription for its future.

Selfishness had also underlay his other behavior. It was the
only explanation for his frequent abandonment of honor to
press attentions on her. Pleasure and passion were not excuses.
No gentleman would behave thus. But he had thought of nothing but the moment. And he had ruined her as surely as if he
had ravished her. If she would not return to him, she was
doomed. No other man would accept her to wife.

But that was not behind his continued campaign to win her
back, for his thinking was changing. He still needed her desperately, so selfish desire played a role. But he would make no
attempt to coerce her in the future. She must eventually consent to talk to him. He would state his case calmly, without
pretense, then accept her decision as final. If she refused him
again, he would somehow learn to cope. And it would be no
more than his just desserts for all the lies he had told.

He had nearly given up hope of having that opportunity when a missive arrived from Lady Castleton. Fear for Melissa set his hand shaking. But fear turned to cold chills as he read—

Lord Rathbone,

My granddaughter has decided to visit relatives in America. She will be sailing on 29 August from Southampton aboard the *Western Star*, an American ship out of Baltimore. I have the uncomfortable impression that she does not plan to return.

I do not know what caused this rift, but this may be your last chance to repair things. Regardless of her claims, she must regret the current situation. Though she has refused every letter and will not speak your name, I still hear her crying long into the night.

Lady Castleton

I despise you! Her voice echoed, as it had done thousands of times since that quarrel. Was it true, or was pride driving her away? This might be her way of circumventing a weakened will. If she felt she might give in, it was conceivable that she would run instead. She was as stubborn a miss as he had ever encountered.

But he loved her so . . .

He was at least as stubborn as she, he reminded himself grimly. This was his chance. And so he laid his plans.

A thump awakened Melissa from her slumbers. It took a moment to identify her surroundings. A louder thump reverberated through the floor, accompanied by creaking. Her bunk lurched.

They were under sail, she realized, gingerly rising. Another lurch tumbled her into the washstand, her fingers clawing at the raised edges until she regained her balance. Could she endure two months of this?

It was a little late to ask that, she admitted as her stomach turned over. She touched one white cheek, staring into the mirror. Fear blazed in her eyes. It was going to be a long trip.

Another lurch sent her hand back to the washstand. The face in the mirror stared accusingly, recrimination evident in every pore. Her vision blurred. Gasping, she looked again. A pale face. Two faces. She was losing her mind. Dizzily blinking, she focused once more. Nothing had changed. Beyond her own ghostly image floated one of Charles.

"Melissa?" he whispered.

She whipped around, nearly falling as the floor tilted.

He would swear her eyes lit with joy before she clamped her face into anger. His heart soared.

"What are you doing here?" she demanded harshly.

"Sailing to Baltimore."

"Why?" She clutched her throat in terror.

"Because the only lady I can ever love is going there." He sighed. "We must talk, Melissa. If you won't discuss it now, I swear that some time in the next two months you will." His heart was pounding so hard he thought he might faint, but he kept a tight rein on himself. Neither anger nor passion must intrude if he hoped to win.

"Why must you hound me?" she cried.

He winced. "Melissa, I love you more than life. Without you I am nothing. I have no desire to hurt you. But we need to go back to the beginning and discover how we reached this pass. Afterward, if you still wish me to Hades, I will never disturb you again."

"How? It would seem I'm stuck with you for two months."

"You needn't be." He had to force the words out. "This ship stops at Le Havre before crossing the Atlantic. I can be gone by tonight."

She relaxed, sending fear through his soul. The boat dipped and she stumbled against him, his arms closing automatically around her. Dear God, she felt so good!

"No!" she glared, pulling away. She had feared seeing him again, for he could cajole her into anything. But he was right. If there was a chance that she had misjudged him, she must explore it. "If it is a discussion you want, then we will talk. But you will not touch me again. It distorts reason." Dear Lord, how well she knew that, but if he kept his distance, she could think.

He sighed. "Sit down, Melissa." He pointed to the bunk, seating himself in the chair, far enough away that he could not reach her.

"How did you get in here?" she demanded, sipping water to moisten her suddenly dry mouth. Now that she was over the initial shock, she could see the changes. He was thinner, with new marks of pain and unhappiness marring his face. They resurrected the worst of her own pain, but she stifled her emotions, determined to judge impartially.

"I booked as Mr. Sharpe to get the adjoining cabin," he admitted, pointing to a door that she had assumed was a wardrobe.

"More deceit?" She sighed.

"No more than yours, Mrs. Sharpe," he countered.

She blushed. "Touché."

"Tell me of your brother's house party," he said quietly. "That is the real beginning, isn't it? Matt admitted what he did, and you mentioned Heflin's advances once before. Now I want to know the rest."

"Very well." She related the entire sorry tale.

"So that is why you were traveling as Harriet Sharpe."

"Yes. I feared that Toby would be so desperate that he would try to follow and drag me back. I had left a note implying that I was going home with Beatrice, and we believed that the other charade would protect our escape. Beatrice's mother was born Harriet Sharpe. It made the names seem more natural."

"So you were not trying to trick me," he murmured.

"Of course not!" she snapped. "Why would I? I knew nothing of you when we first met."

"You knew about the Willingfords," he reminded her.

"I had forgotten." She shrugged. "It wasn't until the next morning when you talked about your accident and mentioned the estate that I remembered the gossip. If I had not already given my word, I'd have turned you down then. The last thing I needed was to fall into the clutches of another Heflin."

"How did you learn of Lady Willingford's character?"

"She trapped me into covering her affair with a neighbor when I was thirteen. I had been studying with their daughters—my only means of acquiring any social training. But after months of listening to her threats and enduring her husband's inquisitions, I quit the lessons and gave up all thought of becoming a proper lady."

"You have been badly used by everyone, it seems," he admitted, shaking his head. "But we digress. You were traveling as Harriet Sharpe to escape your brother. But you had already eluded him. Why continue the deceit with me?"

"Do you honestly think that any well-bred female could accept the charade you were demanding?" she asked. "No one not three sheets to the wind would even have suggested it. How did I know I could trust you? My reputation would be in shreds if it came out. Lady Melissa would have starved in a ditch before agreeing, but Harriet Sharpe could do it, for afterward she would disappear like the myth she always was."

"I had not considered it in that light," he admitted with chagrin.

"Your only consideration was money," she reminded him.

He sighed. "I was a fool."

"Yes, you were. Your grandmother would have gladly advanced you enough to set Swansea to rights had you asked her. And she would have thought better of you if you had."

He stared. "Dear Lord. I never even considered it. The only reason I ignored the estate was because there was nothing I could do for it. I had always planned to renovate it when she passed on."

"Surely you knew what store she set by accomplishment. Even I know that, and I only met her during those few days at Lanyard Manor."

"All right. I'm a bigger fool than I thought. I had too much pride to beg. But why did you hide your identity in London? Do you hate me so much?"

It was her turn to stare. "What ever gave you that idea?"

"It was the only explanation I could devise, Melissa. You knew how much I needed the money, yet you hid the one fact that could have helped me."

"As I thought. It always comes back to money, doesn't it, Charles? I remain what I have been from the first night in that inn, a means to acquire a fortune. I cannot live like that." She rose as if to push him out.

"Please, my love," he pleaded. "Why? The money means nothing. It is you that I want, but I cannot understand your continued deceit."

She made the mistake of looking at him. Pain twisted his face, filling his eyes with tears. She shuddered.

"I never meant to deceive you, Charles," she said, sighing as she returned to the bunk. "When Grandmama insisted on bringing me out, I was terrified. I had never considered the possibility, for I thought she was as poor as we were. It was another thing that would have stopped me from helping you. But I had no choice. The thought of seeing Heflin again made me ill, but I hoped to avoid him, as he was not received. Then there was you. You could destroy me with a word, and after the way we parted, I saw no reason to doubt you would. It was a relief to find you from town. Thinking you were in mourning, I had relaxed, so when you turned up at Castleton House that day, I nearly died of fright. But you refrained from mentioning the past. I decided you were going to be gentlemanly about it and let the subject drop. It wasn't until some time later that I realized you didn't recognize me."

"How could I, Melissa? You had changed so much I still have trouble believing you are Harriet."

"It is a family trait," she shrugged. "Your grandmother was exactly the same. In fact, that is probably how she discovered my identity. She had a picture painted when she was eighteen in which she looked remarkably like me—I was eighteen when you found me."

He grimaced, remembering his remark about nobody believing she could be eighteen.

"The painting in the gallery was done when she was nineteen."

"It also looks like you. But I never saw the earlier portrait. And I never got a good look at you that entire fortnight. When I started searching for you after Grandmama died, I sketched a likeness to show to coachmen and innkeepers. Your cousin was easy, but I could not capture you. I would have been hard pressed to recognize you even if you had not changed. Between illness and fever, I was half out of my mind at Lanyard. Besides, that horrible bonnet hid your face outdoors, and inside you seemed enamored of darkened rooms."

She shuddered. "I had to be. Betsy dyed my hair before we left Drayton, but the coloring was so dull and lifeless—to say nothing of unevenly applied—that it would have been obvious in good light."

He burst out laughing, and she joined in. "Another thing I had never considered," he admitted when he caught his breath. "How did black-haired Harriet evolve so rapidly into golden Melissa? But why did you continue the charade after you learned that I had to find Harriet?"

"Again we return to money," she snorted, but resumed her tale. "I did not know the provisions of Lady Lanyard's will," she reminded him. "I thought you already had the inheritance. As I mentioned before, I had no interest in tying myself to a wastrel like my father and brother. I still don't.

When I mentioned your supposed betrothal to keep you at a distance, I was then forced to account for how I knew of it. I could hardly use it as a weapon while admitting that I was she."

"You gave me a shock that day. I had never considered that Grandmama might tell others."

"I doubt she did. Lady Beatrice knows nothing of it. Lies breed more lies, as we have both discovered this past year." She sighed. "I was forced into several more, as I am sure you recall. I was horrified to discover that you had to marry Harriet."

"Because you thought I recognized you?" he asked.

"In part. But it went beyond that. If I then admitted to being Harriet, it was tantamount to throwing myself at you. Even hoydens like me have been taught from birth that no lady would do such a thing. I remained uncertain whether I wanted to wed you. Admitting I was Harriet and then turning you down would have been the worst sort of taunting. And there was another problem. I could easily convince you that I was Harriet, but she does not exist. How could I convince a solicitor? I had changed so much that no one at Lanyard would recognize me. Few people spent time with me, and none in good light except your grandmother. I had no idea she had identified me. It seemed better to refuse your hand and allow you to make your own way in the world. The frustration of losing the fortune would destroy us both."

"So why did you ultimately accept me?" he asked softly.

"You know why," she challenged him, but the look in his eye forced her to continue. "Because I love you, of course. I am accustomed to living on nothing. You finally convinced me that you were content. You believed that Harriet existed, yet you chose me." She shrugged.

"I still choose you, my darling," he murmured, rising to go to her, but her hand stayed him. "I want only you, Melissa. We will give the money to charity as Grandmama directed."

She stared. "What game are you playing now, Charles?"

"No game, my love. If the only way to convince you that you are essential to my life is to live in poverty, then we shall live in poverty." He reached into his jacket and drew out a letter. "Here, my love. This is no sudden decision. It is something I have been trying to tell you for weeks. This is the first letter I sent you. The others are but variations on it."

She hesitantly broke the seal and read. He had spoken truly.

The words leaped from the page. *You may have returned my ring but you still hold my soul . . . would gladly live in a ditch if you were at my side . . . Let her treasure help others. We can help ourselves.* "You feel that strongly?" Melissa breathed.

"Always." Hesitantly, he moved closer.

The look in his eyes ignited her desire. Her nipples hardened into taut nubs, pushing against the bodice of her gown. His eyes gleamed at that telltale sign, his heart soaring in gladness. She held out her hand to his.

"Dear Lord, Melissa," he sobbed, pulling her into his arms at last. Starved for the sweet taste of her mouth, his lips crushed against hers, his tongue reveling in her velvety depths.

"Oh, Charles, I have missed you so," she cried when he bent his head to nuzzle her shoulder. This was where she belonged, where she would have been weeks ago if her stubborn pride had not interfered. Her longing increased, building tension, concentrating it.

"We will marry immediately," he choked.

"Arrogant toad—," she began teasingly.

The ship lurched, twisting her stomach with it. She pushed him away and dropped heavily to the bunk.

"What now?" he demanded.

"Leave me for a while, Charles," she begged, paling to chalk white. "I fear I am about to be sick."

"My poor darling," he murmured, grabbing the basin and sitting beside her.

She had no time to repeat her request. He held her head, whispering soothing words in her ears and holding her shaking, clammy body close when she was through.

Melissa drifted in a hazy sea, unwilling to return to awareness where she would have to cope with the scene he had just witnessed.

"Drink this," Charles commanded, pulling her back to consciousness by thrusting a glass into her hand. It contained a generous dollop of brandy, and she realized he had been to his own cabin while her senses floated. The basin was gone, replaced by another.

"No!" she protested as the boat again lurched.

"I guarantee you'll feel better," he insisted, holding the glass to her lips.

She gagged on the first swallow, nausea again attacking, but she fought it down and drank. Warmth exploded through her body.

"I am so embarrassed," she sobbed.

"Don't be, my love," he murmured. "This was nothing compared to what I put you through that first day. Now let me back away from arrogance and do this right. Will you marry me?"

"Not yet, Charles. There are other things we need to discuss first," she choked out, her face again paling sharply.

He sighed. "In that case, you had better rest, Melissa. You're looking worse again. Lie down. It's at least another eight hours to France so there's no rush."

She tried to protest but he stretched her out on the bed, first opening the tapes of her gown. She shivered as he slid it off—and not with cold.

She was not the only one. He had to exert rigid control on himself. She was weak, exhausted, and needed sleep. But he could not resist smoothing her shift before drawing a coverlet over her.

"Oh, God," he breathed as his hand encountered the slight swelling of her abdomen. "It wasn't just *mal de mer*, was it, love?"

She turned her face to the wall, tears glittering in her eyes even as new sobs tore from her throat. The brandy's heat had turned to ice.

He pulled her gently into his arms, sitting beside her on the bunk and holding her in a tender, protective embrace. "No wonder you decided to flee to America." He sighed. "You must have been terrified. And that explains Mrs. Sharpe. Did you believe I would hate you?"

"No, but you would have felt obligated to offer for me."

"Never obligation, my love," he swore, tilting her face until she met his eyes. "I hope you know that now. And while there will be a few raised brows, I could not be more pleased." His face reflected the truth of his words, shining with love and awe.

Her fear faded, leaving only love in her eyes.

"Will you marry me, my dearest Melissa? Not for money. Not because a moment of weakness produced consequences. But because we love each other. I am only half a man without you."

"And I am merely half a woman. Yes, Charles, I will."

"Thank God," he breathed, cradling her gently and stroking her hair as her arms moved around his waist. "Sleep now, my love," he urged.

"In a moment. I need to savor the wonder. I feel as though heaven has suddenly wrested me from the bowels of hell." She reached up to touch his face.

"It does feel like that." His arms tightened and he laid his cheek against her forehead.

"I wasn't really terrified," she murmured softly into his cravat. "Just thankful that I would still have part of you to love and cherish."

His arms tightened. "I have a special license—I prepared for all possible contingencies, you see."

She smiled. "Excellent. We will seek out a vicar as soon as possible." She snuggled closer into his arms.

"As soon as possible. Don't tempt me, love," he added as her hand slid under his jacket. " This time we are doing everything right. I am trying to become a pattern card of responsible, respectable behavior."

"Yes, Charles," she agreed, planting one soft kiss on his cheek before sliding beneath the coverlet. "See? I'm practicing to be a conformable wife."

"Don't change," he begged, dragging the chair close to the bunk. "I love you just the way you are, sharp tongue and all. Now go to sleep before I forget myself. I need you desperately, but I am determined to wait."

"No more lies, Charles," she admonished him. "There are enough ladies panting for your body to keep even the most lecherous gentleman satisfied."

He turned her face to his, holding her eyes squarely with his own. "Never another lie," he swore seriously. "There will be no more deceit. And there has been no one else since I first proposed. The thought of making love to another makes me sick."

Her tongue ran across suddenly dry lips as Beatrice's words returned. He really did love her. She smiled.

"Oh, God," he groaned, running frustrated fingers through his hair. Several deep breaths restored his composure.

"I'm sorry, Charles." And she truly was. "But you needn't give up your grandmother's fortune," she added as he tucked the coverlet more securely around her and laid a hand on her shoulder. "I've been terribly childish over that. Your tenants should not have to pay for my insecurities. It was never the money, you know, but a question of your motives."

"Perhaps half," he suggested. "It is what she designated

for marrying someone else, and I had already renounced Harriet."

"As you wish."

"Never doubt my love, Melissa. And I cannot blame you for your fears. I have learned more about your home and family in recent weeks. There has been no one you could trust."

"I trust you, Charles," she murmured softly, turning to kiss his hand before slipping into a deep sleep, the first she had had in weeks.

He remained at her bedside, his heart at peace, his mind already planning their future.

"Did you really borrow Heflin's coach to escape his clutches?" Charles laughed as he fastened her gown. They would be landing at Le Havre within minutes.

She giggled. "We did indeed. He never suspected a thing. I don't know how they thought we had escaped with a trunk and three valises. Toby had nought but a dogcart left in the stable."

His hands rested on her shoulders, their two images gazing back from the mirror. "I still don't know why Grandmama put us through this. Why did she not expose us both at Lanyard?"

"Do you not, my love?" She smiled at his reflection. "Your grandmother was quite a matchmaker. She decided we would suit and took steps to see that we did."

"By attaching her fortune to you?"

"In part. But she also delayed telling you where to find me until I had finished growing up. That's what the codicil was for, of course."

"The old witch." He chuckled. "And I suppose she ordered me to town for the Season so you wouldn't marry someone else in the meantime."

"It worked. If you hadn't kissed me at the Wharburton masquerade, I'd have accepted George." They both shuddered.

"I hope you don't mind immediately recrossing," he said, changing the subject. "I've booked passage back tonight. Willis has your luggage ready. We've an appointment with the vicar in the morning." He gave her a quick squeeze.

"And what names are we using this time?"

"Lord and Lady Rathbone, of course. I knew if we ever sat down to talk calmly, your intelligence and good sense would prevail. Or my charm and seduction." He leered suggestively.

"Arrogance, Charles," she chided him, turning to smile directly into his eyes. "We must do something about that. Later," she added, pulling his head down for a searing kiss.